THE LOCKWOOD FAMILY

LAURA BEERS

Chapter One

England, 1813

A burden.

That is what her uncle had called her. A troublesome burden. Lady Edwina Lockwood knew that she shouldn't be eavesdropping on a private conversation, but she couldn't help herself. Seated just beyond her uncle's study, she overheard him discussing her and her future.

Did she even have one?

When her father was alive, she had a promising one. But now she didn't know what her future would hold. It frightened her, to say the least.

"What would you have me say, Catherine?" her uncle shouted. "There aren't enough funds available to give Edwina a Season."

Her aunt responded in a hushed voice, "Shh. Keep your voice down. Do you wish for everyone to overhear our conversation?"

"Why should I care what they think?" her uncle asked,

albeit in a more reserved voice. "Do you wish to deprive our twins, Elodie and Melody, of their first Season?"

"No, but we can manage with a lot less to ensure Edwina has a Season. I am sure we can find a way—" her aunt attempted.

Her uncle spoke over her. "You say that now, but how is that fair to our daughters? Besides, I doubt Edwina would attract a suitor anyway. She is pretty enough, but she is very mousy."

"Mousy?" her aunt questioned.

"I do believe that Edwina is afraid of her own shadow," her uncle clarified.

Edwina rested her head against the wall, releasing a sigh. *Mousy*. Just another word that her uncle described her as. The worst part is that he wasn't entirely wrong. She was reserved, far more than she should be, but she was struggling. Her life had been taken from her in a blink of an eye when her father had died, nearly four months ago, and now Brockhall Manor felt no more like a home, despite her growing up here.

Once her uncle had inherited her father's title of the Marquess of Dallington, he moved his family into Brockhall Manor and immediately went about making changes. He even brought along his own butler.

In a firm voice, her aunt declared, "Edwina is a delightful young woman, and any gentleman would be lucky to have her as a wife." Her words were spoken as if she were daring her husband to contradict her.

Edwina always found solace in her aunt's unwavering support. Having an ally made her feel less isolated, a comforting presence in the face of loneliness.

Her older cousin's baritone voice came from above her. "What are you doing, Edwina?" Bennett asked, his voice holding more curiosity than censure.

Bennett stood tall, his dark hair brushed forward, looking

very much the part of a dashing earl. In his eyes, she found the reassuring kindness that had become a familiar trait.

She brought her finger up to her lips, indicating he should be quiet. She didn't want to get caught by her uncle.

Bennett crouched down next to her and lowered his voice. "I would be remiss if I did not remind you that a lady should not eavesdrop." He paused, a smile playing on his lips. "At least, you shouldn't get caught."

Edwina dropped her hand. "Your father is discussing my future," she explained. "I had little choice in the matter."

With a glance at the open door, Bennett asked, "What is my father saying this time?"

"There aren't enough funds to give me a Season since Elodie and Melody will be debuting this Season," Edwina replied.

Bennett looked displeased by what she had revealed. "What did my mother say about that?"

"She is trying to convince your father otherwise, but he is rather adamant about it."

"My father is many things, but his frugality knows no bounds. The coffers aren't as full as he would like, but we can tighten our purse strings," Bennett said. "I shall talk to him and get this matter resolved. You need not worry."

But Edwina did worry. If she didn't have a Season, what would become of her? Would she be relegated to the role of a companion or, even worse, a governess?

Bennett placed a comforting hand on her shoulder. "I know that look," he started, "but everything will work out."

"How?" she asked. "If I don't have a Season, what will I do?"

Withdrawing his hand, he replied, "Take it from me, your much older- and wiser- cousin, don't try to grow up too fast."

"Says the man who is nearly thirty and still unwed," Edwina retorted.

"Yes, but that is by choice," Bennett said with a sly grin.

Before either of them could say more, her uncle shouted, "Edwina is not my daughter! You will not make me feel guilty about this."

"No, but she is your niece and giving her a Season is the right thing to do," her aunt pressed, her voice rising. "That is what Richard would have wanted us to do, considering he left her a dowry of fifteen thousand pounds. Besides, Edwina has already delayed her Season once because of her father's illness. I will not make her wait any longer to debut."

Bennett rose and extended his hand towards her. "Come, let us go for that ride now," he urged.

Edwina slipped her hand into his and allowed him to assist her in rising.

As Bennett dropped his hand to his side, he said, "Do not fret. My mother can be very persuasive."

"Uncle called me a 'burden,'" she admitted.

Bennett's jaw clenched. "That was wrong of him to do so," he said. "You, Cousin, are no burden. I hope you know that."

Edwina wanted to believe him, yet there were times when she felt like an interloper in her own home. She longed for the days when her father was alive, a time when she was truly happy.

Her cousin regarded her with compassion, perhaps tinged with a hint of pity. "Do not let my father's words upset you," he encouraged. "He is just under a lot of pressure since he inherited his title."

Mustering a smile to her face, Edwina said, "Very well." She knew there was no point in arguing with her cousin. He was trying to comfort her, but she was not used to people making disparaging remarks about her.

"If we don't hurry, we shall be late for breakfast," Bennett remarked.

While they walked towards the stables, Edwina retreated to her own thoughts, a habit that was all too familiar now. Her heart ached, and she doubted that time would soften it. She just felt so alone, despite being surrounded by family.

Bennett arrived at the door of the stables and opened it. "After you," he encouraged.

Edwina made her way down the central aisle until she reached her horse's stall. A genuine smile graced her face as she approached, extending her hand to pet the chestnut gelding. Her father had gifted her the horse on her eighth birthday, and they had been inseparable ever since.

"Hello, Sorrel," she greeted. "How have you been?"

Bennett offered her an amused look. "Sometimes I am not sure if you expect your horse to actually answer you."

"It would be nice," Edwina joked.

A familiar groom stepped forward. "Would you like me to saddle your horse, my lady?" Jack asked.

"I can do it," Edwina responded.

Jack didn't look pleased by her remark. "Your riding habit is too fine to be mucking around in the stalls," he said. "Allow me to do it."

Bennett nodded his head in agreement. "Jack is right. Besides, a lady shouldn't saddle her own horse."

Edwina bit her tongue. Why couldn't she saddle her horse? She had been able to do so when her father was alive. But now, the rules were different. Everything, it seemed, was different.

Stepping back, Edwina watched as Jack led her horse out of the stall and began saddling him.

Bennett came to stand by her. "You are angry."

"No, not angry, just frustrated," Edwina admitted.

Turning towards her, Bennett explained, "I know your father allowed you to saddle your own horse, which was progressive of him. However, my father holds a different view, as does Society. You must know that."

"Why does it matter?" Edwina asked.

"It matters greatly, I'm afraid. You are a lady, and must act like one," Bennett responded.

Edwina approached Sorrel and ran her hand down his neck. The only time that she felt free from this oppressive life was when she was riding her horse. At least her uncle couldn't take that away from her.

Jack stepped forward. "Allow me to help you onto your horse," he said.

Once she was seated atop Sorrel, Edwina grasped the reins and guided her horse out of the stables. She pointed Sorrel towards the woodlands and spurred him into a swift gallop. Her carefully arranged chignon unraveled, allowing her dark hair to dance freely in the wind.

She urged her horse to go faster, not bothering to wait for her cousin to catch up. She knew that Bennett would chide her on her recklessness, but she did not care. That was only when she stopped. And for now, she had no intention of doing so.

Once she reached the path's end, she reined in her horse and waited for Bennett to approach her. She gently patted her horse's neck, anticipating the forthcoming reprimand.

As Bennett drew near, a frustrated look marred his features as he demanded, "Do you wish to break your neck?"

"No, that was not my intention," Edwina responded with a shake of her head.

"What was, then?" Bennett asked. "Your horsemanship is excellent, there is no denying that, but you can't keep riding your horse like that. It is far too dangerous for a lady."

Edwina pressed her lips together, refraining from asking if it was equally perilous for a gentleman, but she didn't want to upset him any further.

"I'm sorry," she said.

Bennett's face softened. "I apologize, too. I should be accustomed to your riding by now. I just worry about you. Sometimes I am not sure if you care whether you live or die."

"I do not wish to die," Edwina admitted. That much was true.

"Just be careful, Cousin," he said. "I know you are hurting now, but life has a way of getting better. You just have to hold on."

Edwina turned her attention towards the open fields, grappling with her emotions. She wanted to believe what Bennett was saying was true, but uncertainty lingered within her.

Before her father died, she had always embraced life to the fullest, seeing no reason to ever doubt her life would be anything but extraordinary. How naive she had been. That life had been ripped away from her when her father had died from a long, lingering illness.

Edwina wanted someone to pay for his death, but there was no one to blame.

And that was the problem.

She could only blame herself for her misery.

Bennett's voice interrupted her thoughts. "Are you all right?" he asked.

It was the same question she was asked repeatedly, but she didn't dare answer truthfully. She didn't want anyone to know how much she was hurting. What could they do for her anyway?

"Yes," she replied. "I was just woolgathering."

It looked as if Bennett were going to press her, but thankfully he let it drop. Instead, he said, "I wanted to tell you that my friend will be joining us for a fortnight."

"Wonderful," Edwina responded, feigning interest. Why did it matter to her if Bennett invited a friend to Brockhall Manor? She would no doubt go out of her way to avoid this person.

With a glance up at the sky, Bennett remarked, "We should return home now. I do not want my father to chide us for being late to breakfast."

"Good point," Edwina said. "Lead the way."

Bennett gave her a knowing look. "Why bother?" he teased. "Your horse will just overtake mine. You should go first but do try to have some restraint."

"If you insist," Edwina said with a smile.

As she urged her horse into a run, Edwina knew that something had to change in her life. Happiness seemed elusive, and the uncertainty gnawed at her. No one truly grasped the depth of her emotions.

But today was a new day, and Edwina hoped that something would usher in the change she so desperately needed.

Miles Burke, Earl of Hilgrove, regretted his decision to accept his friend's invitation to visit Brockhall Manor. He had no desire to smile and pretend all was well. He just wanted to be alone. Yet, somehow, Bennett had convinced him otherwise.

Perched atop his horse, he trailed his coach down the winding gravel driveway lined with ancient trees. The sun bore down on him, beads of sweat tracing a path down his spine. Though uncomfortable, the open air was a welcome alternative to being cooped up inside of the coach.

In the distance, a grand manor emerged on the horizon, a sprawling brick residence adorned with dormer windows, a steeply gabled roof, and ivy gracefully climbing its walls. The picturesque scene was completed by the meticulously tended garden encircling the manor, where vibrant flowers and precisely trimmed hedges added to its idyllic charm.

Miles had the strangest urge to turn his horse around and leave this place. It was perfect, almost too perfect. The manor's flawless façade triggered memories of his late wife's countryside estate, casting a shadow of sadness upon him.

The very air around him seemed to grow heavy and he found himself struggling to catch his breath.

Why had he thought this was a good idea, he grumbled to himself.

The coach rolled to a halt in front of the manor, and Miles guided his horse to a stop nearby. Footmen swiftly emerged from the main entrance, hastening towards the coach to retrieve his trunks. With a dismount, Miles handed over the reins to a waiting footman.

Bennett exited the main door and descended the steps to greet him, a triumphant grin on his face. "Well, as I live and breathe, you did come," he exclaimed. "I had my doubts, but I remained optimistic."

"You are too blasted optimistic," Miles retorted.

Undeterred, Bennett's grin shifted into a smirk. "In this case, I was right," he said. "How was your journey from Grimsby?"

"Tolerable."

His friend's smirk persisted. "I see you are your rather pleasant self this afternoon," he observed, gesturing towards the manor. "Come, let's get you settled. Perhaps you require a rest from your travels."

Miles found Bennett's remark to be rather absurd. He was not one to waste the day away in bed. "I do not require a nap," he said. "The journey here was hardly perilous."

"A drink, then?"

"Yes, a drink would be much more preferable," Miles replied.

As they made their way towards the main entrance, Bennett said, "I had one of the guest bedchambers readied for you. Did you, by chance, bring your valet with you?"

"I did," Miles informed him. "He was my batman in the war."

Bennett nodded. "Very good."

Once they arrived in the opulent entry hall, Miles dreaded

this visit already. Bennett's perpetual cheerfulness had always grated on his nerves, and it seemed to have only intensified since their carefree days at Cambridge.

Miles' gaze roamed over the entry hall, lingering on the Corinthian columns that adorned the entrance with intricate golden motifs. The polished marble floor beneath his feet expanded the grandeur of the space, while a sweeping staircase graced the far wall.

Bennett's voice broke the silence, filled with a quiet reverence. "It is grand, is it not?" he asked. "My grandmother worked with the architect to design this hall."

"It is rather impressive," Miles admitted.

"Come, let me show you to the study," Bennett said, holding his hand out. "We will have that drink I promised you."

While they walked towards the rear of the manor, Miles inquired, "I know you were close with your uncle. How have you fared since his death?"

Bennett shrugged. "The pain still lingers, but it gets easier with time."

Miles fell silent. He understood the lingering pain but couldn't fathom the idea that time could bring any reprieve. If anything, his grief seemed to only intensify with each passing day.

They entered a masculine room adorned with dark wood paneling and walls lined with bookshelves. Bennett approached the drink cart, picked up a decanter, and poured two drinks. Walking over to Miles, he handed his guest a glass.

"Thank you," Miles acknowledged as he accepted the glass.

Bennett eyed him with concern. "Dare I ask how you are faring?"

"I have been better," Miles admitted. "But I do not wish to talk about that."

"You never do."

"And yet, you persist in prying," Miles remarked. He wasn't upset with Bennett; he knew his friend meant well. Nevertheless, he believed he could handle things on his own. It was a lie he told himself and, deep down, he wasn't sure if he believed it.

"Well, I hope you are ready to be thoroughly entertained during your visit," Bennett said. "I have our days planned with pall-mall, angling and shooting."

"Marvelous," Miles muttered, lifting the glass to his lips. He recognized his friend's attempt to divert him from his grief. But it had proven ineffective in the past, so why would this occasion be any different?

He had just taken a sip of his drink when an attractive young woman entered the room, clad in a black gown. She had a slender frame, and her dark hair was fashioned into a loose chignon at the nape of her neck. Her green eyes, set deep and framed by high cheekbones, held a familiarity that he couldn't explain.

A small squeak escaped her as she noticed them, quickly lowering her gaze. "My apologies," the young woman said. "I hadn't realized your guest had arrived yet. I will go."

Swirling gracefully on her heel, the young woman moved to leave but Bennett's voice stopped her retreat. "Wait, Edwina," he called out.

She reluctantly turned back around, casting an expectant gaze upon him.

Bennett placed his hand out towards the young woman. "Allow me the privilege of introducing you to my cousin, Lady Edwina Lockwood."

Miles executed a bow. "My lady," he greeted.

Edwina responded with a deep curtsy, her gaze seemingly fixed on the open door, as if contemplating her imminent escape.

Bennett lowered his hand, proceeding with the introductions. "Lord Hilgrove is a good friend of mine and we housed together during our time at Cambridge."

"My lord," Edwina murmured, looking entirely unimpressed with what her cousin had just revealed. He was accustomed to women reacting with admiration upon learning of his title, but her lack of such a response intrigued him. It was a reaction he found rather refreshing.

Edwina held his gaze for the briefest of moments before it turned downcast. "If that will be all…" Her voice trailed off, as if looking for permission to leave.

"You had a purpose for visiting the study, did you not?" Bennett asked.

With a quick glance at the bookshelves, Edwina remarked, "I was going to collect a book, but I can return at another time."

"You mustn't change your plans on our account," Bennett insisted. "Do not let us deter you from your original purpose."

Edwina nodded, turning towards the nearest bookshelf. Her fingers traced along the spines until she found one to her liking, which she promptly retrieved and tucked under her arm. "Thank you," she said softly.

Bennett lifted his brow. "Are you interested in estate management, Cousin?"

Her brow puckered. "No, why do you ask?"

"The book you chose is on farmland equipment and techniques," Bennett replied. "I doubt you would find it very engaging."

"Oh," Edwina said. "Perhaps I shall select something else."

Bennett gave her an encouraging look, appearing as if he had expected her response. "Take your time. You are not inconveniencing us."

Edwina proceeded to return the book to its rightful place, her eyes wandering over the array of titles.

Facing Miles, Bennett inquired, "How is your sister?"

"She is well," Miles replied. "I hardly see her now that she is married and has two little ones to keep her busy."

"That is not a day that I long for," Bennett admitted.

Miles tightened the hold on his glass. His wife had been increasing when she had grown ill. It was a devastating blow to not only lose her but the child as well. "It is not for everyone," he muttered.

Edwina turned around from the bookshelves with a book in hand. "I found one," she said, her voice not much more than a whisper.

"Which book caught your fancy?" Bennett asked.

"*Robinson Crusoe*," Edwina replied, tucking the book under her arm.

"But you have read that one, multiple times," Bennett pointed out.

Edwina retained the book, responding, "Indeed, but Mr. Warren has not. I thought he might enjoy it while recovering from his fall."

"I wasn't aware he had hurt himself," Bennett said, turning to Miles to explain. "Mr. Warren was the butler here before my father arrived. He has since retired to one of the cottages on the estate."

"Yes, but Mrs. Warren says he remains in good spirits, despite hurting his ankle," Edwina shared.

"It's not broken, is it?" Bennett asked.

Edwina shook her head. "The doctor does not believe so but has advised him to stay off of it for a few days."

"How did he manage to fall?"

A faint smile graced Edwina's lips. "He was tending to his goats and one butted him in the backside."

"Those blasted goats," Bennett said with a teasing lilt to his voice. "They get into more mischief than we did at Cambridge."

"Mr. Warren does love them, though, much to his wife's

chagrin," Edwina shared. "If she had her way, they would have gotten rid of them long ago."

Miles observed Edwina, noting the lively sparkle in her eyes as she spoke about the goats. He wondered what it would take to elicit a genuine smile from her.

Sensing his gaze, Edwina looked over at him and, catching his scrutiny, averted her eyes. "Excuse me," she murmured, then gracefully left the study.

Bennett offered him an apologetic look. "I do apologize, but Edwina is rather timid around people she doesn't know."

"She seems pleasant enough," Miles acknowledged.

His friend agreed with a slight nod. "She used to be different before her father's passing, but she's still grappling with grief."

"Aren't we all?" Miles asked.

"Sometimes I wish she would stop running from the grief and face it," Bennett admitted. "But she is not ready to do so yet."

Miles placed his glass down onto the table. "Grief isn't that simple. It consumes you, body and soul."

Bennett smiled. "This conversation has grown much too serious for my liking. Allow me to show you to your bedchamber."

"I don't need a nap," Miles reminded his friend.

"Shall we go riding, then?" Bennett asked. "You can use one of the horses in our stables so your horse can rest."

Miles shifted uncomfortably in his stance. "I am not sure if I am ready to get back into the saddle," he confessed.

Bennett seemed to consider him for a moment before suggesting, "How about a game of chess? I haven't defeated you in ages."

"I seem to recall our chess games quite differently," Miles retorted.

"Then your recollection would be inaccurate, although in

all fairness, you did take quite a few hits to the head playing cricket," Bennett quipped.

Miles released an exasperated breath. "That was one time, and you aimed at my head."

"You could have ducked."

"I was preoccupied."

A knowing smile came to Bennett's lips. "Yes, I remember," he said. "That was the day I was finally introduced to Arabella."

The memory of that moment weighed heavy on his heart, causing Miles' expression to grow somber. "It was a good day," he expressed.

Bennett strolled over to the drink tray, setting his glass down. "I still can't fathom what Arabella saw in you. Surely it wasn't your lackluster cricket-playing skills."

"I don't know either, but I was most fortunate that she did," Miles expressed.

"Perhaps she hit her head one too many times, as well," Bennett joked.

Miles let out a heavy sigh. "You make it nearly impossible to be your friend," he said. "I don't think I have met a more bacon-brained person than you."

Bennett simply laughed in response. "You can't shoot the messenger," he retorted.

"I think I may need a nap now since our conversation has exhausted me," Miles declared, feigning annoyance.

Bennett gestured towards the door. "Come, let us adjourn to the parlor where we can play a game of chess."

"You will lose, just like old times," Miles remarked.

"Maybe I will surprise you," Bennett responded, leading the way out of the study.

Miles followed his friend from the room, but he hoped he would beat Bennett rather soundly in chess. He had grown wary of surprises, as they tended to be more bothersome than a delight in his experience.

Chapter Two

Edwina walked down the dirt path, running her fingers over the wildflowers that bordered the trail. As she tilted her head towards the sun, she welcomed the soothing warmth, appreciating the contrast to the usual cloudy weather.

During moments like these, she almost forgot that her life was in utter shambles. She needed to find a way to move forward and let go of the lingering heartache of her past.

But it was proving to be entirely too difficult.

The Warrens' cottage emerged on the horizon, and accompanying the sight was the distinct sound of a goat's bellow resonating from overhead. Lifting her gaze, she spotted Matilda perched on the lower branches of a nearby tree.

Edwina let out a laugh. "What are you doing up there, Matilda?" she inquired, amused by the goat's antics.

In response, Matilda let out another resounding bellow, as if offering an explanation for her lofty perch.

Continuing towards the modest cottage, Edwina reached out and knocked on the door. After a brief pause, the door swung open, revealing the welcoming figure of Mrs. Warren, a short and portly woman.

A warm smile graced Mrs. Warren's face. "Lady Edwina, what a pleasant surprise," she greeted. "Do come in."

Returning the smile, Edwina stepped inside and inquired, "How is Mr. Warren today?"

Mrs. Warren let out an exasperated sigh. "He is awful. Just awful. Despite the doctor's advice to stay off his feet for a few days, he keeps trying to get out of his chair."

Edwina, holding up the book in her hand, suggested, "I hope a book might distract him then."

"One can only hope," Mrs. Warren responded. "Would you mind sitting with him while I finish preparing our supper for this evening?"

"I would be happy to," Edwina replied.

As Mrs. Warren headed towards a room off the corridor, Edwina followed and found the tall, heavy-set Mr. Warren seated on a chair, his right leg propped up by a bench. His once vibrant black hair that adorned his head had started to fade, now marked with streaks of white.

"Look who came to visit," Mrs. Warren announced cheerfully.

Mr. Warren glanced up, his kind eyes crinkling around the edges. "My lady," he said.

Edwina took a step forward, extending the book towards Mr. Warren. "I brought you a book that I thought you might enjoy."

Accepting the book, Mr. Warren studied it for a moment. "Thank you," he acknowledged. "I haven't read *Robinson Crusoe*."

"I had hoped that was the case," Edwina said.

Gesturing towards a nearby chair, Mr. Warren offered, "Please sit. I could use the company."

Mrs. Warren interjected, "I will return shortly."

Mr. Warren's gaze followed his wife's retreating figure until she disappeared out the door. Then, in a hushed voice, he turned towards Edwina and said, "I think my wife is trying to kill me."

Edwina eyed him warily. "Pardon?"

"She is trying to kill me with boredom," Mr. Warren joked, a mischievous glint in his eyes. "She won't let me leave this chair."

"That is per doctor's orders," Edwina reminded him.

Mr. Warren reclined back in his chair. "You sound like my wife," he said with a wry smile.

"Good, because she is a very wise woman," Edwina stated, daring him to contradict her.

"I am a smart enough man to not disagree with that remark," Mr. Warren said. "How have you been faring?"

Mustering up a small smile, she replied, "I am well."

Mr. Warren didn't look convinced. "I would prefer the truth, if you don't mind."

Edwina should have known that Mr. Warren would have seen through her facade. "To be honest, I am not well. My uncle says there aren't enough funds for me to have a Season alongside my cousins."

"He told you this?"

With a slight hesitation, she admitted, "No, but I may have overheard it in passing."

Mr. Warren gave her a knowing look. "You mean you were eavesdropping."

"Perhaps," she said, seeing no reason to conceal the truth.

"What does your aunt say?" Mr. Warren questioned.

Edwina smoothed the delicate folds of her black gown. "She is adamant that I am to have a Season, but I do not wish to upset my uncle."

"You have always put other people before yourself, which is admirable, but not at the expense of your own future," Mr. Warren counseled. "You deserve to have a Season."

"What if I have a Season and I don't get an offer of marriage?" Edwina asked.

Mr. Warren shrugged, throwing his hands up. "And what if you marry a prince?" he inquired. "You don't know what the future holds for you."

"I don't aspire to marry a prince."

"My point is, it is all right to be a little selfish every now and then."

Edwina's gaze drew downcast as she admitted, "My uncle considers me a burden."

"Did he say this to you or did you overhear it?"

"Does it matter?" Edwina asked.

With displeasure in his voice, Mr. Warren said, "Since I am no longer in Lord Dallington's employ, I can speak freely, and tell you that he was wrong to say such a thing. You are not a burden."

"But he said it none the less."

Mr. Warren shifted in his seat to face her. "Your father loved you, more than life itself. I have never seen a father dote on his child more than he did on you," he remarked. "He would be furious by the ill-treatment that you are receiving from his brother."

"Uncle isn't entirely unkind to me," Edwina admitted. "I know he is under immense pressure since he assumed my father's title."

"That does not excuse his behavior."

Edwina clasped her hands in her lap. "I just wish things were different," she murmured.

"Don't we all?" Mr. Warren questioned. "But you can't look for your future in your past. You must move forward."

"And if I can't?" Edwina asked.

"Then you shall have a life of misery, not being able to let go of what once was," Mr. Warren said. "Your father wouldn't have wanted that for you."

Edwina grew silent. Mr. Warren's words resonated with truth, but the challenge of putting her past behind her felt overwhelming.

"But enough of me preaching to you," Mr. Warren said, his tone lightening. "I would prefer to speak on something else. Anything else, really."

Grateful for the change in conversation, Edwina shared, "I did see Matilda up in a tree on my way here."

"Of course you did. I can hardly get her down from there," Mr. Warren remarked, a touch of pride in his voice.

"I did not see Baxter though."

Mr. Warren turned his head towards the window and said, "Baxter is sleeping just outside the window. Mrs. Warren won't let him come inside to sit by the fire."

"Well, she is right in doing so since he is a goat."

"Shh," Mr. Warren urged, putting a finger to his lips. "Don't let Baxter hear you say that. He doesn't realize he is just a goat."

A laugh escaped Edwina's lips and she brought her gloved hand up to cover her mouth.

Mr. Warren lowered his hand and informed her, "Your cousin came by a few days ago to look in on us."

"He did?" Edwina asked, surprised by her cousin's thoughtfulness.

"Yes, which I was most grateful for, but I was surprised he didn't send one of his servants to complete the task," Mr. Warren replied.

"I am surprised as well," she admitted.

"Lord Dunsby has always treated us with kindness."

"I must admit that my cousin has made these past few months bearable for me," Edwina said.

Mr. Warren nodded. "He is a good man, there is no questioning that, but I am concerned about you. You seem troubled."

Not wanting to delve deeper into the conversation, she abruptly rose. "I should be going. I do not wish to take up too much of your time."

"You can run all you want, but when you eventually come to a stop, just remember that I will be here," Mr. Warren said.

Edwina offered him a grateful smile. "Thank you."

Mrs. Warren entered the room as she dried her hands off on the apron that was tied around her waist. "Did you have a nice chat?" she asked.

"We did," Mr. Warren confirmed.

Turning to face her, Mrs. Warren inquired, "Would you care for a biscuit before you depart?"

"That is kind of you to offer but I should leave now so I can prepare for dinner," she replied. "My cousin invited his friend to Brockhall Manor and he will be dining with us."

Mrs. Warren's eyes twinkled. "Is he handsome?"

An image of Lord Hilgrove came to her mind. Undoubtedly handsome, he possessed a square jaw, a straight nose, and dark hair that framed his face. But it wasn't solely his appearance that captivated her. No, it wasn't that at all. It was his eyes. They harbored a depth of sorrow, much like her own. And she knew there was a story in them, waiting to be told.

"He is tolerable, I suppose," Edwina lied.

"Well, you could use a handsome suitor, or two," Mrs. Warren said. "You are much too beautiful to go unnoticed for much longer."

Edwina appreciated Mrs. Warren's kind words, but she knew that she was no great beauty. With her brown hair and slightly tanned skin, she was forced to acknowledge that she didn't embody the traditional beauty associated with debutantes. At least, she wasn't entirely unfortunate to look upon.

Mr. Warren spoke up, drawing back her attention. "You look just like your mother did at this age."

"I wish I had known her," Edwina admitted.

"Your parents waited years to finally have you, and were overjoyed when your mother was expecting," Mr. Warren said. "It was a shame that she died so shortly after you were born."

Mrs. Warren placed a comforting hand on Edwina's shoulder. "Your mother was kind and generous, and she would be proud of the woman that you have become."

"Thank you, Mrs. Warren," Edwina said, touched by her words.

Dropping her hand to her side, Mrs. Warren remarked, "Do not let us keep you. We would talk to you for hours if we could."

Edwina tipped her head at Mr. Warren. "I shall call upon you shortly to see how you are enjoying that book."

"I will be looking forward to it," Mr. Warren acknowledged.

Wearing a stern expression, she asserted in the firmest voice she could muster up, "And do not leave that chair for any reason until the doctor says you can."

Mr. Warren saluted her, his eyes holding mirth. "Yes, my lady."

"Good," Edwina said. "Then my work here is done."

Mrs. Warren gestured towards the corridor. "Allow me to walk you to the door."

While they approached the main door, Edwina said, "I hope I was able to convince Mr. Warren to remain in that chair a little while longer."

"I hope so," Mrs. Warren responded.

Edwina stepped out of the cottage and said, "Good day."

With a warm smile gracing her lips, Mrs. Warren informed her, "You are always welcome in our home. I hope you know that."

"I do."

Mrs. Warren waved her hand in front of her. "Now, off with you. Go enjoy dinner with that handsome gentleman."

"I never said he was handsome."

"You didn't need to," Mrs. Warren said as she closed the door.

Edwina started down the path, wondering what Mrs.

Warren was thinking saying such an outlandish thing. It didn't matter that Lord Hilgrove was handsome. She had no interest in spending any more time than she had to with him.

Standing in front of a mirror, Miles meticulously adjusted his cravat before his valet helped him into his jacket. Bailey had been his batman during the war and they had fought side by side with one another on countless missions.

However, those days felt like a lifetime ago.

An image of Arabella flashed in his mind, and he quickly banished it. Dwelling on the past served no purpose. His wife was gone. Why couldn't he just accept it and move on? Yet the pain remained, taking hold of his heart and making him utterly miserable.

Bailey took a step back and asked, "Will there be anything else, my lord?"

"Not at this time," he replied. "You may go."

After Bailey had departed from the room, Miles walked over to the window and stared out into the gardens. He sighed as he dropped his head. It was a blessing and a curse to fall in love. He had created beautiful memories with Arabella, but in the end, he was just left with an empty heart.

Faintly hearing the dinner bell ringing, Miles knew it was time to put his mask on once more. If anyone saw how much he was hurting, they would pity him. And he didn't want anyone's pity. He was doing just fine on his own. But even he couldn't fathom his own lie.

Miles crossed the room and left his bedchamber. As he started down the corridor, he saw Edwina emerging from her own bedchamber. She was wearing a black gown and her hair was elegantly swept up into an elaborate chignon. She really was a pretty thing, but that hardly mattered to him. He had no more interest in looking for a wife than chewing glass.

He noticed the moment she caught sight of him, as her eyes widened, and she started fidgeting with her hands in front of her.

"My lady," Miles acknowledged.

Edwina tipped her head. "My lord," she murmured.

Miles came to a stop next to her, knowing the polite thing to do would be to escort her to the dining room. But was that what Edwina would want? He didn't want to do anything that would make her feel uncomfortable.

That was one thing he appreciated about Arabella. She was unapologetically forthright. He always knew where he stood with her because she would speak her mind. It was just one of the many reasons why he loved her so much.

He decided to try a different approach with Edwina. "Seeing as we are going in the same direction, would you mind showing me where the drawing room is?"

Edwina nodded, albeit weakly. "Yes, of course. It would be my privilege."

They started walking down the corridor and he stole a glance at Edwina. Her eyes were downcast, and she appeared withdrawn.

He should have been satisfied with the silence, yet an odd feeling tugged at him. He typically favored solitude, but now he found himself desiring to engage in conversation with Edwina.

"Did Mr. Warren appreciate the book you selected for him?" he asked. There. That was a safe question.

"He did," Edwina said, keeping her gaze straight ahead.

"I haven't read *Robinson Crusoe* in years, at least not since my days at Eton," Miles admitted.

Edwina spared him a glance as she revealed, "My father used to read it to me before bedtime. It was a time that I greatly cherished."

Taken aback by what she shared, he asked, "Dare I ask how old you were?"

"I was eight."

Miles gave her a curious look. "Was your father not concerned by the serious nature of the book?"

Edwina didn't seem concerned by his question. "My father encouraged me to think for myself and to find my own voice. He did not shy away from books that required much discussion on moral or cultural issues."

"Your father seems rather progressive."

"He was," Edwina agreed. "He felt education was important for a young woman to possess and would often sit in on my lessons with my governess." She paused before adding, "But I am still proficient at the usual pastimes for a lady."

"I had no doubt."

While they descended the stairs, Miles shared, "My parents sent me to Eton as soon as I came of age. My older brother was already there, but he refused to speak to me. He pretended as if I didn't exist."

"How awful," Edwina murmured.

Miles shrugged. "John had his group of friends and I had mine. It wasn't until we attended university that we became close, at least, somewhat."

"It must have been nice to have a brother, someone to rely on," Edwina said. "I always wished for a sibling to play with."

"Be careful what you wish for," Miles teased. "John used to put frogs down the back of my trousers whenever we were by the stream by our country home. He thought it was hilarious the way I would have to shake my legs to get the frogs out."

Edwina looked horrified by what he revealed. "What a terrible trick to play on one's own brother."

Miles grinned, finding amusement in that recollection. "That was tame in comparison to what John usually did."

"I can't imagine."

They stepped down onto the marble floor and headed

towards the drawing room. He didn't truly need Edwina's assistance to locate the drawing room, but he was glad that he had asked her. She conversed with him, despite being reluctant to do so. But that had been enough… for now.

As they stepped into the drawing room, Miles saw Bennett conversing with his mother in the center of the room.

When Lady Dallington saw him, her eyes lit up. "Miles, it is so good to see you," she exclaimed. "It has been far too long."

Miles bowed. "Yes, it has, my lady." He had always enjoyed spending time with Lady Dallington. She not only exuded a welcoming warmth but also had a talent for making everyone in her presence feel cherished. There had always been a slight pang of envy towards Bennett, considering Miles had lost his own mother at a young age.

Lady Dallington shifted her attention towards Edwina. "You look lovely, my dear."

Edwina offered her an appreciative glance. "Thank you," she replied before moving to stand by her aunt.

Bennett approached him and said in a hushed voice, "I was rather surprised to see you enter with my cousin. Did she show you the way to the drawing room?"

"She did," Miles replied, choosing not to disclose that he had known the way all along. He was just being a gentleman.

"Did Edwina actually speak to you?" Bennett inquired.

"Yes, and we had a nice conversation," he admitted.

Bennett gave him a look of surprise. "That is rather interesting, considering my cousin is not one to talk with strangers."

"We aren't exactly strangers, as I was properly introduced to her," Miles pointed out.

"I recall since I was the one who introduced you two," Bennett said, a smirk playing on his lips. "Dare I ask what you two spoke about?"

Miles shook his head, trying to brush off the prying question. "Aren't you being rather intrusive?" he asked.

"More intrigued than anything else," Bennett replied.

Sighing, Miles gave in. "If you must know, we spoke about John."

Bennett's brow lifted. "You don't speak of John too often."

"No, I don't," Miles agreed, hoping to put an end to this line of questioning. Talking about his brother's death was far too painful.

However, Bennett either didn't care or didn't notice his discomfort. "I have thought of John often these past few months."

Miles scoffed. There wasn't a day that went by that he didn't think about his brother or Arabella. "Would you like a medal?" he grumbled.

He knew he was being rude but he couldn't seem to help himself. Opening up meant risking what he might reveal, and vulnerability was not something he could afford at the moment. Not here. Not now.

Undeterred by his brusque remark, Bennett persisted, "I hope you know you aren't alone in this. Many people share in your grief."

Miles stared back at his friend in disbelief. Bennett couldn't possibly understand the agony of losing a wife, an unborn child, and a brother, all within a few months of each other. His friend might offer sympathy, but the depth of pain Miles endured every single day went beyond anyone's comprehension.

His unrelenting grief had led his commanding officer to strongly advise him to sell his commission, citing distraction. It wasn't just the loss of his family. He had lost his career, something he had worked diligently to obtain. And it was all gone in one fell swoop.

As he debated on the words that he would unleash on his

friend, Lord Dallington entered the room and greeted him. "Welcome to our home, Miles."

"Thank you, my lord," Miles said, hoping his words sounded cordial enough.

Lord Dallington approached his wife and kissed her on the cheek. "You look enchanting this evening, Wife."

Lady Dallington smiled, murmuring her thanks.

The warmth in Lord Dallington's voice seemed to diminish as he turned to acknowledge his niece. "Edwina," he said in a curt tone. "How did you occupy your time today?"

Edwina clasped her hands in front of her. "I called upon Mr. and Mrs. Warren at their cottage. Mr. Warren had a terrible fall and injured himself," she shared.

Lord Dallington barely seemed to listen as he spoke over her. "Good, good." He returned his attention back to Miles. "I was rather pleased when Bennett told us you would be visiting for a fortnight."

Miles gave a polite nod. "I appreciate you opening up your home to me," he said.

Growing somber, Lord Dallington remarked, "I was deeply saddened to hear that you lost John so closely to your wife." He paused. "Fortunately, with you inheriting a title, you were able to leave that blasted war behind."

Miles tensed as he worked to keep his voice steady. "Inheriting an earldom is not why I left the war," he asserted.

With a bob of his head, Lord Dallington replied, "Yes, but your influence will be much greater in the House of Lords than on the battlefield."

Miles struggled to keep a polite mask on his face as he revealed, "I have yet to take up my seat in the House of Lords."

Lord Dallington gave him a pointed look. "You must take your duty to King and Country much more seriously. You are an earl now and that comes with certain responsibilities."

Lady Dallington spoke up. Her soft voice carried a

warning as she addressed her husband. "Lionel, you are being terribly inconsiderate to our guest, considering his situation."

"Forgive me," Lord Dallington said, his expression softening as he turned to his wife. "I often become overly passionate on a subject that is dear to me."

The butler stepped into the room and announced dinner was ready to be served.

Lord Dallington extended his arm to his wife and led her from the drawing room.

Bennett offered Miles an apologetic look. "I apologize for my father. He can be rather blunt in his assessment of things."

"I remember," Miles said. "And you have nothing to apologize for. Lord Dallington isn't wrong. I should take up my seat in the House of Lords."

"You need time to grieve…"

Miles put his hand up. "Enough talk about this," he said, speaking over his friend. "I am famished."

Bennett's eyes held compassion as he tipped his head. "Very well." He turned back towards Edwina. "May I escort you to the dining room, Cousin?"

Edwina stepped forward. "Thank you," she responded.

Miles remained rooted in his spot as he watched them depart from the drawing room. He wished he could say that Lord Dallington's reaction to the death of his loved ones was uncommon, but it wasn't. It was all too familiar. He had endured too many conversations where people dismissed his grief as inconsequential or couldn't comprehend why he was still grieving.

All he yearned for was not to feel so broken. How he could achieve that, he wasn't quite sure.

Chapter Three

Edwina sat at the dining table as she listened to the conversation going on around her. She felt no need to interject her thoughts, not that they would be welcomed by her uncle, who appeared to barely tolerate her as of late.

She sat alone on her side of the table, which was preferable to her. Her cousin and Lord Hilgrove sat across from her, while her aunt and uncle occupied the opposite ends of the table.

Edwina took her fork and moved the food around her plate. Her uncle hadn't always treated her with such disdain. Growing up, she had always enjoyed being around him, but everything changed when he inherited the title from her father. He grew distant, almost cold, a stark change in his demeanor towards her.

She had often asked herself why the sudden change. Had she done something wrong to earn his ire? If so, she wished she knew what it was so she could fix it.

Her aunt's voice broke through her musings. "Are you not hungry, Dear?"

Realizing she had been caught woolgathering, Edwina

lowered her fork to the plate and replied, "I'm afraid not, but the food was delicious."

"That it was," her aunt agreed.

Her uncle cleared his throat, drawing her attention. "You should be more present in the conversation, especially when we have guests dining with us," he chided.

"Yes, Uncle," Edwina acknowledged.

"You mentioned calling upon someone earlier," her uncle said. "Who was that again?"

Edwina wasn't surprised that her uncle had dismissed what she had said earlier as unimportant. "Mr. and Mrs. Warren," she replied.

Her uncle gave her a blank stare. "Why would you wish to call upon your father's old butler?"

Edwina went to reply, but Bennett spoke up. "Mr. Warren is a good man and served Uncle Richard dutifully."

"Yes, well, now he is living off my good graces," her uncle grumbled. "I do not know what the blazes Richard was thinking about when he willed one of our cottages to the Warrens."

Bennett reached for his glass as he shared, "I find it admirable how Uncle Richard made sure to take care of the Warrens even after he passed."

Her uncle's expression was stern as he countered, "He still was a servant."

"That is very high-handed of you, Father," Bennett stated. "Besides, Mrs. Warren was a delightful housekeeper who always made sure I had plenty of biscuits during our visits."

The tension in the room rose as her uncle leaned forward in his seat. "There is a line that must be drawn with servants, but it seems Richard believed that line could be blurred."

Edwina knew her next words would not be well received by her uncle, but she said them anyway. "My father treated the Warrens like family."

"That is rubbish!" her uncle exclaimed. "By doing so, the Warrens would never have learned their place."

She bristled at her uncle's words, her back stiffening in response. She knew it was pointless to argue with him since he was an incredibly stubborn man who seemed to revel in disagreements. But he was wrong. Her father cared more about the people working around him than following what Society dictated.

Lord Hilgrove spoke up, his voice calm but firm. "I do believe it says a lot about a man by the way he treats his servants, or people that are less fortunate than himself."

"I am not for tar and feathering the servants, but I do think it is important that they know their place," her uncle insisted. "We have worked too hard to be lumped in with commoners. It is our birthright."

Lord Hilgrove seemed to take her uncle's words in stride as he shared, "I rather enjoyed serving in the Army, because no one seemed to care that I was a son of an earl. They only cared that I did my job, a job that many lives depended on."

Her uncle settled back in his seat. "I have no doubt that you served honorably in the war but life is much different on English soil."

"I wholeheartedly agree to that," Lord Hilgrove said.

Edwina leaned to the side as a footman stepped forward to retrieve her plate. With only dessert remaining, she anticipated retiring to her bedchamber for the evening, looking forward to her nightly routine of reading by the crackling fire in the hearth.

Her aunt redirected her focus towards Lord Hilgrove. "Have you been to Town since you have returned from the war?"

"No, I'm afraid my country estate has commanded much of my attention, and I have little time for frivolous things," Lord Hilgrove responded.

"That is a shame. Everyone deserves to have fun, once in a while," her aunt said.

"I'm afraid my brother didn't spend the time necessary to make our estate profitable and it has taken much work to bring it up to snuff," Lord Hilgrove shared.

Her aunt smiled. "Elodie and Melody will be arriving any day now and they will be pleased to see you once more," she said. "They refused to leave their boarding school a day earlier than required."

"I do not blame them, considering I only have fond memories of my time at Eton," Lord Hilgrove shared.

Bennett chuckled. "Only fond memories?" he joked. "What about the time our headmaster punished us for sneaking out for a night swim at the stream? Or when we caused a mouse invasion?"

"Mouse invasion?" Edwina asked.

"Yes, we had the ingenious idea of storing food in our dormitories, despite it being against the rules," Bennett said. "For a few days, we thought we had outwitted our headmaster and we feasted on food late into the evening."

Edwina leaned forward in her seat. "What happened?"

Bennett's lips curled upward. "The mice arrived in droves and ate through everything. It was awful, and it didn't take a genius to figure out who the culprits were. We were severely punished and I couldn't sit down for days."

"How awful," Edwina murmured.

"No, what is awful is sharing a bed with mice," Lord Hilgrove added. "They went after the crumbs in my bed, and it didn't matter that I was occupying it."

Edwina shuddered. "I can't even imagine how awful that would be."

A somber expression crossed Lord Hilgrove's face. "As awful as that was, it was nothing compared to the numerous rats we encountered on the Continent."

"I'm sorry," Edwina said, a sense of inadequacy lingering in her words.

"No, it is me that should apologize," Lord Hilgrove remarked. "I should not have broached the subject of the war over supper, particularly with ladies present."

Finding herself curious, Edwina asked, "What was the war like?"

Apparently, that was the wrong thing to ask because Lord Hilgrove stiffened, his once open countenance cloaked by the shadows of memory, and his eyes grew guarded. "I cannot explain in detail the depravity that I saw and the lives that were lost, some in such a senseless manner."

Before Edwina could respond, her uncle interjected with a stern rebuke, "What were you thinking, Edwina? You can't just ask someone about the war. That was rather thoughtless of you, considering ladies do not speak of such things."

Edwina's eyes grew downcast as she tried to pretend that her uncle's words didn't affect her so deeply. He was always so quick to chide her, too quick.

"Lady Edwina did nothing wrong, and I didn't mean to imply as much," Lord Hilgrove stated, coming to her defense. "War is a fascinating topic yet a harrowing subject, and I could understand why it piqued her interest."

Bringing her gaze up, Edwina couldn't quite believe what had just happened. This man she hardly knew had just defended her. In a soft voice, she said, "Thank you, my lord."

Their eyes met again, and Edwina saw a kindness in his expression that carried over into his eyes. Though not quick to smile, there was a genuineness to him that she found captivating.

"Well, shall we eat our dessert?" her aunt asked.

Edwina lowered her gaze, feeling a subtle warmth creeping up her cheeks for having held Lord Hilgrove's gaze for so long, as she reached for her spoon.

"We are playing a game of pall-mall tomorrow. Who would care to join us?" Bennett asked the table.

"We are?" Lord Hilgrove inquired.

Bennett nodded with enthusiasm. "Indeed, we are going to make you have fun here, whether you want to or not. We are a fun family."

"I have a series of meetings all day tomorrow," her uncle shared.

"And I have a fitting session with the dressmaker," her aunt informed them. "Perhaps I shall join you, depending on the time you play."

Bennett sighed theatrically. "It would seem that we are not as entertaining as we believe. We should be dubbed the 'I am too busy to properly enjoy myself' family."

With a brief glance at Lord Hilgrove, Edwina said, "I will join you."

"Wonderful," Bennett declared. "However, we will need one more person to join us. Do you think your friend, Miss Bawden, would be interested in joining us?"

"I can ask," Edwina responded.

"We shall play at dawn," Bennett announced, emphasizing each word with a dramatic sweep of his hand.

"Dawn?" Lord Hilgrove raised an eyebrow in disbelief. "You don't actually expect us to partake in a game at such an early hour?"

Bennett feigned a mock expression of disapproval. "Very well. We shall play after breakfast so my dandy friend here can sleep in."

"I never said I sleep in," Lord Hilgrove said.

"Don't forget to don a cap this evening to preserve your impeccable hair," Bennett teased. "We wouldn't want your locks tousled for our pall-mall game."

"You are a muttonhead," Lord Hilgrove muttered.

Bennett placed a hand over his chest. "You insult me in

front of the ladies?" he asked. "That isn't very gentlemanly of you."

"Well, I am sure they already know what a muttonhead you are," Lord Hilgrove retorted.

A laugh escaped Edwina's lips at their banter, and she brought her hand up to cover her mouth.

Pushing back his chair, her uncle declared, "I think it is about time for a glass of port. Gentlemen, would you care to join me?"

As her cousin and Lord Hilgrove followed suit, her aunt caught Edwina's gaze and inquired, "Did you plan to read this evening?"

"I did," Edwina replied. "Is that all right?"

Her aunt's expression softened. "You don't need my permission. You are welcome to read anytime you wish."

"Thank you," Edwina expressed as she pushed back her chair. "Goodnight, Aunt Catherine."

"Goodnight, my dear," her aunt responded.

While Edwina departed from the dining room, she found herself eager for her nightly routine. There was a particular joy in changing into something more comfortable and indulging in her favorite pastime- reading. These quiet times reminded her of how she used to spend time with her father.

The sun had just peeked over the horizon as Miles sat atop his horse on a hill that overlooked Brockhall Manor. He had always enjoyed waking up early, giving him the opportunity to take time for himself without all the distractions. Although, as of late, his thoughts stewed in his mind, making it rather unbearable to find solace even in the quiet dawn.

He shouldn't be here, he thought. He should be back at his estate, working on his accounts and ensuring his tenants were being taken care of. Why was he wasting his time here? Bennett was trying to help him, but he was past hope. Broken. No one could help him overcome what he had been through.

A sudden movement in the distance diverted his troubled thoughts. He watched as Lady Edwina raced across the fields with poise, despite her breakneck speed. She didn't slow her horse as she veered towards the woodlands.

Miles gripped the reins tighter in his hands, concerned for her safety. The woodlands were treacherous, even with a marked trail, and such reckless speed could lead to injury. At least, that was his experience of the woodlands on his lands.

But it was none of his business. How Edwina rode her horse shouldn't matter to him so why did his eyes remain on the path that she had taken?

Botheration.

He should return his horse to the stables and leave well enough alone. However, he was unable to do so. He felt compelled to ensure that Edwina was well. An unforeseen desire to protect her seemed to cloud his judgment, leaving him with one option.

Miles kicked his horse into a run and headed towards the woodlands. Once he arrived at the trail where Edwina had disappeared, he eased his horse into a slower pace entering the woods. The trees formed a natural canopy overhead, casting dappled shadows that heightened the contrast between light and darkness in the early morning.

Moving along the path, Miles couldn't help but be entranced by the serene beauty that unfolded around him. Sunlight filtered through the foliage, creating a mesmerizing dance of shadows on the forest floor.

Up ahead, he saw Edwina's horse before he saw her. She was sitting on a large rock, her gaze fixed on a gently meandering stream. She remained unaware of his presence, lost in contemplation with her back turned towards him.

Now that he confirmed that Edwina was safe, the sensible

choice would be to leave and allow her the tranquility of the moment.

But something stopped him, and it was that something that caused him to dismount his horse.

Keeping a firm hold on the reins in his hand, he walked towards Edwina, a keen awareness of the potential consequences if anyone discovered them alone in the woodlands.

Edwina didn't seem to notice his presence as he approached. He didn't want to scare the poor girl, so he said in a soft voice, "Lady Edwina."

She gasped as she quickly moved off the rock, creating more distance between them. "What are you doing here?" she demanded.

"I saw you entering the woodlands and I wanted to ensure you were all right," Miles said, knowing how absurd he sounded at the moment. Why had he thought this was a good idea?

"As you can see, I am well," Edwina stated. "You may go."

Miles nodded. "I would be remiss if I did not tell you that you ride your horse far too recklessly and I would encourage you to use some restraint, especially when entering the woodlands."

She offered him a shy smile. "You wouldn't be the first person to tell me so, but I do thank you for your concern."

"How did you learn to ride like that?" Miles asked.

"My father said I was in the saddle before I could walk," Edwina shared. "I have always had a fascination with horses."

Miles studied Edwina for a moment. She seemed much more forthright than usual, as if the woodlands gave her strength.

Edwina furrowed her brow. "What is it?"

"You are not as reserved as you usually are," Miles observed.

"I suppose I'm not," Edwina said.

Miles' eyes roamed over his surroundings and acknowledged, "I think you might have found the most picturesque place I have ever seen."

Turning her attention back towards the stream, Edwina remarked, "This was my father's favorite place to come and sit. He would do so for hours. When I want to feel close to him, I come here and try to remember his voice. He said my name in a way only a father could, a way that I knew meant love."

"I am sorry for your loss," Miles said, knowing his words were wholly inadequate.

Edwina acknowledged his words with a subtle tip of her head, choosing to remain silent. Not that he blamed her. He had heard that same phrase offered countless times after the deaths of his wife and brother. He couldn't help but wonder if people uttered these words out of genuine empathy or merely as a societal obligation.

They lingered there, time stretching out before them. Miles sensed he should depart, yet against his own judgment, he inquired, "How long has it been?"

"A little over four months now," Edwina sighed. "Everyone said that it gets easier with time, but they are wrong."

"That they are. No amount of time will fill the void that was left when your father died. It festers, robbing life of its joy."

Edwina regarded him with curiosity. "You speak from experience." Her words carried a weight of knowing, as if she had already assumed his answer.

"I do, regretfully so," he admitted, reluctant to disclose more.

"That person must have meant a great deal to you," she prodded gently, her words laced with sympathy.

Miles felt his back grow rigid at her words. "They were very dear to me." That was all he wished to say at the moment.

Thankfully, Edwina seemed to sense his discomfort and

did not press him. Instead, she said, "My uncle thinks I should just move on from my father's passing, just as he has so easily done."

"Everyone grieves differently," he attempted.

"I don't think my uncle grieved at all." Her hand shot up to her mouth. "Forgive me. That was—"

Miles interjected, "The truth."

She lowered her hand and responded, "Yes, but I shouldn't have said such a thing."

"You need not fear. I will not betray your confidence," Miles assured her.

Edwina offered him a grateful look. "How is it that you are awake at such an early hour?" she asked. "I thought you preferred to sleep in."

"No, Bennett implied such, but I enjoy waking up before dawn and being alone with my thoughts," he said.

"The mornings are the only time that I feel as if I am able to breathe."

Miles led his horse to the stream to drink. "I do apologize for intruding on your solitude. That was rather thoughtless of me."

Edwina's expression softened. "I know it may sound contradictory, but it is nice to not be alone." She hesitated before adding, "I am sorry that I asked you about the war. That was callous of me."

Miles grew somber. "The war was my life. Until it wasn't. Now I am left a broken man with nothing to show for it." The weight of his words hung in the quiet air, as the stream continued its peaceful murmur.

"I share your sentiments, except for the war part. My father was my whole world. Until he wasn't," she remarked.

Edwina grew silent, and he feared he might have unintentionally upset her. As he was about to express his concern, she spoke up. "I should be going. We wouldn't want to risk being seen with one another, considering the circumstances."

"I had a similar thought as well."

She bit her lower lip before saying, "It was nice to have someone to talk to. I grow tired of everyone looking at me with pity."

Miles knitted his brows together, genuinely puzzled. "Why would anyone pity you?"

Her gaze grew distant. "Why, indeed?" she asked. "I am an orphan and I have to rely on my uncle for support."

A sympathetic frown formed on Miles' face. "That is your uncle's duty to do so. I must assume he is your guardian."

"He is, but I do not wish to be 'a duty,'" Edwina responded with a bitter undertone. "My uncle barely seems to tolerate me these days."

Miles felt a surge of empathy for Edwina's plight. "I do not know what I can say that could help you."

Edwina's shoulders drooped, no doubt weighed down by her troubles. "That is the thing. I don't know what you could say either. It is the plight of being a female, I suppose."

Miles wished he had the perfect words to offer solace, to dispel the sadness not just from her eyes but from the depths of her soul. However, he felt useless to help. He couldn't even seem to help himself. Why would he think he could help another?

He watched as Edwina went to retrieve her horse and lead him back to the large rock. In a swift motion, she used the rock to climb onto her saddle.

"I could have helped you," Miles pointed out.

"You could have, but I have learned to manage on my own," Edwina said, a tinge of vulnerability in her voice.

Miles stepped closer to her horse and placed a hand on its neck. "I will have you know that your cousin loves you very much."

Edwina bobbed her head. "I love Bennett. He has been a saving grace to me ever since my father died. Without him, and my aunt, I don't know how I would have survived these past few months. He understands me without words and offers unwavering support. It has been nice to have such an ally by my side."

"What of Lord Winston?"

"He is in London, working as a barrister. He is determined to prove himself as more than just a second son," Edwina shared. "He came home for my father's funeral but departed shortly thereafter. I do believe he is expected home when Elodie and Melody return from boarding school."

"Are you close with your other cousins?"

A wistful smile played on Edwina's lips. "I am. They used to come spend the summers at Brockhall Manor and we would have such fun. It was a time that I greatly cherish."

"That sounds perfect."

"It was," Edwina agreed, her eyes reflecting the fond memories. "We would stay up late, wake up early, and go swimming in the pond, much to my father's chagrin. It was rather idyllic, at least while it lasted. We all seemed to grow up much too fast."

"I do believe that is a common sentiment."

Edwina adjusted the reins in her hand, her fingers tracing the contours thoughtfully. "I tried to convince my father to send me to the same boarding school as Elodie and Melody, but he was adamant that I have a governess. I think he wanted to keep me close."

"Do you blame him for that?"

"No, especially now," Edwina replied. "I'm glad that I was able to spend so much time with him, not knowing how long it would last."

Miles took a step back. "If only we had more time with our loved ones. Sometimes they are taken much too early."

"I agree, wholeheartedly."

An unusual calm settled upon him, and he found himself drawn to linger in Edwina's presence. It felt as if his soul could finally breathe again. It was unnerving, and yet, all he felt was calm. Peace. It was a feeling that he hadn't felt for some time.

Unsure of why she had elicited such a reaction in him, Miles remarked, "I should not keep you any longer, but I have enjoyed conversing with you."

"And I, you," Edwina responded. "I shall see you back at the manor."

Miles gave her a chiding look. "Do try to avoid riding at such a breakneck speed."

"What is the point, then?" Edwina retorted.

He chuckled. "I see that stubbornness is a family trait," he joked.

Edwina laughed, a beautiful sound that momentarily stole Miles' breath. "Yes, the Lockwood family is known for our stubbornness. It has been passed down for many generations."

Miles cleared his throat, forcing himself to look away. "Good day, my lady."

"Good day, my lord," Edwina responded before she urged her horse forward.

As he watched Edwina disappear down the path, Miles was forced to recognize that his initial impression of her had been incorrect. She was reserved, given the right circumstances, but she also could be rather pleasant to converse with. He usually found most conversations with young women to be tedious, but Edwina was different. She was purposeful in her thoughts. A trait that he greatly appreciated.

Nevertheless, he would be mindful to keep his distance. He had no intention of delving deeper into more of an acquaintance with Edwina.

Chapter Four

Reining in her horse in front of Brockhall Manor, Edwina gracefully dismounted and handed off the reins to the waiting footman.

She murmured her thanks before she headed up the stairs towards the main door. The lanky butler, White, stood to the side, his impeccable black hair slicked back and glistening in the sun.

With a subtle nod, he acknowledged her presence as he held the door open. Edwina entered the entry hall, casting a thoughtful glance at White's stoic expression. She wondered if there was a chance to witness a smile on his face, a rare sight since he took charge as the butler.

"Did you have an enjoyable ride, my lady?" White asked.

"I did," Edwina replied. "I shall go change and come down for breakfast."

White closed the door as he said, "Very good."

Edwina turned on her heel and made her way towards the stairs. Her gaze swept over the entry hall, a space her uncle had left untouched. Yet, it seemed so different now that her father wasn't here.

As her hand touched the cool iron railing, she began

ascending the stairs, reflecting on the vulnerability she had shown Lord Hilgrove in the woodlands earlier. She questioned what he must think of her, having exposed so much of herself. However, she did believe him when he assured her that he wouldn't betray her confidence.

The depths of trust she placed in a man she hardly knew puzzled her, yet she couldn't deny it. There was an unspoken connection in their shared grief that resonated with her, providing the courage to confide in him- a rare occurrence since her father's passing. Few cared to know the true extent of her thoughts and pain, but with Lord Hilgrove, she felt heard.

Edwina proceeded down the corridor until she arrived at her bedchamber, opening the door. Inside, her silver-haired lady's maid was busy organizing the vanity table in the corner.

Martha, who had once served her mother in the same capacity, greeted Edwina with a warm smile. "How was your ride?" she asked.

"It went well," Edwina replied as she closed the door behind her.

"You are back much earlier than I was expecting," Martha noted.

Edwina didn't dare admit that Lord Hilgrove had been the reason she hadn't tarried as long as she usually did in the woodlands. "I didn't wish to be late for breakfast," she offered. At least that much was true.

Martha eyed her curiously. "Since when do you care about being on time to breakfast?"

"Since we have a guest residing with us," Edwina explained. "I do not wish to give my uncle any reason to chide me."

"Your uncle cares for you," Martha attempted.

Edwina huffed in disbelief. "He used to," she replied. "But ever since he inherited my father's title, he chides me for the tiniest infraction."

"Perhaps he does care too much about what you do," Martha responded as she walked over to the wardrobe. "Shall we change you out of your riding habit?"

"I suppose that would be for the best."

Martha removed a black muslin gown from the wardrobe. "What are your thoughts on Lord Hilgrove?"

"I have none," she rushed out.

"Not even one?"

Edwina shook her head. "I do not think upon Lord Hilgrove at all," she replied. "He is *Bennett*'s guest, not mine, and his appearance does not matter to me, especially since I don't plan to spend more time with him than necessary."

Martha seemed like she wanted to delve into the topic further, but thankfully chose to leave well enough alone. "We should hurry if you want to be on time for breakfast," she suggested.

Edwina had no desire to talk about Lord Hilgrove. He was a nice enough man, but that is all it was. In a fortnight, he would go his way and she would go her way. He was just a guest in their home, and her politeness was solely for Bennett's sake. Nothing more.

Once she was dressed, Edwina departed from her bedchamber and hurried towards the dining room. She stepped into the room and saw Bennett and Lord Hilgrove sitting at the long rectangular table. They both stood as she entered, and she waved them back down.

"Good morning, Cousin," Bennett greeted. "You are remarkably punctual for breakfast today." His words carried a hint of playfulness.

As a footman pulled out a chair for her, Edwina sat down. "I deemed it prudent to be on time since we have a guest."

Bennett shifted in his seat, turning towards Lord Hilgrove. "Edwina has a tendency to be fashionably late for breakfast due to her morning rides in the woodlands. She always seems to lose track of time."

"Is that so?" Lord Hilgrove inquired, his gaze fixed on Edwina.

Edwina leaned slightly as a footman placed a plate of food before her. "Bennett is prone to exaggeration."

"That he is," Lord Hilgrove agreed.

Bennett smirked. "But in this case, I do not exaggerate," he said with a hint of amusement. "There is a stream deep within the woodlands that Edwina loves to escape to. She will just sit on a large rock and retreat to her own thoughts for what feels like hours."

"Perhaps Lady Edwina is attempting to ignore you, but you aren't clever enough to take the hint?" Lord Hilgrove suggested.

Edwina grinned, her hand instinctively covering her mouth.

Bennett chuckled. "Who wouldn't relish in my company?"

"Lots of people," Lord Hilgrove promptly replied, raising an eyebrow. "I am sure our teacher from Eton, Mr. Maddocks, would agree."

"That is because he couldn't take a joke," Bennett defended himself.

"Or it had something to do with the fact that you put a hedgehog into his bed and laughed when the headmaster informed you that Mr. Maddock had been attacked," Lord Hilgrove retorted dryly.

Bennett merely shrugged, a glint of mischief still present in his eyes. "Exactly, *he* couldn't take a joke."

Lord Hilgrove looked heavenward. "My friend is an idiot."

"You choose to associate with me. What does that say about you?" Bennett joked. "Besides, Edwina loves my company, don't you?"

Edwina lowered her hand to her lap. "I do." Her voice held a hint of teasing before adding hesitantly, "Some of the time."

With a shake of his head, Bennett feigned hurt. "You have betrayed me, Cousin."

Lord Hilgrove gave her an approving nod. "Well done, my lady," he praised. "You have managed to knock Bennett down a peg or two."

Edwina resisted the urge to smile at Lord Hilgrove. Instead, she masked her amusement with a demure sip of her tea. She reached for her fork and began to eat her breakfast.

"Will Miss Bawden be joining us on the lawn today for our game of pall-mall?" Bennett inquired.

She swallowed the bite of food before replying, "Yes, I received word early this morning."

"Wonderful," Bennett said with enthusiasm. "I have played with Miss Bawden before and she isn't completely incompetent at pall-mall."

"That is quite the compliment coming from you," Lord Hilgrove quipped.

Bennett nodded. "Unfortunately, you are easily the worst player of the group and you will no doubt embarrass yourself in front of the ladies."

Lord Hilgrove's brow furrowed in annoyance. "I doubt that."

"No, it is true," Bennett insisted. "I suspect you haven't picked up a mallet since your interests have been elsewhere."

"You mean the war?" Lord Hilgrove asked incredulously.

Bennett waved his hand in front of him. "A true gentleman never abandons his beloved game of pall-mall, no matter the circumstances," he joked with dramatic flair. "Instead of fighting with muskets, you could have brought mallets and balls with you and played on the battlefield."

Lord Hilgrove sat back in his chair, appearing unimpressed by his friend's antics. "Do you even know how war works?"

"It can't be overly complicated since you participated in it," Bennett remarked with a teasing smirk.

Lord Hilgrove let out an exasperated sigh. "Why am I friends with you again?" he grumbled.

"Because I am without a doubt the most entertaining person you know," Bennett responded.

"No, that is most assuredly not it," Lord Hilgrove said.

Edwina couldn't help but smile as she watched the banter between her cousin and Lord Hilgrove unfold. Their playful teasing was a welcome distraction from the tense atmosphere that had surrounded her since her father's passing.

Turning towards her, Bennett asked, "What say you?"

She dabbed at the corners of her mouth with her napkin before inquiring, "About what, exactly?"

"Do you know why Miles is friends with me?" Bennett questioned.

With a quick glance at Lord Hilgrove, she answered carefully, "I cannot presume to know his reasonings."

"You are of no use, Cousin," Bennett joked, his words softened by a smile. "You should be on my side, not Lord Hilgrove's."

"I am on no one's side," Edwina said.

Just then, her aunt stepped into the room and the men stood. "Well said, Edwina," she praised. "I have learned to stay out of Bennett's spats with his friends."

"It is not a spat, Mother," Bennett clarified. "We are having a serious conversation about why Lord Hilgrove is friends with me."

After her aunt settled back into her seat, the men resumed their positions. "I have often wondered how you two ended up friends," her aunt mused, her eyes flickering between Lord Hilgrove and Bennett. "Lord Hilgrove has always had a seriousness to him, and Bennett, well, is Bennett. He is special, in more ways than one."

Lord Hilgrove smiled. "I couldn't agree with you more, my lady."

Her aunt's attention shifted towards Edwina. "I understand that Miss Bawden will be joining you for your game of pall-mall today," she said.

"It is true," Edwina confirmed.

Her aunt turned to Bennett again, giving him a pointed look. "Miss Bawden would make a fine choice for a bride, considering she is the granddaughter of an earl," she said.

Bennett's expression tightened at his mother's words. "Mother…" Bennett started.

Placing her hand up, Lady Dallington spoke over him. "You are nearly thirty years old. It is time for you to take a wife."

"In due time," Bennett responded.

Lady Dallington took a sip of her drink. "You say that, but you have made no effort in finding one. I had four children at your age."

"Our situations are vastly different," Bennett argued, his voice rising in frustration. The lines on his forehead deepened as he tried to make his point.

Her aunt reached for her fork, a glimmer of mischief dancing in her eyes. "And that, my dears, is how you can successfully goad Bennett into silence," she teased.

Edwina couldn't contain her laugher at her aunt's playful antics.

"Now, let us enjoy our meal before you all must run along to play your rousing game of pall-mall," her aunt encouraged with a warm smile.

After breakfast, Miles descended the stairs of the manor and made his way towards the sprawling lawn. The sun was already high in the sky, casting its warm rays upon him, making him deucedly uncomfortable. He had no desire to play a game of pall-mall, but he didn't dare disappoint Edwina.

He had enjoyed speaking with her this morning in the woodlands, far more than he should have. She seemed more open and talkative, yet he could still sense that she held a part of herself back from him. He understood that feeling all too well.

As Miles reached for a mallet, a gloved hand swooped in and took the one he had wanted. He turned around to see a tall, redheaded young woman with a mischievous smile on her face.

"I always get the mallet with the blue stripe on it," the young woman declared, her voice carrying a hint of playful competition. "Blue has been my lucky color as of late."

"Is any color truly lucky?" Miles questioned.

She laughed. "For me, it is," she replied confidently. "I have won every match the last few times that I have played with this mallet, and I don't intend to break my streak today."

While Bennett approached them, he chimed in, "I do believe introductions are in order. Lord Hilgrove, allow me the privilege of introducing you to Miss Bawden, the eldest daughter of our esteemed vicar."

Miles bowed. "The pleasure is all mine."

Miss Bawden dropped into a curtsy, her grip firm on the coveted mallet. "My lord," she murmured.

Bennett stopped next to them and warned, "Just so you know, Winston is Miss Bawden's archenemy."

At the mere mention of Winston's name, Miss Bawden groaned. "Your brother is simply terrible, absolutely dreadful," she declared.

Bennett chuckled and turned to him, saying, "Winston and Miss Bawden have been constantly at odds for many, many years now."

"I dreaded whenever Lord Winston came to visit Brockhall Manor. He would make my life utterly unbearable for the short time he was here on his visits," Miss Bawden stated.

Miles opened his mouth to inquire why that was, but Bennett spoke first. "Do not ask any questions," he urged, a teasing lilt in his voice. "Trust me, you don't want to get caught up in the tangled web of their longstanding feud."

Edwina's soft voice chimed in from behind them. "Bennett is right. The list of grievances between them is long and cumbersome."

"That is only because Lord Winston can't handle being proven wrong," Miss Bawden muttered under her breath.

"Neither can you," Edwina teased.

"You make a fair point," Miss Bawden reluctantly admitted. "But it is only because I am so rarely in the wrong."

Edwina smiled. "I see that you have your lucky blue mallet," she said, gesturing towards the mallet in Miss Bawden's hand.

"Mallets, themselves, cannot be lucky," Miles interjected.

Miss Bawden looked amused. "I see you are not a believer, but you will be. Once I beat you soundly, you will believe in the magic of the blue mallet."

"Magic does not exist," Miles argued.

"So say *you*," Miss Bawden retorted.

Miles shook his head, finding this conversation to be utterly ridiculous. "So says everyone."

Bennett's laughter rang out. "You are not going to win this argument, Miles," he said. "Miss Bawden would rather fall on her own sword than admit defeat."

"That is only because I have right on my side," Miss Bawden stated. "But enough of this talk, it is time to play pall-mall."

Reaching for a mallet, Bennett asked, "Shall we play doubles?"

Miss Bawden held her mallet up. "I will partner with Lord Dunsby," she announced. "Together, we will be an unstoppable team."

Bennett tipped his head at Miss Bawden before saying, "That means that Miles will be partnering with Edwina."

Miles turned to face Edwina. "I hope you have no objections about partnering with me."

"I have none," she responded.

As Miles reached for a mallet, his hand suddenly stilled and he asked with curiosity, "Dare I ask if you have a lucky mallet, as well?"

Edwina's eyes lit up with amusement. "I do not."

He retrieved a polished mallet and extended it towards her. "I hope this one will suffice."

"It will do quite nicely," Edwina said graciously. "I feel as if I should warn you that I am not nearly as competitive as Miss Bawden."

Miles shifted his gaze towards Miss Bawden and noticed that she was gracefully stretching with the mallet in her hands. "What is she doing?" he asked.

Edwina followed his gaze. "Miss Bawden takes pall-mall very seriously. She always stretches before a game."

"That is rather unconventional," Miles commented.

"You have seen nothing yet, I'm afraid," Edwina said. "Sometimes Miss Bawden will even crouch down and speak to her ball."

"What does she say?"

Edwina shrugged. "She mostly encourages it to go through the arch."

Miles selected a mallet for himself and said, "That would be a sight to behold."

"You should consider yourself lucky that you have never witnessed a game where Miss Bawden and Winston are playing," Edwina said. "It is pandemonium."

"Surely it can't be that bad," Miles remarked.

Bennett, who had been silently observing the conversation, stepped closer to them and lowered his voice. "Edwina is right. They both are far too competitive for their own good."

"Then why partner with Miss Bawden if she is so competitive?" Miles inquired.

A determined gleam came into Bennett's eyes. "To win, of course," he responded.

While Bennett walked away, Edwina asked, "What is our plan?"

"A plan?" Miles questioned. "Do we truly need one?"

Edwina bobbed her head. "We will surely lose if we do not have an effective strategy," she urged in a serious tone. "Do we want to plan our shots in advance or attempt to block our opponent?"

Miles couldn't help but grin at her insistence. "When did pall-mall become so complicated?"

"There are bragging rights to whoever wins pall-mall, and my family takes those very seriously," she explained. "If Bennett wins, then…"

"He will be more unbearable than he already is," Miles said, finishing her thought.

"Precisely," Edwina responded.

Miles shifted his gaze towards Bennett and Miss Bawden, who were engaged in hushed conversation near the refreshment table. No doubt planning their own strategy.

A moment of nostalgia washed over him as he remembered the last time he had played pall-mall was with Arabella. It was a sunny day much like this one, although the circumstances were vastly different. Arabella had been terrible at pall-mall- the worst he had ever seen. But she didn't let that stop her from playing with boundless enthusiasm. Nothing could dampen her spirits.

He couldn't do this. Quite frankly, he had no desire to participate in this game of pall-mall with the memories of Arabella still so vibrant in his mind.

Miles returned the mallet to its holder and took a deep breath. "I'm sorry, Lady Edwina. I can't do this."

Concern etched across her features as she gazed up at him. "It will be all right," she reassured him. "It is just a game. No one truly cares who wins or loses."

Knowing he owed her an explanation, Miles responded, "The last time I played pall-mall was with my late wife."

Her eyes filled with compassion. "I understand, more so than you know, considering my father loved pall-mall. He was the one who taught me how to play."

"Then how is it that you can play pall-mall without the memory of your father haunting you?" Miles inquired.

Edwina looked thoughtful for a moment before replying, "I never thought about it that way. To me, I am simply doing something that we both loved, and it brings back pleasant memories."

"Arabella was terrible at pall-mall. She could never quite hit the ball with the right amount of force," Miles admitted. "But winning wasn't important to her. She simply found joy in playing the game." He paused. "She used to say that she only came for the food."

With a glance at the refreshment table, Edwina said, "I do enjoy the food, as well."

"So you see why I can't play?" Miles asked.

Edwina brought her gaze back to his as she replied, "I don't, actually."

Taken aback by her response, he asked, "I beg your pardon?"

"I feel that you shouldn't stop living and enjoying the little moments just because your wife has passed on," Edwina explained, her voice gentle. "She wouldn't want you to avoid doing things you used to enjoy."

Miles' brow shot up. "Surely you cannot be serious?" he asked. "You presume to know what my wife would have wanted?" His words came out much harsher than he had intended.

Edwina winced. "I know it isn't my place—"

He spoke over her. "No, it isn't," he said. "Am I supposed to take advice from you- someone who only lost a father? I lost my wife and brother! It is not the same and do not try to pretend that it is."

Miles could see a flicker of emotion pass over her features, but he couldn't quite decipher what it was. Was it anger? Annoyance? Or something else entirely different? But it was evident that he had gotten a rise out of her.

"Forgive me," she murmured as she returned the mallet to its holder. "I do not feel much like playing anymore." Her eyes glistened with unshed tears as she spun on her heel. Hurrying up the pathway leading to the manor, she disappeared within its walls.

Miles felt a wave of guilt wash over him. He had been so insensitive, not considering how his words would affect her.

Bennett's inquiring voice came from behind him. "Where did Edwina go?" he asked.

Shifting uncomfortably in his stance, Miles admitted, "I'm afraid I upset her."

"What did you do?" Bennett asked, his words accusatory.

Facing his friend, Miles couldn't help but feel ashamed. "I may have insinuated that Edwina's grief is less than my own."

Bennett drew his brows together. "That is rather unfair of you to say."

"I know," Miles responded, knowing that is all he could say. He was in the wrong, and it pained him to admit that to himself.

Miss Bawden placed the mallet down. "Perhaps I should go see if Edwina is all right. Please excuse me," she said before she headed towards the manor.

Bennett's arms were crossed tightly over his chest, his eyes glinting with barely contained anger. "Do you care to explain yourself?" he demanded.

"No."

"Well, try anyways," Bennett stated.

Miles decided it would be best if he just told his friend the truth and hoped he would understand. "The last time I played pall-mall was with Arabella," he shared. "I informed Lady Edwina of this, and she encouraged me to still play."

"And?" Bennett prodded.

"That is all."

"So you responded by insulting her?"

"It wasn't my finest moment," Miles admitted.

Bennett uncrossed his arms, his expression softening slightly. "No, it wasn't," he agreed. "One cannot measure or compare the weight of grief of another."

Miles knew his friend was right, but Bennett didn't understand. No one could possibly grasp the immense depths of pain that consumed him each and every day. He was broken, a mere shell of the man he once was.

Turning his attention towards the manor, Bennett continued, "There may be one person who understands, but you pushed her away when she only wanted to offer her support."

In a steely voice, Miles said, "I do not need- or want- Lady Edwina's help."

With a shake of his head, Bennett countered, "Regardless, the next time you hurt my cousin, I will have no choice but to challenge you to a duel."

Miles resisted the urge to laugh. "You would lose. I am a trained soldier and sharpshooter."

"Most likely, but I love my cousin and I won't have her dishonored in her own home," Bennett declared in an unyielding and resolute tone.

"For what it is worth, I am sorry," Miles said, feeling contrite. "It was not my intention to dishonor Lady Edwina."

Bennett gave him a knowing look, conveying both understanding and disappointment. "I am not the one that you owe an apology to," he stated before making his way towards the manor.

Miles waited until his friend disappeared into the manor before he hung his head. What he had said to Lady Edwina was terribly unfair. Now he found himself in the uncomfortable position of having to apologize to her and make amends for his thoughtless words.

Chapter Five

Edwina hurried up the stairs as she fumed about her conversation with the arrogant Lord Hilgrove. He was truly insufferable, and his audacity to claim that his grief somehow ran deeper than hers only infuriated her more.

Who was he to tell her how *she* should feel?

As she entered the library, Edwina approached the tall windows that overlooked the sprawling estate. Lord Hilgrove was still standing on the lawn, clutching a mallet in his hands as he spoke to Bennett. He had a deep furrow etched between his brows, giving him an air of utter misery.

Lord Hilgrove's gaze shifted towards the window and Edwina quickly crouched down, ducking out of sight. She didn't want Lord Hilgrove to think that she had been spying on him- which she most definitely was not.

Her friend's amused voice came from the doorway. "What, pray tell, are you doing down there?"

Remaining in her low position, Edwina replied, "I did not want Lord Hilgrove to see me from the lawn."

"But why were you watching him in the first place?" Miss Bawden asked.

"I wasn't," Edwina insisted.

Miss Bawden's smile only seemed to widen. "But you were peering out the window at him."

"No, I came to the library, and I just happened to see him out there," Edwina clarified. "It was all very innocent, I assure you."

Stepping closer to the window, Miss Bawden said, "You can stand now. Lord Hilgrove is no longer on the lawn."

"Good," Edwina replied, rising and smoothing out her gown. "With any luck, he decided to shorten his trip and return home."

Miss Bawden studied Edwina's expression. "You are angry."

"I am," she confirmed, her jaw set in a determined line. "Lord Hilgrove said the most maddening thing. He said that the loss of my father wasn't as terrible as the loss of his brother and wife."

Miss Bawden raised an eyebrow. "Why should his opinion matter to you?"

"It doesn't."

"It appears as if it does," Miss Bawden pointed out. "You are clearly upset about it."

Edwina shrugged. "How can I not be? My father died and he tried to minimize my feelings."

Crossing her arms over her chest, Miss Bawden spoke gently but firmly. "Lord Hilgrove doesn't have the power to tell you how to feel; only you do."

"I should have known that you would take a practical approach to this," Edwina muttered.

Miss Bawden laughed. "Do you want me to hate Lord Hilgrove?" she asked. "Just say the word and I will do it."

"No, I don't want you to hate Lord Hilgrove. I don't even hate him," she reluctantly admitted.

"You seemed to get along nicely before he said something so bacon-brained," Miss Bawden remarked.

"We did," Edwina said. "He isn't awful."

"If that is true, then perhaps he just misspoke," Miss Bawden suggested.

"No, he spoke plainly enough."

Uncrossing her arms, Miss Bawden asked, "So we are back to disliking him?" Her eyes held a mischievous glint to them.

"No, I don't dislike him either. I am just angry at him," Edwina admitted. "Who tries to compare one's grief with another?"

Miss Bawden gave her a knowing look. "Someone who is hurting."

"I am hurting, too."

"It isn't a contest," Miss Bawden said. "Grief is a lonely walk alone. People will be there to try to help, but it is something that you must do on your own. In time, hopefully, you will come to your own peace."

"Does that excuse his behavior?"

Miss Bawden shook her head. "No, but it gives you some perspective," she replied. "Try to have some compassion towards his plight."

Edwina let out a frustrated sigh. "Whose side are you on?"

"Yours, and I always will be," Miss Bawden replied. "That is why I am telling you all these very intelligent things, if I do say so myself."

She had to admit that her friend did have a point. "Your advice isn't awful."

Miss Bawden beamed. "I daresay that I have been listening to my father far too much. Being a vicar's daughter does have some benefits."

"Your father is a good man."

"He is, but he doesn't know what to do with me," Miss Bawden shared. "He thinks I am far too outspoken."

"Which you are."

Miss Bawden gave her a look of innocence. "No more than any other young woman in the village."

Edwina laughed. "That is entirely untrue."

"Now whose side are *you* on?" Miss Bawden asked, using Edwina's words against her.

A knock came at the door, interrupting their conversation.

Turning her head, Edwina saw Lord Hilgrove standing in the doorway, his piercing gaze fixed upon her. "May I come in?" he asked, a hint of vulnerability in his baritone voice.

Edwina wanted to send him away, but something was holding her back. And it was that something that wanted to know what he had to say. "You may," she replied.

Lord Hilgrove stepped into the room. His tall frame and sharp features were softened by the sunlight that flooded through the windows. "I was hoping to speak to you, privately, if you don't mind," he said.

"I'm afraid that is impossible, my lord—" Edwina started.

Miss Bawden spoke over her, speaking quickly and confidently. "It is entirely possible, if I remain in the library for propriety's sake." She walked over to the chair in the far corner and settled into it gracefully. "I will sit right here, but I can't promise I won't eavesdrop. It is a terrible habit that I hope to overcome one day."

As Lord Hilgrove took a step closer to Edwina, she could feel her heart pounding in her chest. He lowered his voice, making her lean in slightly to hear him better. "I wanted to apologize to you for what I said earlier. It was wrong of me."

Edwina had no desire to make this easy on Lord Hilgrove. He had hurt her deeply with his words, and she needed to know his reasonings behind them. "Why did you say it, then?"

"Because I was being thoughtless," Lord Hilgrove admitted.

"That you were, but you meant it," Edwina said firmly. "Did you not?"

The silence hung heavy between them before Lord Hilgrove spoke up again. "Does it matter if I did?" he asked.

"It does to me," Edwina replied.

"I thought I did, but I was wrong to think so," Lord Hilgrove confessed. "I cannot measure your grief, just as you cannot measure mine."

Edwina could hear the sincerity in his voice, and she couldn't help but feel a sense of empathy for him. "I am sorry to hear about your wife and your brother," she said softly. "That must have been very hard to lose two people so closely together."

"It was," Lord Hilgrove replied, his voice thick with emotion. "And thank you."

"For what?"

Lord Hilgrove's lips tightened into a thin line. "Not looking at me like I am broken."

"Who thinks you are broken?" Edwina asked.

His shoulders slumped slightly. "Everyone," he declared dejectedly, the weight of his struggles evident in his tone.

Edwina cocked her head, studying him intently. "But you aren't broken," she reassured him. "You do know that."

A flicker of disbelief crossed Lord Hilgrove's features before he let out a slight huff. "You are wrong. I am terribly broken," he finally admitted, his voice slightly strained.

"Why?"

He gave her a baffled look. "Pardon?"

"Why do you think you are broken?" Edwina pressed.

Lord Hilgrove's eyes grew guarded and she knew that she had pushed him too far. "Do you accept my apology, my lady?" he asked, his voice taking on a formal tone.

"I do," Edwina replied without hesitation.

"Then this conversation is over," Lord Hilgrove declared, turning to leave.

Edwina reached out and touched his sleeve, stilling him. "I have never thought you were broken, my lord," she said. She wanted him to know that. Quite frankly, she *needed* him to know that.

Lord Hilgrove glanced down at her hand on his sleeve and

she quickly withdrew it, mortified by her brazen action. But she couldn't bear the thought that he was hurting. She wanted to show him that there was someone who believed in him.

He tipped his head in acknowledgment but not before she saw his burdens still weighing heavily on him. His suffering was evident in every line of his face and every spark of emotion in his eyes.

As Lord Hilgrove's figure retreated from the library, a deep sadness settled over Edwina. She saw him as a man who believed himself to be broken, a feeling she knew all too well.

Miss Bawden came to stand next to her, her voice carrying a playful lilt. "Do we still like Lord Hilgrove?" she asked.

"We do," Edwina said, turning to face her friend. "He is hurting, deeply so."

"As are you," Miss Bawden noted.

"Yes, but I want to help him."

Miss Bawden gave her a curious look. "How do you plan on doing that?" she asked. "After all, he does not strike me as the type that would welcome any assistance."

"No, he does not," Edwina agreed. "Which means I will have to go about it sneakily."

The corners of Miss Bawden's lips twitched upward in amusement. "You, sneaky? I never thought I would hear those words used to describe you," she teased.

Edwina straightened her back and put on a determined expression. "I can be sneaky."

Miss Bawden let out a laugh. "Let's say you have your moments of sneakiness. What is your plan?"

Hesitating for a moment, Edwina admitted, "I don't have one yet."

"Well then, we are off to a good start," Miss Bawden joked.

Edwina grew quiet. What could she say- or do- to help Lord Hilgrove? She wanted him to know that he wasn't alone in his grief. She understood, all too well. She knew the pain and struggle of rebuilding oneself after she had lost her father. In fact, she would never truly be the same after the suffering she had endured. The weight of her own sadness settled heavily on her heart.

Miss Bawden's expression tightened with concern as she gently suggested, "Perhaps it would be best to focus on your own grief for now. I can see how it is weighing heavily upon you."

"I have done nothing but focus on my own grief for what feels like an eternity," Edwina replied. "But I believe I am in a position to help Lord Hilgrove."

Miss Bawden didn't look convinced. "Even if what you are saying is true, why would he accept your help?"

Edwina squared her shoulders and met Miss Bawden's doubtful gaze. "I have to at least try," she said in a determined voice, feeling a newfound sense of purpose blossoming within. Maybe, just maybe, her own experiences could help Lord Hilgrove through his pain.

She had tried everything to ease her grief, but to no avail. But now, with this new endeavor, she hoped that by focusing on another's pain, hers would lessen. Perhaps even become tolerable.

As Miles made his way towards the gardens, he couldn't quite believe the audacity of Lady Edwina. She had been far too bold with him in the library. They were hardly acquaintances and she had tried pestering him with questions, questions that he did not want to answer. He couldn't.

Why couldn't everyone just leave him be? He wanted to wallow in his grief and misery, yet it seemed like every person he encountered wanted to help him. Memories of happier times still haunted him, taunting him with what he once had and lost. It was all gone now, snatched away in one swift and cruel blow.

He just needed to be alone. If he was smart, he would saddle his horse and leave this manor without concern for social niceties. It would be a great insult to depart early, but he was at his wits' end. He didn't want to pretend that all was well when he was struggling. Deeply.

Miles had just passed by the open study door when he heard Edwina's name being mentioned in a hushed and somber tone. His steps faltered in the corridor as his curiosity was piqued. He could not resist stopping to listen to what was being said about her.

Lord Dallington's voice carried through the study walls. "What am I supposed to tell her?" he asked, gruffly.

Another voice, unfamiliar to Miles, responded, "Tell her that there are no funds available for her."

"That isn't true though, is it?"

The unfamiliar voice remained steadfast. "It is true enough, at least as far as she is concerned."

Lord Dallington let out a deep sigh. "I suppose you are right," he conceded. "Although, on the other hand, do I even need to say anything? She is none the wiser about these funds."

"I will leave that decision up to you, my lord," the man said. "I shall see my way out."

Realizing that he needed to leave before he was caught eavesdropping, Miles quickly retreated down the corridor and slipped out the back door into the gardens.

He glanced back at the manor as his mind raced with thoughts of what he had overheard. What funds was Lord Dallington referring to? It almost sounded as if Edwina was being cheated out of some money.

Regardless, it wasn't his place to say or do anything. He was just a guest here. And he had no desire to intrude where he wasn't wanted.

Botheration.

Could he just stand back and say nothing, knowing that Lady Edwina was being treated unfairly? He let out a groan. Why had his curiosity gotten the best of him and he listened in on Lord Dallington's private conversation?

Miles knew that he had to do what his conscience dictated or else he would have more regrets. And he already had far too many of those.

Bennett's voice sounded beside him. "Miles," he said. "Is everything all right?"

Turning to face his friend, Miles asked, "Yes, why do you ask?"

"I have been calling your name, but you appeared deep in thought," Bennett replied. "Or you were just trying to ignore me."

"Yet, you didn't take the hint," Miles said lightly.

Bennett grinned. "I never do," he responded. "I thought we could ride into the village and have a drink at the pub."

"That sounds like a fine idea."

"You will discover that I am full of them."

Miles smirked. "You are full of something," he joked.

As they started walking towards the stables, Miles knew it was the perfect opportunity to discuss the conversation that he had just overheard. But how did he broach the subject? It was an odd question for him to be asking.

Miles just decided to say what needed to be said and be done with it. "Did Lady Edwina's father leave her an inheritance?" he asked.

Bennett looked over at him in surprise. "Why do you care?"

"I don't, but just humor me."

With a curious expression, Bennett divulged, "No, but my uncle did leave her a dowry of fifteen thousand pounds."

"That is a substantial dowry," Miles responded.

"It is," Bennett agreed. "Are you, by chance, interested in my cousin?"

Miles shook his head vehemently. "Absolutely not! I do not intend to marry ever again," he asserted. "I was merely curious."

"Well, I think it is a brilliant idea. If you were to marry Edwina, we would be family. Forever," Bennett teased. "You would never be able to get rid of me."

Miles shuddered at the thought, emphasizing his point. "How terrifying."

"Lots of people would want me as their family," Bennett said. "I have been told that I am rather charming."

Miles huffed. "Whoever told you that is lying to you."

"Only a true friend would be so honest," Bennett quipped.

They continued to make their way towards the stables, but Miles couldn't shake off the feeling that there was more to the conversation than what he had overheard. He replayed the words in his mind, wondering if he had missed something important. Or perhaps he was reading too much into it. After all, he had only caught a brief snippet of their discussion.

"Come on," Bennett encouraged before stepping into the stables.

Miles followed his friend inside and saw the gelding that Edwina had ridden into the woodlands earlier. He approached the horse and said, "This is a magnificent horse."

"It is," Bennett agreed. "Edwina adores Sorrel, but I fear for her safety sometimes. She can be quite reckless."

"I saw a glimpse of that when I caught sight of Edwina riding her horse this morning," Miles shared.

Bennett came to stand next to him and ran a gentle hand down Sorrel's neck. "Sometimes I am not sure if Edwina cares if she lives or dies."

Miles empathized with his friend's concern. "I understand that feeling all too well."

Bennett grew somber. "Quite frankly, I don't know how to

help my cousin. She is hurting and I feel helpless to do anything about it."

Miles offered him a reassuring look. "You are helping her by being there."

His friend looked grateful for his words, but still appeared troubled. "It isn't enough," he pressed, his tone filled with guilt.

"You mustn't look at it like you are failing. You are making a difference, one day at a time, by chipping away at the grief."

Bennett removed his hand from Sorrel's neck and turned to face him. "Could you talk to her?"

"Me?" Miles replied in surprise.

He nodded earnestly. "You understand grief, more so than I ever could. I've tried talking to Edwina but she won't listen to me."

Miles frowned, unsure if he was the right person to comfort Edwina. Or anyone, for that matter. "I don't know. How do you know she will listen to me?"

"Why wouldn't she?" Bennett grinned. "You are very personable."

"I used to be, but not anymore. Those days are long gone," Miles admitted.

A mischievous glint came into Bennett's eyes. "I know. I remember growing tired of your incessant chatter when we were younger."

"That was you," Miles retorted.

"Perhaps," Bennett conceded with a shrug, "but I know how much you love to hear your own voice."

Miles glanced heavenward with mock exasperation. "Again, that is *you*."

Bennett gripped his lapels and said, "You are right. And what a glorious voice I have. It can make the ladies swoon."

He was tired of this pointless conversation so he attempted to steer the conversation back to Edwina. "Regardless, I do believe that your cousin is still angry at me," Miles said.

"Did you not apologize?"

Miles winced. "I did, but the apology went awry rather quickly."

Bennett's expression remained unperturbed by what he had just revealed. "I suspected as much, knowing how stubborn both of you can be. Edwina may be reserved at times, but she can be rather feisty, given the circumstances."

"I have witnessed that firsthand."

His friend continued down the aisle and stopped by a stall that housed a black horse. "This was my uncle's horse," he revealed. "Hercules won't let anyone ride him now that my uncle is gone. I know because I have tried, multiple times, in fact."

"Horses can be finicky," Miles attempted.

"My father wants to sell Hercules, making it someone else's problem, but I have refused to do so," Bennett said. "I see a kindred soul in this horse."

Miles approached the black horse and studied it. "You could fetch a pretty penny selling this horse."

"Some things are more important than the money."

"Well said," Miles agreed. "Hopefully, with time, Hercules will begin to trust you, eventually allowing you to ride it."

Bennett looked unconvinced. "That might take some time."

"Do you have something else that is more pressing?" Miles asked.

"I am an earl."

Miles shrugged. "Who isn't?" he quipped.

Reaching into a bucket, Bennett retrieved an apple and held it up to the horse. "I never asked for this, you know."

"Neither did I," Miles said.

"Yet, here we are," Bennett responded. "Now I can't go anywhere without women batting their eyelashes at me. I don't think they see me as much as the title. It is unnerving."

Miles nodded his understanding. "No one cared about me

when I was the second son of an earl." He paused. "Well, except for Arabella. She loved me for who I was, not my position in Society."

"Arabella was good for you."

Miles offered him a weak smile. "She was the best part about me," he said. "I couldn't quite believe she agreed to go with me to the Continent."

"She was an extraordinary woman."

"That she was," Miles said, his voice growing hoarse with emotion. "I was grateful for the time I was able to spend with her."

The groom cleared his throat behind them. "Pardon the interruption, my lords, but your horses have been readied."

Bennett put his hand out, indicating that Miles should go first.

As Miles headed towards his horse, he worked hard to bury the familiar emotions that were threatening to rise to the surface. He would ride to the village, drink some watered-down ale and try to forget. Just as he always did. But it never seemed to work.

Chapter Six

As Edwina descended the grand staircase, her eyes caught sight of her aunt standing in the entry hall. The wide brim of a straw hat sat slightly askew on her head.

Her aunt had always been a striking woman with her blonde hair and fair skin, but the lines on her face were starting to mark her advancing age. But it wasn't just her face that made her beautiful. It was the way she was quick to smile or offer a comforting embrace.

"Where is your hat?" her aunt asked.

Edwina came to a stop on the bottom step. "I forgot it," she said sheepishly.

Her aunt didn't chide her but rather turned towards the butler who stood nearby. "Will you retrieve Lady Edwina's hat?" she requested.

White nodded with a bow. "Yes, my lady," he responded before he departed to do her bidding.

"Thank you," Edwina acknowledged.

Her aunt smiled. "You can't very well go into the village without a hat. What are you, a ruffian?" she teased.

Edwina returned her aunt's smile. "Good heavens, I think not."

"There it is," her aunt said. "I have missed your smile. I daresay you have been far too serious as of late."

"I suppose I have," Edwina admitted.

Her aunt stepped forward and placed a comforting hand on her sleeve. "You are loved. I hope you know that."

"I do," she replied, grateful for her aunt's kind words.

"Good, because we will get you through this," her aunt said, lowering her arm. "We can't have you moping about when we arrive in London for the Season."

Edwina lifted her brow in surprise. "I thought I was not to have a Season."

"Who told you that?" her aunt asked, tilting her head curiously.

Pressing her lips together, Edwina didn't wish to reveal that she had been eavesdropping on their conversation.

Her aunt gave her a knowing look and lightly chided her for it. "You have been eavesdropping again."

"I did, but only because you were speaking about me," Edwina admitted.

"If you had stayed around a little longer, you would have heard your uncle relenting and agreeing to let you have a Season," her aunt said with a hint of amusement in her voice.

Edwina stared at her aunt in disbelief. "How did you manage to convince him?" she asked incredulously.

Her aunt's expression softened. "My dear, you didn't truly think I was going to stand by and deprive you of a Season, did you?" she asked.

"But Uncle was so adamant."

"As was I. But my powers of persuasion are not to be underestimated," her aunt responded. "Besides, you do have a dowry of fifteen thousand pounds. That is not something to scoff at."

White approached them with a black bonnet in his hand, extending it to Edwina.

Edwina accepted the bonnet with a gracious nod and

murmured her thanks before placing it on over her loose chignon.

"Shall we?" her aunt asked, gesturing towards the front door where their coach awaited.

A knock came at the door and the butler went to open the door, revealing the tall, silver-haired Mr. Stanley. He had been her father's man of business for as long as she could remember, and now he worked in the same capacity for her uncle. His warm smile immediately put Edwina at ease, just like it always had when she was a child.

Stepping into the entry hall, Mr. Stanley bowed. "Lady Dallington. Lady Edwina," he greeted. "What a pleasant surprise."

"We were on our way to the village to do some shopping," Edwina shared.

"Very well, do not let me stop you," Mr. Stanley said as he stood to the side.

Lady Dallington gave him a pointed look. "I expect your business with my husband will conclude before our supper."

Mr. Stanley nodded. "I shall ensure that it does, my lady."

"Thank you," Lady Dallington said.

Turning his attention towards Edwina, the concern was evident in Mr. Stanley's voice as he asked, "How are you faring, my lady?" His brown eyes bored into hers, searching for any signs of discomfort or stress.

Edwina mustered up the most convincing smile that she could. "I am well."

Mr. Stanley didn't look convinced, but thankfully he did not press her. Instead, he remarked, "It is a lovely day to go shopping."

"It is," Edwina agreed, trying to match his enthusiasm.

Her aunt interjected, "We must depart if we want to enjoy our time shopping at a leisurely pace. We can't very well be late to supper, now can we?"

Edwina eyed her aunt warily. "How long do you intend to shop for ribbons?" she asked.

"All day, if I have my way," her aunt declared as she gracefully exited the manor. "Come along."

With a tip of her head at Mr. Stanley, Edwina followed her aunt out and stepped into the waiting coach.

After they were situated, her aunt broke the comfortable silence. "It has been far too long since we went into the village for some shopping," she said with a contented sigh.

"It has been," Edwina agreed.

Her aunt studied her with a discerning eye before saying, "I saw you on the lawn with Lord Hilgrove earlier. You two appeared to be getting along quite well."

"Appearances can be deceiving," Edwina replied.

"Lord Hilgrove is hurting, just as you are," her aunt gently reminded her. "It is often beneficial to surround yourself with others who understand what you are going through. It helps in the healing process."

Edwina adjusted the strings of her bonnet under her chin, considering her aunt's words carefully before revealing, "I have decided that I am going to help Lord Hilgrove."

Her aunt lifted her brow. "How exactly are you going to do that?"

"I don't know all the particulars yet, but I can sense his pain," Edwina admitted. "I want to do something meaningful with my life instead of wallowing in grief."

"An admirable goal, my dear, but if I may point out, you are still struggling yourself," her aunt remarked.

Edwina understood her aunt's concern but she was determined to follow through with her plan. "That is precisely why I need to look beyond my own heartache and help another."

Her aunt looked doubtful but didn't argue further. "Lord Hilgrove is not one to ask for help, and he may not appreciate your intentions."

"I know," Edwina replied determinedly. "But I have to at least try."

A heavy silence hung in the air as her aunt grew silent. Finally, she spoke. "Did you know that I was married before your Uncle Lionel?" Her words were tinged with sorrow.

Edwina reared back, surprised by this revelation. "You were?" she asked. "Why haven't you said anything before now?"

"I didn't think it was prudent to do so. It was in my past, and my future is with Lionel," her aunt explained, her eyes growing reflective. "Hugh was the fourth son of a marquess, and thus his chances of inheriting were unlikely. He chose to pursue a career in the Navy instead."

Her aunt's voice softened as she reminisced about her late husband. "He was the most handsome man and he was a wonderful, ardent kisser."

Edwina couldn't help but giggle at her aunt's unexpected remark.

"But he died shortly after we were wed when his ship was attacked," her aunt said, her tone turning somber. "Fortunately for me, my wedding contract specified that my dowry would be returned to me in case of his untimely death. However, my father wasted no time in negotiating a marriage contract between Lionel and me."

The sadness in her aunt's words was palpable. Edwina couldn't hold back her curiosity any longer. "Did you even want to marry Uncle Lionel?"

"Not at first," her aunt replied with a wistful sigh. "Lionel was kind to me but I had loved Hugh with all my heart. That kind of love just doesn't go away. But Lionel was persistent in his affection, and it was almost impossible not to fall in love with him over time. It was unexpected, but not unwanted. There is a difference."

"Why was your father so adamant that you were wed again?" Edwina asked.

Her aunt let out a frustrated huff. "Why, indeed? I suppose he didn't think I was capable of taking care of myself," she said.

"But you had your dowry."

"True, but maintaining a household is expensive," her aunt replied. "And as for my father, he simply could not understand why I wouldn't just move on from Hugh. But I think we both know that grief is not something one can simply move on from. Is it?"

"No, it is not," Edwina agreed, understanding all too well the weight of loss and heartache.

Her aunt leaned forward in her seat, her eyes filled with empathy. "I know Lionel may seem impatient and aloof at times, but that doesn't mean he loves you any less. He is just struggling to cope with his own pain."

Edwina's lips formed a thin line, unconvinced by her aunt's words.

"I don't expect you to believe me immediately, but it is the truth," her aunt insisted. "Lionel may try to deny or ignore it, but the death of his brother has deeply affected him. And he is hurting."

Edwina turned her head towards the window, gazing out at the passing countryside. She remembered when her uncle used to be kind and patient with her, before her father's death had changed everything. "I wish it could go back to the way it was, back when Uncle Lionel used to tolerate me," she said pensively.

Her aunt gave her an understanding nod. "Your uncle does love you, but he is doing a poor job of showing it."

Edwina arched an eyebrow. "He is doing a terrible job."

With a laugh, her aunt conceded, "That is fair."

The scent of freshly baked bread drifted through the open window as they approached the village. Edwina turned her head to take in the picturesque cottages with thatched roofs that lined the road. In the distance, she could hear the faint bleating of sheep grazing in nearby fields.

How she missed traveling to the village with her father. He would make an adventure out of it, just as he always did with everything. He had had a way of turning even the most mundane tasks into something enjoyable.

The coach came to a stop next to the pavement and her aunt remarked, "Bennett mentioned he was taking Lord Hilgrove to the pub for a drink. Since it is close to the ribbon shop, I wonder if he will come shopping with us." Her words were light, playful.

"I doubt it, especially since I do not think Lord Hilgrove cares much about ribbons," Edwina joked.

"No, he does not," her aunt readily agreed.

The coach door opened and Edwina accepted the hand of the footman as she stepped down onto the pavement. She withdrew her hand and smoothed down her black gown as she waited for her aunt to join her.

"Before we begin our shopping, I was hoping we would get a treat from the bakery shop across the street," her aunt said.

"I would never refuse such an offer," Edwina responded as she stepped off the pavement and into the cobblestone street.

As they made their way across the street, the air was filled with the deafening sound of hooves pounding against the uneven stones. Panic seized Edwina's heart as she realized a horse was charging towards them. She stood frozen in fear, unable to move despite seeing her aunt run for safety.

In the next moment, a strong hand grabbed her arm and yanked her out of harm's way, causing her to stumble and fall into the firm embrace of Lord Hilgrove.

Miles held Edwina tight against his chest, her small frame trembling in his embrace. The thundering sound of the horse's hooves faded away. When he had seen the horse barreling down on her, he had felt a fear unlike any he had ever known.

He gazed down at Edwina, taking in the panic and shock etched on her delicate features. He couldn't quite believe how close she had come to serious injury or even death.

Bennett's voice cut through the tense air. "You can release my cousin now," he said firmly, stepping closer to them.

Reluctantly, Miles loosened his grip but remained close enough to feel Edwina's quick breaths against his skin. He searched her eyes for any sign of harm. "Are you all right?" he inquired.

A mixture of emotions flickered across her face before she finally answered with a shaky voice. "Yes… no," she admitted.

"You will be just fine," he encouraged, not knowing what else he could say to provide her with comfort.

Lady Dallington placed her hand on Edwina's arm and gently turned her to face her. The concern was evident on her face as she seemingly searched Edwina's eyes for answers. "You had me so worried," she exclaimed. "What were you thinking, freezing up like that in the middle of the street?"

Edwina's gaze dropped to the ground. "I wasn't," she murmured.

Without hesitation, Lady Dallington pulled Edwina into a tight embrace, relief flooding over her features. "Thank heavens for Lord Hilgrove," she declared. "If he hadn't come to your rescue when he did…" Her voice trailed off. "I don't even want to think about what could have happened."

As Lady Dallington embraced her niece, Miles couldn't help but notice the growing crowd around them as people stopped to gawk and whisper. He knew they needed to move quickly before the situation became even more bothersome.

Fortunately, Bennett must have had the same thought

about their circumstances because he suggested, "Perhaps we should depart for the manor."

Lady Dallington released Edwina as she attempted to regain her composure. "You are right," she said. "We should return home at once."

A finely dressed gentleman broke through the crowd, his brow furrowed. "Is everyone all right?" he asked.

"We are," Lady Dallington confirmed.

The man relaxed slightly. "I don't know what spooked my horse, but I am terribly sorry for the distress that it caused."

Bennett's eyes narrowed as he took a commanding step towards the man. "You need to learn to control your horse better. The consequences could have been dire if not for my friend, Lord Hilgrove."

The man nodded, guilt and remorse evident on his expression. "Yes, my lord," he said, lowering his gaze. "It won't happen again."

"It better not," Bennett snapped.

Miles knew that emotions were running high, but it was just an unfortunate accident. He stepped forward and placed a calming hand on Bennett's shoulder. "Let us go collect our horses," he suggested.

Bennett took a few deep breaths, no doubt in an attempt to compose himself before speaking again. "Very well," he growled.

Lady Dallington guided Edwina towards the coach and Bennett, ever the gentleman, hastened to open the door for them. Miles stood back slightly, not quite sure what he should do.

Edwina paused in front of the coach and turned around to face Miles. She spoke, her voice barely above a whisper but filled with genuine gratitude. "Thank you," she said, her gaze speaking volumes.

A fluttering feeling stirred in Miles' chest as he held her gaze and he couldn't help but feel drawn to Edwina. Which was rather odd, considering his heart had been irrevocably broken after his wife had died. No, it was impossible. Surely, he must have imagined it. It was nerves; that is all that it was.

The ladies stepped gracefully into the coach and Miles stood on the pavement, watching it drive away. Bennett came to stand next to him, breaking the silence.

"Have I thanked you yet?" Bennett asked.

"There is no need..." Miles started to say.

Bennett turned to face him. "There is," he insisted, speaking over him. "If you hadn't saved Edwina when you did..." His voice cracked and he struggled to hold back his emotions. "I'm sorry. I just shudder at that thought."

"Well, it is over now," Miles reassured him. "Lady Edwina is safe and that is what matters."

"Yes, because of you."

Miles put his hand up, deflecting his friend's praise. "I am just thankful I was there to lend a helping hand."

Bennett grew uncharacteristically solemn. "Thank you for what you did," he said.

"You are welcome," Miles responded. "Can we drop it now?"

A grin slowly spread across Bennett's face. "We should have a parade for you," he joked. "The villagers would love that."

"That seems like a lousy reason to have a parade," Miles remarked dryly.

"I think you are worth it," Bennett said. "The war hero, turned saver of lives."

Miles looked heavenward, feigning exasperation. "You make it almost impossible to like you," he sighed.

Bennett chuckled. "It would be fun. We could have fireworks and a whole theatrical show," he teased.

"Clearly, you do not know how parades work."

"And you do?"

Miles nodded. "I was in a military parade before I left for the Continent."

"Were there fireworks?" Bennett inquired.

With a huff, Miles replied, "A military parade is a serious affair. We are not there to entertain people, but to show off our strength."

Bennett looked unimpressed by his remark. "I would rather watch a bear at a circus," he said. "Or a bear setting off fireworks. Now that would be a sight to behold."

"Are you drunk?"

"No, I am entirely sober," Bennett replied. "Why, are you drunk?"

Miles started to walk away from his friend. He'd had enough of this ridiculous conversation and he suspected he had gotten dumber because of it.

Bennett caught up to him and matched his stride. "I see that you are in no mood to joke around," he said. "What if I only said serious things from now on?"

"You can't quite seem to help yourself, can you?"

Bennett smirked. "No, only because I know it goads you."

A man wearing a brown jacket with a matching waistcoat approached them from the opposite direction. As he passed Bennett, he deliberately leaned in and brushed his shoulder, causing Bennett to stumble off balance.

"Watch where you are going," Bennett snapped as he regained his footing.

The man performed an exaggerated bow, his hand resting mockingly on his chest. "My apologies, my lord," he drawled. "I should be more careful around such greatness."

Bennett knitted his brow in confusion. "Do I know you?"

"You should," the man replied, the contempt evident in his voice. "I am one of your tenants, but you don't pay attention to those types of things, do you?"

"I do, but I am still learning the names of our tenants," Bennett said. "What is your name?"

The man scoffed. "Why, so you can evict me?"

"I have no intention of evicting you," Bennett assured him. "I am just trying to understand why you hold such disdain for me."

Stepping forward, the man said, "You think so little of me and the other tenants."

Bennett reared back. "That is wholly and emphatically not true."

"You can deny it all you want, but ever since you and your father came around, nothing has happened," the man declared. "You store your money in your coffers and you let us suffer."

With a frown, Bennett said, "I have no idea what you are referring to."

The man took a step back. "Be warned, my lord, you are nothing without this village and its people. I would remember that," he advised before spinning on his heel and hurrying down the pavement.

Miles gave Bennett a questioning look. "What was that about?"

"I haven't the faintest idea, but I intend to find out," Bennett replied. "I think it would be best if we go speak to Mr. Stanley, my father's man of business. His office is just around the corner here."

Both of them seemed to retreat into their thoughts as they rounded the corner and entered a two-level brick building. Miles trailed behind Bennett to a door on the first level and waited as he rapped his knuckles against it.

"Enter," came a voice from inside the office.

Bennett opened the door and stepped inside, revealing a silver-haired man sitting behind a large desk. The office was spacious, lined with bookshelves filled to the brim with books. A single window provided light and overlooked the garden below.

The man rose from his seat and greeted them with a warm

smile. "Lord Dunsby, welcome," he said, motioning them to enter. "Please come in."

Miles recognized that voice. It had been the voice of the man speaking to Lord Dallington earlier in the study.

Bennett gestured towards Miles, providing the introductions. "Mr. Stanley, allow me to introduce you to Lord Hilgrove."

Mr. Stanley bowed respectfully. "My lord." He turned his attention back to Bennett, curiosity evident in his expression. "Now, what do I owe this unexpected pleasure to?"

Bennett's demeanor shifted, becoming more serious. "I just had an interesting conversation on the pavement with one of my tenants."

"May I ask which one?" Mr. Stanley asked.

"I don't know," Bennett replied. "He wouldn't give me his name."

Mr. Stanley gave him a blank stare. "That is rather odd. Did he say as to why that was?"

Bennett shrugged. "He seemed afraid that I was going to evict him."

"For what purpose?" Mr. Stanley inquired.

Bennett leaned closer, placing his hands on the chair's back for support. "He implied that our tenants weren't happy since my father took over the estate."

"That is ludicrous, and not the least bit true," Mr. Stanley declared.

"But why would he even say such a thing?" Bennett pressed.

Mr. Stanley picked up a stack of papers and rifled through them. His brows were furrowed in concentration as he searched for a specific document, finally removing it from the pile and holding it up for Bennett to see. "I think I know what it might be," he shared. "There have been a few families that haven't been paying their fair share and I threatened them with eviction. But that takes time."

Bennett accepted the paper and his eyes skimmed it. "Is there a particular reason why these families haven't been paying?" he questioned.

"The crops were not as plentiful this year as past years have been, and I'm afraid some of your tenants are struggling to make ends meet," Mr. Stanley said, his tone sympathetic.

Bennett extended the paper back to Mr. Stanley. "Does my father know this?"

"He is aware," Mr. Stanley replied. "But times are tough for everyone, and it isn't fair to pass the burden on to your father."

"I suppose not," Bennett reluctantly admitted. "But rather than evict, what can we do to help them?"

"Help them, my lord?" Mr. Stanley repeated incredulously.

"Perhaps we can buy new machinery to help aid with the crops next season," Bennett proposed. "By doing so, we can continue to collect rent and our tenants can produce more crops."

Mr. Stanley lowered the paper back onto the desk and rubbed his chin thoughtfully. "I will go speak to your father and see if he is opposed to such an idea."

"Thank you, Mr. Stanley," Bennett said.

"Do not thank me just yet," Mr. Stanley acknowledged. "This is your father's decision, not mine. I can only make suggestions."

"I understand," Bennett said before excusing himself from the office.

Once they were alone in the dimly lit corridor, Miles asked, "Do you feel better?"

"No, but that is only because I don't know what I can do to help these families," Bennett replied, a troubled look in his eyes. "The thought that they are struggling does not sit well with me. But I intend to speak to my father about this at once."

"You are right to do so," Miles remarked.

Bennett bobbed his head, a determined look in his eyes. "But for now, we should head back to the manor. It is almost time for your nap. I wouldn't want you to miss it," he said playfully.

Miles could tell that his friend was trying to lighten the mood, but it wasn't working. Bennett was troubled by what had been discussed with Mr. Stanley.

Chapter Seven

Edwina sat on the chair in her bedchamber, gazing out at the gardens. The recent brush with death still lingered in her mind and it sent shivers down her spine. She could feel her heart thudding against her chest at the mere thought of it. If not for Lord Hilgrove, she might have met her end. What a morbid and petrifying realization.

There was so much of life that she still wanted to accomplish. Marriage, children, growing old with a true love- these were all dreams she held close to her heart. But perhaps there was even more she could do, like taking up a new hobby. Almost losing everything gave her a newfound appreciation for every moment and opportunity that life had to offer. This second chance was not something to be squandered or taken for granted.

A soft knock sounded at the door before it was gently pushed open, revealing her lady's maid. "I thought you were resting," she said.

"I couldn't sleep," Edwina admitted. "Every time I close my eyes, I see the horse barreling down upon me and I panic."

Martha's eyes held compassion. "That is to be expected, but those feelings should fade with time."

Edwina could only hope that was true. "Everything seems to take time, does it not?"

"Anything worth having does," Martha replied with a smile.

Reaching up, Edwina tightened the blanket around her shoulders. "This brush of death has me thinking."

Martha came to sit across from her. "About what?"

"I want to be happy."

"You will be, in due time," Martha encouraged. "You are still grieving the loss of your father and there is no shame in that."

Edwina glanced down at her mourning clothes, feeling suffocated by their weight on her heart. After a moment of contemplation, she made a decision. "I want to go into half-mourning and stop wearing all black."

Martha's brow shot up. "Are you sure, my lady?"

"I am," Edwina responded confidently. "It is time that I accept the fact that my father is gone and I need to make something of myself."

"It has only been four months…" Martha trailed off.

Edwina put her hand up to stop her words. "Yes, and my father would have wanted me to move on, without him."

Martha's expression softened. "That he would have."

A spark of hope ignited within Edwina, a glimmer of a second chance at happiness. It was time for her to start living again.

Rising, Martha walked over to the wardrobe and pulled out a maroon gown. "I daresay that your aunt will be happy that you are finally wearing these gowns."

A flash of movement in the gardens caught Edwina's eye, drawing her attention towards the window. Her eyes fixated on her cousin and Lord Hilgrove making their way towards the archery targets, each holding a bow in their hands. A sudden desire to join them overtook her.

Martha came to stand next to her, the gown draped over her hand. "What are we looking at?"

"I think I will join Bennett and Lord Hilgrove on the lawn," Edwina replied as she rose. "It would be much more enjoyable than wasting away my afternoon in here."

With a concerned look, Martha said, "There is no shame in resting, given the circumstances."

"I am tired of resting. That is all I seem to do now," Edwina remarked.

Martha tipped her head. "Very well," she conceded. "Let's get you dressed so you can spend time with the handsome Lord Hilgrove."

Edwina feigned confusion. "Is Lord Hilgrove handsome?" she asked. "Perhaps I could see his appeal to *some* women but he is much too..." Her voice trailed off as she thought of the right word. She didn't dare admit that she found him to be extremely handsome or Martha might wrongly assume she had interest in him.

Knowing that Martha was still waiting on a response, Edwina settled on, "Earlish."

"'Earlish'? What does that even mean?" Martha asked, clearly perplexed.

Edwina inwardly scolded herself for blurting out such a nonsensical word. But she couldn't back down now and risk exposing her true feelings. "He looks and acts the part of an earl," Edwina said.

Martha looked unsure. "Is that not a good thing since he is, in fact, an earl?"

"It is, I suppose, for some people, but not for me," Edwina replied with a slight shrug of her shoulders.

"To clarify, you don't like people that act the part of being titled. Or is it just earls you have a complaint against?" Martha questioned.

Edwina winced, knowing how utterly ridiculous she sounded. "I am not explaining myself well, but I have no interest in Lord Hilgrove."

"I never implied that you did," Martha said.

"Good, good," Edwina muttered. "Because just the thought of us two together is absolutely ludicrous. We are such different people."

Martha bobbed her head. "I believe you."

"Yes, well, that is settled then," Edwina said. "I'm glad that we are in agreement."

"We are," Martha said, holding up the dress. "But do you plan on spending your time with me or would you rather go join the 'earlish' Lord Hilgrove?" Her words held amusement.

Edwina slipped the blanket off her shoulders and draped it on the back of the chair. "I am going to spend time with Bennett, who happens to be with Lord Hilgrove at the moment," she clarified.

"My apologies," Martha said lightly. "Why would you want to spend time with a handsome, unattached lord?"

"Because he is just Bennett's guest," Edwina stated.

Martha shook her head. "Just promise me that you won't close yourself off from the idea."

Edwina knew that her lady's maid was only trying to help, but she had no intention of even entertaining the thought of pursuing Lord Hilgrove. He may have been her hero earlier, but that is all that he was- a fleeting hero in the moment of danger. No matter how calm and familiar his gaze felt when it met hers.

She decided to respond with what her heart dictated. "I know you mean well, but Lord Hilgrove is not my future. I am sure of it."

"If you say so, my lady."

"I do," Edwina stated confidently.

Martha smiled as if she were privy to a secret. "Very well, then, shall we dress you?"

After Edwina was dressed, she departed her bedchamber and headed towards the main level. She halfway expected everyone to gawk at her since she wasn't wearing her mourning clothes, but the servants went about their tasks, giving her little heed.

Making her way down the corridor towards the gardens, Edwina heard her aunt's voice call out to her from the study.

Edwina changed course and entered the study. She saw her aunt sitting on the settee, a book in her hand, and her uncle was hunched over his desk, reviewing the ledgers.

Her aunt's eyes gleamed with approval as they swept over Edwina's appearance. "You look lovely, Dear," she praised before turning to her husband. "Doesn't she, Lionel?"

"Yes, lovely," her uncle replied, not bothering to look up.

Pressing her lips together, her aunt shared, "Edwina is wearing a maroon gown."

"Wonderful," her uncle muttered dully.

A flash of annoyance crossed her aunt's face at his indifference. "Lionel!" she exclaimed in exasperation.

Her uncle finally tore his gaze away from the ledgers and brought his gaze up. "What is it?" he asked.

Tilting her head towards Edwina, her aunt prompted, "Doesn't Edwina look nice?"

Her uncle shifted his gaze towards her. "I must agree with my wife. You do look lovely," he declared, his voice holding a touch of sincerity. "I am glad to see that you are no longer wearing all black."

Interjecting, her aunt asked, "May I ask what prompted the change?"

Edwina smoothed down the maroon gown. "My brush with death made me realize that there is still so much I want to accomplish," she explained.

Her aunt nodded understandingly. "You are still young and have a whole life ahead of you."

With a huff, her uncle grumbled, "Life is not as grand as

you make it out to be. The older you get, the more mundane tasks take over and dull the excitement of living."

"You are being rather pleasant today," her aunt remarked, her voice terse as she directed her comment at her husband.

"Would you prefer if I lied to Edwina?" he asked.

"No, but you could be a little more encouraging," her aunt responded.

Waving his hand over his cluttered desk, her uncle said, "I just read a report on soil. It wasn't the least bit riveting, but it had to be done."

Her aunt shifted her gaze towards Edwina. "Do not let us keep you, Dear," she encouraged. "I suspect you would rather do anything else than hear us bicker."

"We are not bickering." Her uncle paused. "Are we?"

Glancing at her husband, she confirmed, "We are."

"Drats," her uncle said.

Edwina took a step back. "I am going to join Bennett and Lord Hilgrove on the lawn. They are practicing archery."

"Wonderful," her aunt said. "Enjoy yourself, but do not be late for supper."

As she made her way out of the study, Edwina had the briefest thought about how Lord Hilgrove would respond to her gown. Which was absurd. Why should she care what he thought about her gown or about anything else for that matter? They were acquaintances, nothing more. Yet, she did enjoy their conversations when he wasn't so contrary. But surely those moments meant nothing.

Brushing aside that thought, Edwina exited the back door and stepped into the gardens. She headed towards the lawn where the archery targets were positioned.

Edwina came to a stop a short distance away and watched Lord Hilgrove release an arrow, its sharp point embedding itself perfectly in the center of the target.

"Well done," Bennett praised. "I see your archery skills have greatly improved since our days at Eton."

Lord Hilgrove lowered the bow to his side and smirked. "And yet, your own abilities seem to have stayed the same."

Bennett chuckled before he turned his head towards her. His eyes widened. "Edwina," he said. "You look different. Good different, though."

Lord Hilgrove leaned closer to Bennett and joked, "That was poorly done on your part."

Holding up his bow, Bennett offered it to Edwina as he asked, "Would you care to join us?"

"I would, thank you," Edwina said as she accepted the bow. "It has been quite some time since I last shot an arrow."

"Not to worry," Bennett assured her with a smile. "You have come to the right teachers."

Edwina reached for an arrow and set it in her bowstring. She pulled back the string with practiced ease and released the arrow towards the target, hitting just next to Lord Hilgrove's successful shot.

Lord Hilgrove raised an impressed brow at her. "It seems like you don't need our help after all," he remarked, his voice carrying a hint of admiration.

Edwina couldn't help but feel a sense of pride swell within her at those words. "No, I suppose I don't," she admitted.

Bennett held his hand out for the bow, breaking the moment between her and Lord Hilgrove. "It would appear that *I* am the one in need of practice," he said.

She grinned at her cousin's playful tone as she relinquished the bow to him. "I didn't want to be the one to say it," she teased.

Lord Hilgrove's deep chuckle rang out and her heart took flight at the sound. Uncertain of why his laugh had elicited such a reaction, Edwina quickly directed her attention back towards the targets, determined not to let Lord Hilgrove's presence distract her.

The faint sound of the dinner bell could be heard as Miles slipped into his tailored jacket and straightened his cuffs. Bailey stood dutifully by his side, ready to assist with any request.

"That will be all," Miles said, dismissing the valet with a wave of his hand.

Bailey bowed and began tidying up the bedchamber.

Miles walked over to the door, his hand resting on the handle. "How is your sister?" he inquired.

"Which one, my lord?" Bailey asked with a smile.

"The one who eloped," Miles clarified.

Bailey's expression grew somber. "It has been some time since then, but she seems to be doing well," he said. "I receive an occasional letter from her."

Miles bobbed his head. "That is good."

"Dare I ask when the last time was that you wrote your sister?" Bailey inquired with a lifted brow.

Letting out a sigh, Miles turned to face his valet. "I must admit that it has been quite some time."

Bailey grinned. "I am well aware since you have me post the letters."

"Then why bother asking?" Miles grumbled.

Reaching down, the valet picked up Miles' riding boots. "Because I wanted you to realize how long it has been," he said with an amused glint in his eyes.

Miles frowned. "Why does it matter?" he asked. "She is married with little ones running around. She doesn't need me."

"But you are her brother, and she writes to you. Typically, people who write letters enjoy receiving a response."

"Yes, but she is happy."

Bailey gave him a knowing look. "And there lies the crux

of the matter," he responded slowly. "I believe that you are envious of her happiness."

Miles huffed, feeling a touch of indignation at the accusation. "I should reprimand you for your impertinence—"

"But you won't because I am right, and you know it," Bailey interjected confidently. He paused. "Just think on it for a while."

Reaching for the handle, Miles pushed open the door and stepped out into the corridor. He wanted to be angry at Bailey but the only person he could truly be angry at was himself. He could pretend all he wanted that he wasn't jealous of his sister, but he was. She had married for love and now they were blissfully happy at their country estate.

He didn't want to tell his sister how he was truly doing or else she might pity him. And he didn't need anyone's pity. Not now.

As he headed down the corridor, he saw Edwina slip out of her bedchamber, dressed in a dark blue gown.

Her eyes grew wide at the sight of him and she quickly dropped into a slight curtsy. "My lord," she greeted him.

"We have to stop meeting like this," he joked.

A small smile tugged at her lips, but she remained quiet.

Sensing her unease, Miles offered his arm. "May I escort you to the drawing room?" he asked.

He could see the hesitation in Edwina's eyes as she glanced down at his outstretched arm, but propriety won out and she gently placed her hand on it. "Thank you," she murmured.

While he led her down the corridor, Edwina glanced over at him. "I wanted to thank you again for saving me from that runaway horse."

"You don't need to keep thanking me."

"I know, but I feel as if I must."

Miles nodded. "Then, please, continue to thank me and perhaps even heap some praise on me around your cousin. I do quite enjoy being called 'a hero,'" he teased with a playful wink.

Edwina lowered her gaze, but not before he saw a charming blush form on her cheeks. Perhaps he did have an effect on her. That was a rather pleasant thought.

Finding himself curious, Miles commented, "I couldn't help but notice that you are no longer clad in black."

She brought her gaze back up. "It seemed appropriate to enter into half-mourning for my father," she explained.

"May I ask what prompted this change?"

With determination shining in her eyes, she answered, "After my brush with death, it made me realize that there was much that I haven't accomplished."

"What is it that you wish to achieve?" he probed gently.

She offered a small, uncertain smile. "I want to marry for love and start a family of my own," she admitted. "You must think I am foolish."

"Not at all. I find it admirable." He hesitated before sharing, "In fact, I married for love and I do not regret that choice." His voice caught on the last word.

Edwina looked up at him, green eyes full of understanding. "But you regret other choices?" she asked.

Miles cleared his throat. "I am a soldier. I have many regrets, I'm afraid, including asking my wife to join me on the Continent. If I hadn't, she might very well be alive."

"You don't know that," she said in a vain attempt to reassure him.

"I do know that she wouldn't have been there when sickness broke out amongst the soldiers, claiming her life in the process," Miles insisted as he worked hard to keep the bitterness out of his tone.

They reached the top step of the grand staircase and Edwina turned to face him. "Your wife's death wasn't your fault."

"Then whose fault was it?" Miles demanded, his emotions laying bare. "I asked her to come."

Edwina's expression grew determined. "Did you force her to come with you?" she asked pointedly.

"No, but Arabella could have remained back in England, where it was safe, had I not asked her," Miles declared.

"I see," Edwina said. "So you are a fortune-teller, then? You can predict the future."

"You don't understand," he scoffed.

Edwina held his gaze. "I do," she replied. "You are blaming yourself for her accompanying you, but what if she had died while you were away? I suspect that you would have blamed yourself for that as well."

Miles grew silent, unable to deny the truth in her words. "Yes, I would have," he reluctantly admitted.

Taking a step closer to him, Edwina said, "Arabella's death was tragic, but you played no hand in it. Sometimes, despite our best efforts, bad things still happen to good people."

He clenched his jaw. "It was my duty to protect her," he said through gritted teeth. "And I failed her."

Edwina placed a comforting hand on his sleeve. "You did all that you could."

"But it wasn't enough," he said, his voice heavy with guilt.

With a soft sigh, Edwina responded, "Life can be terribly unfair at times, but the only thing we can do is accept the things that we cannot change."

Miles glanced down at her hand, finding some small measure of solace from her touch. "I can't accept this."

"Then you will never be able to move forward," Edwina said, withdrawing her hand. "I didn't think I would ever accept my father's passing but it happened all at once."

"When was this?" Miles asked.

"Today, in fact, when you saved my life," Edwina said. "My perspective changed, and it was all because of you."

Miles shifted his gaze away from her. "You make it sound so simple."

Edwina let out a soft, disbelieving laugh. "Simple?" she asked. "No, far from it. I had to almost die to realize that I was living in the past."

"I am not living in the past," Miles said.

"Well, you are certainly not living in the present," Edwina remarked.

Miles grew tense at her words, unwilling to continue this conversation. "I am supposed to take advice from you now?" he growled.

Edwina smiled- actually smiled at him, despite his best attempt at intimidating her. "You can do whatever you want, but just know that I am here for you," she said.

As the words left her mouth, Bennett's voice came from the entry hall, interrupting them. "Are you two still yammering on?" he asked, his voice holding mirth. "I am getting hungry."

Miles remained rooted in his spot as he watched Edwina gracefully descend the stairs, as if having not a care in the world. He wondered what had happened to her. She seemed more confident in herself. Which was a good thing, except when she was lecturing him. Because that is exactly what she was doing. Her advice was wholly unsolicited, but he couldn't seem to brush off her words so easily. The worst part was that she wasn't wrong in her assumptions.

Botheration.

Edwina's words shouldn't have touched him as much as they did. His heart was supposed to be impenetrable, but somehow, her words seemed to soften his heart. Which would not do. He needed to keep his distance from Edwina for now.

Bennett gave him an expectant look. "Are you coming for dinner, Miles?"

"Yes," he replied as he started to descend the stairs. "I

hope I didn't inconvenience Lord and Lady Dallington too much."

"They haven't come down yet, but I expect them shortly," Bennett informed him.

"Then why the rush?" Miles asked.

Bennett grinned. "I suppose I just missed you."

"You are a terrible liar," Miles muttered.

Turning towards Edwina, Bennett acknowledged, "You are looking lovely this evening. That blue color suits you."

"Thank you, Cousin," Edwina said. "I suppose I should return the compliment by saying your waistcoat suits you."

Bennett chuckled. "That was a terrible compliment. I expect better from you next time." He glanced up at the stairs. "I wonder what is taking my mother and father so long."

"Perhaps they have grown tired of you," Miles joked.

"That is absurd," Bennett retorted. "That couldn't possibly be the reason since I am their favorite," Bennett said.

Edwina cocked her head. "I would have thought Winston was their favorite."

"No, Mother always tells me that I am her favorite," Bennett remarked.

Lady Dallington's amused voice came from behind them. "Oh, dear. I tell all my children that they are my favorite. A mother should not have a favorite child."

Bennett went to kiss his mother on her cheek before asking her, "But if there was a scenario where you had to save one child from a bear attack, which one would it be?"

With a thoughtful look on her expression, Lady Dallington inquired, "What are the circumstances?"

"We are at the circus and a bear breaks loose from its restraints and it is headed straight for us. Certain death is imminent," Bennett said. "Which child do you save?"

Lady Dallington smiled at Bennett. "Most assuredly, I would save you. You are my favorite, after all."

Bennett gave Miles a smug look. "I told you- everyone loves me."

Miles resisted the urge to chuckle. "Your mother is clearly lying to you. By her own admission, she has no favorite child."

"Yes, but that is just to make the others feel better about themselves," Bennett remarked. "Isn't that right, Mother?"

Lady Dallington's lips twitched. "Precisely, but it might be best if you don't tell your brother and sisters that."

As she finished speaking, Lord Dallington descended the stairs and joined them in the entry hall. "Shall we adjourn to the dining room?" he asked.

"Finally," Bennett declared. "Trying to get you all to assemble is like trying to herd squirrels."

"That is quite an interesting analogy," Lady Dallington remarked. "Have you tried herding squirrels before?"

Bennett simply shrugged. "No, but it is a common expression."

"I have never heard anyone say that before," Miles insisted.

"Then, perhaps, you don't associate with the right people," Bennett retorted.

Miles let out an exasperated sigh. "Or maybe you are surrounded by idiots."

"Says the person that is standing right next to me," Bennett joked. "Who is the idiot now?"

Edwina laughed, the sound echoing through the entry hall. "I thought you were hungry, Bennett?"

"I am," Bennett said, offering his arm to his cousin. "Allow me to escort you to the dining room."

Miles trailed behind everyone as they made their way to the dining room. He wanted to hold on to his anger but his resolve was starting to slip away. And that thought troubled him more than he cared to admit.

Chapter Eight

Edwina descended the servants' staircase, her footsteps light and careful as she made her way towards the bustling kitchen. The familiar scent of warm bread and roasting meat wafted through the air. She spotted the portly cook, the woman's back to her, standing by the hearth and stirring something in a large pot.

On the counter next to her was a large basket, overflowing with an assortment of foods- fruits, cheeses and meats.

As Edwina reached for the basket, she asked, "Is this the basket for the Warrens?"

Mrs. Meek turned around and faced her with a smile "It is, my lady," she replied. "Be sure to give them my regards."

"I will," Edwina said, slipping the handle of the basket onto her arm.

While Mrs. Meek wiped her hands on the apron that hung around her neck, she inquired, "How are you faring with Lord Dunsby's house guest?"

This was the last thing that she wanted to talk about, but she couldn't be rude to someone who had shown her kindness since she was a child.

Mustering up a smile, Edwina replied, "I am well. Lord

Hilgrove is a pleasant enough man." There. That much was true. If she was lucky, that would end this line of questioning.

But she wasn't so lucky.

Mrs. Meek stepped closer and lowered her voice. "I have heard Lord Hilgrove is rather handsome."

Edwina resisted the urge to roll her eyes. Not this again. Why was everyone so fixated on how handsome Lord Hilgrove was? It was maddening.

With a shrug, Edwina said, "I suppose he is tolerable."

"Tolerable?" Mrs. Meek questioned, clearly not impressed with her response. "That is not how the maids describe him."

Knowing she was going to come to regret this, Edwina asked, "Dare I even ask how they are describing Lord Hilgrove?"

Mrs. Meek grinned. "The general consensus is that he is handsome beyond all measure."

And she already regretted asking the question.

Edwina held up her arm that held the basket. "As riveting as this conversation is, I really must deliver this basket before breakfast."

"Very well," Mrs. Meek said with a wave of her hand. "But I must say, your handsome meter is broken."

Taken aback by this odd comment, Edwina asked, "My 'handsome meter'?"

A look of amusement played on Mrs. Meek's face as she responded, "Lord Hilgrove is clearly a very handsome man, but you only find him 'tolerable'? Either your handsome meter is broken or you are lying to yourself. Which one is it?"

Giving a resigned sigh, Edwina replied, "Neither, I assure you. I really must be going now."

Mrs. Meek tipped her head. "Good day to you, my lady."

After she murmured her goodbyes, Edwina departed from the servants' entrance and looked up at the sky. Why was everyone so insistent on discussing Lord Hilgrove with her?

They were merely acquaintances, not even friends, although that line was beginning to blur.

She started walking down the path leading towards the Warrens' cottage and saw a horse approaching in the distance. It only took her a moment to recognize the rider.

Lord Hilgrove.

Panicking slightly and looking for a place to hide, Edwina realized she was too far from the safety of the woodlands to make a quick escape. Her heart raced as he drew nearer, and she tried to pretend he didn't cut a dashing figure on his horse.

Lord Hilgrove reined in his horse and raised his hand in greeting. "Lady Edwina, what a pleasant surprise."

"Yes, it is," Edwina said. "How was your ride?"

"Delightful. Did you not ride this morning?" he inquired, dismounting his horse.

Edwina nodded. "I went at dawn," she informed him. "I find it is the most peaceful time to sit and reflect."

Lord Hilgrove grew thoughtful. "I must admit that our conversation from last night has been weighing heavily on my mind."

"You mean when Bennett thought he was his mother's favorite?" Edwina asked, attempting to lighten the mood.

He chuckled. "No, but that conversation was rather entertaining."

Edwina smiled. "I have long suspected Winston is my aunt's favorite since he is a barrister. He can out-argue anyone and it can be quite frustrating to be in a debate with him, even if you have right on your side."

"I can only imagine," Lord Hilgrove said, returning her smile.

As they stood there, smiling at one another, Edwina couldn't help but admire the chiseled features of Lord Hilgrove's face. His strong jawline and piercing blue eyes were enough to make any woman swoon, but she shouldn't be noticing such things about her cousin's guest. Lord Hilgrove was here for Bennett, not her. And she needed to be mindful of that. He would leave soon and she had no desire to pine after him.

Her smile faltered as she raised the basket in her hand. "If you will excuse me, I must deliver this basket to the Warrens."

"If memory serves me right, Mr. Warren used to be your father's butler," Lord Hilgrove remarked.

"Yes, and Mrs. Warren was our housekeeper," Edwina shared. She was rather impressed that he remembered their conversation.

A flicker of uncertainty passed over Lord Hilgrove's usually confident expression. "May I accompany you?" he asked quickly, almost anxiously. "If it wouldn't be too much trouble."

It was on the tip of her tongue to refuse him, but she saw the vulnerability in his eyes and it touched her, more than she cared to admit. "I would greatly enjoy that," she replied. And that was the truth. Which frightened her even more.

Lord Hilgrove held his hand out for the basket. "May I?"

Edwina relinquished her hold on the basket, and they began to walk down the path. She wanted to say something clever, but she was at a loss as what to say. In fact, she couldn't think of anything to say. Her mind was befuddled with him standing so close.

Fortunately, Lord Hilgrove seemed more at ease and spoke up. "I hope you do not mind, but I rode to your special spot in the woodlands."

"It is not mine," she responded. "It is a place for anyone to enjoy."

"You are most gracious." He tilted his head back to admire the clear blue sky. "It is shaping up to be a beautiful day, is it not?"

"Yes, quite lovely," she readily agreed. The weather was a safe and mundane topic of conversation.

Lord Hilgrove brought his gaze back to meet hers. "I was

hoping to revisit our conversation from last night." He hesitated before asking, "Do you truly believe that Arabella's death was not my fault?"

The way he spoke his words caused her to pause and something stirred inside of her. They were spoken with such raw emotion, as if he were baring his soul.

Edwina came to a stop and turned to face him. "With my whole heart, I believe it was not your fault."

Lord Hilgrove looked away, but not before she caught a glimpse of deep pain in his eyes. His voice was low and filled with sorrow as he shared, "Arabella was increasing when she died. I didn't just lose her that day… I lost my future."

Unable- or unwilling- to stop herself, Edwina stepped closer and gently placed a hand on his arm. "I'm sorry," she said, at a loss for any other words. He was hurting, and she wished she had the words that would ease his burden.

"No one knew about the baby but us," Lord Hilgrove shared, his eyes growing moist. "It was our secret."

Edwina remained silent, patiently waiting for him to continue if he chose to.

His jaw clenched tightly as he revealed, "It wasn't long after her death that I received word that my brother had died."

"Oh, my," she gasped. "How awful."

"I lost everything I held dear in a short period of time," Lord Hilgrove admitted, his voice trembling with emotion. "And now, I have nothing left to live for."

Before she thought through the repercussions of her actions, she wrapped her arms around his waist and laid her head against his chest. "I understand," she murmured. "But it will get better. You must take each day as it comes."

Resting his chin atop her head, Lord Hilgrove let out a heavy sigh. "I have been trying, but the pain lingers. A constant companion of what I have lost."

"When my father died, I walked around in a haze, unable

to believe that he was truly gone. A part of me had been ripped away and I felt as if I had nothing to give," Edwina shared. "No one could console me, and I felt alone. So utterly alone."

Edwina continued. "My family tried to help me, as did my friends. But grief is a journey that one must make alone. And not everyone comes out a victor."

Lord Hilgrove took a deep breath, his chest rising and falling. "How is it that you are not falling apart right now? Your father only died four months ago."

"Four months and seven days," Edwina murmured. "It is a day that I am unlikely to forget. No one teaches you how to watch your father die. Nor does anyone teach you how to say a final goodbye."

"I held Arabella's hand as she passed, and I continued to hold it for much longer after that. I just couldn't seem to let her go," Lord Hilgrove shared.

Edwina felt tears form in the back of her eyes and she blinked them away. "Moments like those are so monumental that it changes everything."

Lord Hilgrove grew silent. Finally, after a long moment, he said, "You do understand." The relief in his voice was palpable.

"I do," she confirmed, her heart aching for him.

"What a pair we make," he remarked. "Where do we go from here?"

Edwina felt a tear slip down her cheek. "We move forward, remembering the loved ones that are no longer with us."

She could feel Lord Hilgrove bob his head in agreement. "I can do that."

"Good, I am glad you agree," Edwina said with a hint of humor in her voice. "Because I am out of advice."

Lord Hilgrove chuckled, the sound bringing a small smile to Edwina's lips. "It was good advice," he acknowledged.

"But, perhaps, we should deliver this basket now so we are not late for breakfast."

As she recognized the precariousness of their situation, Edwina dropped her arms and took a step back. Her cheeks flushed with embarrassment as she stumbled over her words. "Yes… um… that is a fine idea," she rushed out. "Breakfast is indeed a good thing."

"Yes, it is a very good thing," he repeated with an amused grin playing on his lips.

Edwina felt like a complete fool. Why couldn't she formulate coherent sentences in front of him? But deep down, she already knew the answer. Lord Hilgrove's piercing gaze had a way of disarming her, making her forget all rational thought. And now, against all odds, she had developed feelings for him.

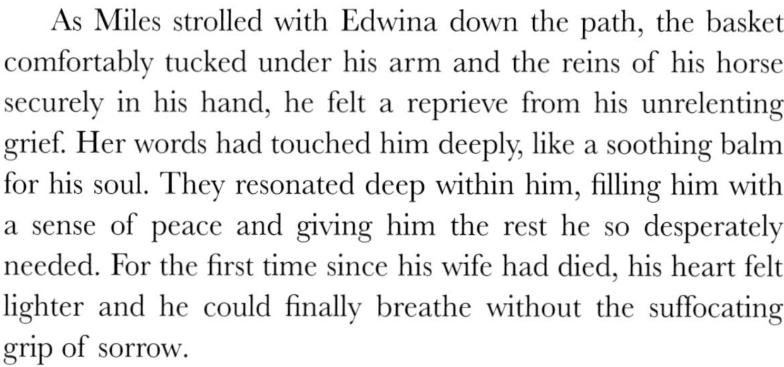

As Miles strolled with Edwina down the path, the basket comfortably tucked under his arm and the reins of his horse securely in his hand, he felt a reprieve from his unrelenting grief. Her words had touched him deeply, like a soothing balm for his soul. They resonated deep within him, filling him with a sense of peace and giving him the rest he so desperately needed. For the first time since his wife had died, his heart felt lighter and he could finally breathe without the suffocating grip of sorrow.

Miles glanced over at Edwina and noticed the solemn look on her lovely face. He had not expected her to embrace him so warmly, but it was a welcome comfort in that moment. And yet, there was something unsettling about the way she fit in his arms so perfectly.

Blazes.

This would not do. He shouldn't have feelings for Edwina,

but he did. And they were starting to make a nuisance of themselves.

Edwina turned her head and caught him staring. He should look away or at least pretend to be embarrassed, but instead he said, "I know very little about you, yet I feel as though we have known each other forever. Is that odd?"

With a shake of her head, Edwina replied, "No, I feel the same."

In that moment, Miles felt an overwhelming desire to learn everything he could about Edwina. "Will you tell me more about yourself?"

Edwina's eyebrow quirked up in amusement. "What exactly would you like to know?"

"Anything and everything," he replied earnestly.

A soft laugh escaped Edwina's lips. "Well then, where shall I begin?" she asked. "I should warn you that I am not very interesting."

"I don't believe that to be true, considering you bested me at archery," he pointed out.

Edwina had a thoughtful expression on her face as she shared, "When I was younger, I had a cat named Cat."

"You named your cat- 'Cat'?" he repeated incredulously.

"I did. 'Cat' was short for 'Catherine the Great,'" Edwina explained. "But we just called her 'Cat' for short."

A mischievous grin spread across his face as he teased, "Dare I ask what you would call a dog?"

Edwina looked amused. "Considering it took me months to name my cat, I would have to think on it."

His grin grew broader. "It took you months to come up with your cat's name?"

She nodded. "I was six. That was the biggest decision I ever had to make up to that point."

"Out of curiosity, why did you name your cat after Catherine the Great?" he asked.

Edwina began to gesture animatedly with her hands as she

explained, "My father read me a book about her, and I found it fascinating that she overthrew her husband to rule Russia. She was strong and independent, as was my cat."

Miles chuckled. "We only had barn cats to catch the mice."

"After Cat died, my father suggested we get another one, but my heart wasn't in it. It felt like betraying her memory," Edwina said.

"She was just a cat," he pointed out.

Edwina pressed her lips together. "No, she was more than that. She was a cherished member of our family."

Miles quickly put his hand up. "My apologies. I did not mean to be insensitive. Forgive me?"

"There is nothing to forgive," she assured him.

His next words slipped out before he could stop them. "Beautiful and gracious," he murmured.

A blush crept up Edwina's cheeks as she lowered her gaze. "You shouldn't say such things, my lord," she chided.

"But it is the truth," Miles insisted.

Edwina brought her gaze back up. "We hardly know one another."

"That may be true, but I already consider you a friend," he confessed. "Do you not feel the same way?"

In a soft voice, she replied, "I do."

"Then with your permission, may I call you by your given name?" Miles asked.

Edwina seemed to consider his words. "I have never given a gentleman leave to call me by my given name before," she remarked.

"I am not just any gentleman," Miles started, "since we have already shared an embrace."

Her eyes went wide at his words. "A true gentleman would never bring that up."

Miles chuckled at her reaction. "I am just merely pressing my point."

After a moment of contemplation, Edwina conceded. "Very well, you may call me by my given name, but only when we are alone."

"And you will call me Miles."

Edwina met his gaze, uncertainty flickering in her eyes. She spoke in a hushed tone, barely louder than a whisper. "And I shall call you Miles."

Feeling a need to tease her, he leaned closer and asked, "What was that?"

Her eyes darted around the path before saying, "Miles."

Miles wasn't prepared for how his heart reacted to her using his given name. It felt right. Comfortable.

Edwina pointed towards a quaint thatched roof cottage just off the path. "This is the Warrens' cottage." She held her hand out. "If you give me the basket, I shall drop it off to them."

"I can deliver the basket to them myself."

"That is wholly unnecessary," she insisted. "You don't need to trouble yourself by coming to the door with me."

His lips twitched. "Why, Edwina, are you embarrassed by me?"

Her mouth dropped. "No, I am not, but you are a lord—"

"And you are a lady," Miles interjected.

"Yes, but you are a stranger to them," Edwina reasoned.

As they stood debating, the door to the cottage opened and a short, rounded woman stood in the doorway. "Lady Edwina, is everything all right?" she called out.

Edwina dropped her hand as she replied in a cordial voice, "Yes, Mrs. Warren. Lord Hilgrove and I were just discussing who would have the honor of delivering a basket to you. It is from all of us at Brockhall Manor."

With a graceful wave, Mrs. Warren encouraged them forward. "Do come in. I have no doubt that Mr. Warren would be delighted to meet Lord Hilgrove."

Miles secured his horse before he followed Edwina inside the cottage, where the scent of freshly baked bread and warm spices filled the air. Once inside, he extended the basket to Mrs. Warren.

Mrs. Warren's face beamed. "Thank you!" she exclaimed. "What a delightful surprise."

Edwina spoke up. "Everyone at Brockhall Manor sends their well wishes for Mr. Warren's quick recovery."

"That is most kind of them, and you," Mrs. Warren replied with grateful sincerity. "Mr. Warren will want to see this basket."

Mrs. Warren turned on her heel and stepped into a room off the small entry hall.

Edwina turned towards him and in a hushed voice said, "I have known the Warrens since I was young, and they are very dear to me."

Miles eyed her curiously. "Are you worried that I won't behave?"

"Just try to not be so earlish," Edwina said.

"'Earlish'?" he repeated back.

"Yes, it is a word," Edwina responded.

He smirked. "I think you made it up."

With a slight shrug of her shoulders, Edwina conceded, "Perhaps, but it still rings true."

Miles leaned in slightly, matching her low tone. "And how does one go about being less 'earlish'?" he asked in mock seriousness.

Edwina perused the length of him. "I don't think it can be done," she admitted.

As he went to reply, Mrs. Warren's voice came from the doorway. "Are you coming, Dear?" she asked.

"Yes, Mrs. Warren," she replied before she made her way into the next room.

Miles followed close behind, passing through a narrow threshold and into a small room. His eyes fell upon a tall, heavy-set man sitting on a chair, his foot propped up on a bench.

Edwina gestured towards him and provided the introductions. "Allow me to introduce Lord Hilgrove. He is a friend of my cousin's," she said.

Mrs. Warren looked upon him with approval in her eyes. "That was most kind of you to escort Lady Edwina here."

"Oh, no. He didn't escort me here," Edwina rushed out. "We met on the path and he offered to accompany me."

"Ah, thank you for that clarification," Mrs. Warren said, a smile tugging at her lips.

Mr. Warren cleared his throat. "I would rise to properly greet you, my lord, but my wife would not approve of such action."

"No, I wouldn't," Mrs. Warren confirmed.

Miles smiled. "Then you must do as your wife says," he responded.

Mr. Warren tipped his head in response. "Indeed, it is always wise to listen to one's wife. At least if you are a sane man, considering they are the ones to do the cooking."

Mrs. Warren laughed. "Don't worry, Dear, I have yet to poison you and I have no intention of doing so in the near future."

Miles glanced at Edwina and saw that her lips were curved into a bright smile as she listened to the Warrens' lighthearted conversation. It was evident in her expression that she felt comfortable here. With them.

Reaching for a book on the table next to him, Mr. Warren addressed Edwina. "I wish to return the book that I borrowed. I greatly enjoyed it."

Edwina stepped forward and collected the book from him. "Would you care for another one?"

"That won't be necessary since the doctor has given me permission to put pressure on my foot starting tomorrow," Mr. Warren revealed.

"But the doctor also said you should take it easy," Mrs. Warren pressed.

Mr. Warren let out an exasperated sigh. "Yes, but the wood still needs to be chopped if we want to eat or stay warm around here."

Miles stepped forward, knowing that was something he could do. "I will do it."

"I cannot ask such a thing of you, my lord," Mr. Warren protested.

"You didn't ask, I offered," Miles remarked. "It would be silly to send for a servant when I am more than capable of wielding an ax."

Mrs. Warren exchanged a look with her husband before saying, "You are kind to offer, my lord, but we do not wish you to trouble yourself. We can manage on our own."

"I'm afraid I won't take no for an answer," Miles said firmly.

Edwina turned towards him and asked, "Do you even know how to cut wood?"

A corner of Miles' lips quirked upward. "It isn't an overly complicated process, but, yes, I do know how," he responded confidently. "It is a skill any decent soldier should possess."

"I thought I recognized a fellow military man when I saw you," Mr. Warren said, his voice reflective. "I served in the Army myself."

"As did I," Miles responded.

Mr. Warren gestured towards the window. "The ax is out back. Just a few logs would do us just fine."

As Miles moved to depart, Edwina placed a hand on his sleeve and said, "I will join you."

"I would like that very much," he replied.

Edwina's gaze lingered on him, her expression a mixture of astonishment and pride. He felt his chest swell with a sense of accomplishment as he watched the admiration in her eyes.

Who would have thought that offering to do such a mundane task would have earned Edwina's approval?

Chapter Nine

As Edwina followed Miles to the rear of the cottage, she couldn't quite believe that he had offered to chop wood, which was a mundane task that was beneath an earl. Yet here they were, standing in front of a neatly stacked pile of logs and an ax propped against them.

Miles came to a stop in front of the ax, his tall figure casting a long shadow on the grassy ground. He removed his jacket and turned to face her. "Would you mind holding this?" he asked with a smile.

"It would be my pleasure, considering you are doing a great service to the Warrens," she replied as she stepped forward to accept the jacket.

Miles reached for the ax. "It is of little consequence," he remarked nonchalantly.

"But it is," she disagreed with admiration in her voice. "You are an earl and I doubt you dirty your hands often."

With an amused look, Miles responded, "You could almost say that I am not acting very 'earlish.'"

She laughed. "Most definitely."

"Good, because above all else, I am a man," Miles said.

"Besides, I used to chop wood all the time when I was younger."

"Did you not have servants to tend to such things?" she asked curiously.

Miles nodded, his expression becoming more thoughtful. "We had servants, but my brother and I used to escape to our hunting lodge in the woodlands. It was just us two and we did what we needed to do to survive," he shared. "It was the best of times."

Edwina could hear the wistfulness in his voice and knew his admission came at a great cost to him.

"Unfortunately, John is no longer with us and the hunting lodge has been vacant for many years now," Miles said.

Miles turned back towards the wood pile and picked up the ax. With a determined expression, he swung the ax in smooth, practiced motions. The sound of wood cracking echoed through the woodlands as he split log after log with impressive precision.

He came to a stop and placed the ax down. He picked up the split pieces of wood and stacked them neatly by the pile.

The sweat glistened from Miles' brow and he wiped it away with the back of his gloved hand. "That should be enough for now," he said.

Edwina could sense the weight of grief and pain that hung around Miles like a cloak. She knew she shouldn't pry, but her curiosity got the best of her. "May I ask how John died?"

Miles' jaw visibly tensed. "In a duel."

"How awful," she murmured.

"It was a needless way to die, but John had always been too cocky for his own good," Miles said. "He never thought anything bad could happen to him. He lived a life with no fear."

Edwina offered him a weak smile, trying to offer comfort

in any way she could. "A little fear is a good thing," she responded tentatively.

Miles' gaze softened as he looked at her, his blue eyes searching hers. "That it is," he agreed. "It reminds us that we have something to live for."

"Does this mean you have found a new purpose for which to live?" Edwina asked.

Miles held her gaze for a moment before answering, his expression giving nothing away. "I believe so," he said.

Edwina felt something stirring in her heart but she refused to acknowledge it. She couldn't. But her treacherous heart didn't seem to listen- or care.

Taking a step closer, Miles asked, "May I have my jacket back?"

Blinking rapidly, Edwina stumbled over her words. "Yes, yes, you can," she managed to say. "I was just holding it for you so you could chop wood."

A smile tugged at the corners of Miles' lips. "And you did a wonderful job."

Feeling flustered and embarrassed by her own behavior, Edwina extended him the jacket. "Yes, well, it was far easier than chopping wood. Which you did brilliantly." Why couldn't she stop yammering on? What must Miles think of her?

Amusement danced in Miles' eyes as he said, "You do not need to heap praises on me for chopping wood."

"When else would I do it, then?" Edwina retorted.

Miles glanced up at the sky. "We must hurry if we wish to join everyone for breakfast. Although, I fear we might already be late."

"Most likely, but I am sure my family will understand."

Miles lifted his brow. "And what would your uncle say about that?"

Straightening her shoulders and adopting a stern tone, Edwina replied, "A lady should never make excuses for being late for breakfast."

He chuckled. "You sound just like him."

"I have had a lot of practice," Edwina said. "I miss Uncle Lionel. He was always so carefree before my father passed away. But now he's burdened with responsibilities and constantly criticizes me."

Miles slipped his jacket back on and gestured towards the path that led to the front of the cottage, indicating she should go first. "He does seem much more serious these days, but he has always been one for propriety."

"That he has been," Edwina sighed. "But it has only gotten worse since he became a marquess."

Miles' gaze turned sympathetic. "I'm sorry."

She glanced over at him as they walked side by side. "There is no need to apologize. This is my lot in life, I'm afraid," she said. "He even called me 'mousy.'"

"Mousy?"

"Yes, I happened to overhear a conversation between my aunt and uncle."

Miles shot her a meaningful glance. "You mean you eavesdropped?"

"Some might call it that," Edwina said with a slight shrug of her shoulder. "But I prefer calling it 'collective listening.'"

"Calling it by a fancy name doesn't change the fact you were eavesdropping," he joked.

Edwina bobbed her head. "You are right. I was eavesdropping."

"Was that so hard to admit?" he asked with a smile.

"It was, actually," Edwina replied.

Miles grew solemn. "It was wrong what Lord Dallington said of you," he said. "I have never considered you 'mousy.' Reserved. Shy. Unapproachable. Those were merely my initial perceptions of you."

Edwina worked hard to keep the displeasure off her expression at his words. "Thank you for your honesty," she muttered.

"But now…" His words trailed off as he turned to face her fully, his expression soft yet intense. "The words I would describe you as are vastly different. Fierce. Loyal. Compassionate. But, more importantly, I am completely and breathtakingly fascinated by you."

Edwina's breath caught, unsure if she could believe his words or if they were simply to flatter her. But the sincerity in Miles' eyes and the conviction in his voice made her want to believe him. "You are kind, my lord," Edwina murmured.

"That is the thing, there is nothing kind about it," Miles said. "It is the way I feel."

As Miles collected his horse, Edwina took a deep breath, trying to steady her racing heart. Could he really mean his words? And if so, what did that mean?

Mrs. Warren stepped out onto the porch. "Thank you again, my lord," she said with genuine gratitude.

Miles acknowledged her words with a tip of his head before he started leading his horse towards the path. Edwina matched his stride and they walked down the path together in comfortable silence. Never had silence felt so poignant.

But it didn't last long.

Miles glanced at her and asked, "Did your father leave you an inheritance?"

Unsure of where this conversation was headed, Edwina replied, "No, just a dowry of fifteen thousand pounds."

"That is a generous dowry, but are you sure that is all your father left for you?" Miles pressed.

Edwina furrowed her brow in thought. "I never read his will, but my uncle informed me that my father made no mention of me in it."

Miles' expression turned solemn as he inquired, "Does that not strike you as odd, considering how much your father doted on you?"

Her brow furrowing deeper, Edwina responded, "Not particularly, since it is my uncle's responsibility to care for me since he inherited my father's title. I'm sure they discussed such matters beforehand."

Miles didn't look convinced as he shared, "I happened to overhear a conversation between your uncle and Mr. Stanley."

"You mean you eavesdropped?" she teased.

He chuckled. "I prefer the term 'collective listening.'" His demeanor grew somber again. "The conversation implied that there may be additional funds that should have been available to you."

"I don't know what funds those could be."

"Perhaps it would be worth asking to see your father's will," Miles suggested.

Edwina's eyes grew wide. "If I were to do such a thing, my uncle would be furious at me for not trusting him. I wouldn't want to anger him."

Miles tightened the reins in his hand. "But what if you are entitled to more than what has been given to you?"

"What if you just misconstrued the conversation?"

"I didn't," Miles replied, his jaw set and his eyes blazing with conviction. "I know what I heard."

Edwina shifted her gaze away from his, her mind racing as she tried to make sense of everything. What was she to do? If she asked to see the will and Miles was wrong, then her uncle would be furious at her. But what if he was right? No. That was inconceivable. Her uncle wouldn't try to cheat her out of an inheritance. The mere thought made her stomach churn with unease.

Would he?

No.

Yes.

Maybe.

The doubt crept in, nagging at her mind, despite her attempts to push it away.

Miles' voice broke through her thoughts. "I can see you

are thinking it over, but just know that I would never lie to you."

"Yet you are asking me to believe that my uncle is lying to me- a man that I have known my entire life," she challenged.

"Is it not worth looking into?" Miles asked.

Edwina felt torn, unsure of who to believe or who to trust. She had a choice to make. Did she continue blindly trusting her uncle or did she trust a man that she only just met? A man who was already stirring inconvenient feelings in her heart.

Brockhall Manor loomed ahead of them as they approached and Edwina suddenly had a thought. What if she didn't have to ask her uncle to see her father's will? Then he would never know that she thought he might be lying to her.

In a determined voice, Edwina asked, "What if I snuck into my uncle's study and read the will when he was away?"

"And what if you don't like what it says?" Miles asked.

Despite the uncertainty that churned within her, Edwina put on a brave face. "I will deal with that when, and if, it becomes an issue," she declared, trying to convince herself as much as Miles.

"All right, I shall help you."

She hesitated, torn between wanting his help and wanting to prove herself capable on her own. "I never asked for your help. Besides, I couldn't ask you to do such a thing."

A smug smirk spread across his lips. "No, but you will need it."

"And why is that?" she challenged.

He came to a stop on the path and turned to face her. "Have you ever broken into a study before?"

Edwina's confidence faltered as she admitted truthfully, "No, but surely it can't be too difficult."

His smirk softened, as did his words. "Trust me, Edwina."

The way he said her name, with such tenderness, she knew- in her heart- that she could trust him. "Very well," she agreed.

Miles looked pleased by her words before he turned his attention back towards Brockhall Manor. "Let us make haste before Bennett comes looking for us."

As Miles escorted Edwina into the dining room, he couldn't help but notice Bennett's disapproving glare from his seat at the long table.

Miles pulled out Edwina's chair and took a seat beside her, bracing himself for Bennett's inevitable interrogation.

"What, pray tell, caused you and Edwina to arrive at the same time?" Bennett asked with a hint of censure in his voice as he addressed Miles.

Miles calmly explained, "I accompanied Lady Edwina to the Warrens' cottage after my morning ride."

Edwina spoke up. "Lord Hilgrove graciously chopped wood for the Warrens," she praised.

Bennett's brow lifted in surprise. "You didn't, did you?" His tone was incredulous as he turned to Miles.

With a slight shrug, Miles replied, "There was a need and I filled it. There is no reason to make a big ado out of it."

"Why didn't you send a servant?" Bennett pressed.

"For what purpose?" Miles asked. "I am more than capable of chopping some wood. And besides, it reminded me of a much simpler time when John and I would go to our hunting lodge. We attempted to live off the land but we were spectacularly bad at it."

Bennett leaned forward in his seat. "Why didn't you have the servants stock food at the hunting lodge?"

"We wanted to hunt our own food," Miles explained with a fond smile at the memory. "Every morning, we would wake up to a fresh kill in one of our traps."

"It sounds like you were successful, then," Bennett acknowledged.

Miles chuckled. "No, far from it," he replied. "Our gamekeeper took pity on us and would always leave us something so we could eat. It wasn't until we were older that he confessed to such a thing."

Bennett clucked his tongue. "I doubt that I would have fared much better," he admitted with a wry smile.

Edwina shifted in her seat to face Miles. "It sounds as if you and your brother were rather close."

"At times, we were," Miles said. "That is why I cherished my time with John at the hunting lodge. It was nice to be together without servants underfoot."

Lord and Lady Dallington stepped into the room and sat at the ends of the table.

"Good morning," Lady Dallington greeted with a warm smile. "I do apologize for our tardiness, but I assure you that it couldn't be helped."

Lord Dallington gave his wife an amused look. "It could have been avoided if you had made a decision on which gown to wear sooner."

"Choosing which gown to wear is no small matter when I am having tea with Mrs. Walker," Lady Dallington said.

Bennett grimaced. "The village gossip," he stated. "Why do you wish to spend time with her?"

"Oh, she is quite a delightful woman," Lady Dallington replied as she elegantly placed a napkin on her lap. "We have much in common."

"You mean, you like to gossip," Bennett teased.

A glint of mischief sparkled in Lady Dallington's eyes. "No, we simply enjoy discussing the happenings of our quaint little village. It's not gossip when it's shared between friends."

"That is precisely what gossip is," Bennett responded.

With a shake of her head, Lady Dallington turned her

attention to Edwina. "Would you care to join us?" she asked. "I am sure that Mrs. Walker would love to see you."

Edwina leaned to the side as a footman placed a plate of food in front of her. "I… um… am busy today," she stammered.

"Doing what, may I ask?" her aunt pressed.

Her eyes darted towards Miles as she no doubt attempted to come up with a believable excuse. "I have a pile of books that I would like to read today," Edwina said quickly. "It will take all day and into the night. I am sure of it."

Her aunt gave her a curious look. "If you are sure…"

Edwina gave a decisive bob of her head. "Yes, these books won't read themselves," she added with a nervous laugh.

Miles resisted the urge to smile at Edwina's uneasy attempt to keep things from her family. She was clearly not cut out for this kind of subterfuge and he couldn't imagine her ever being a successful spy. She wore her emotions on her sleeve. Which was a refreshing change of pace for him.

Deciding it was best to divert the conversation away from Edwina's awkwardness, Miles announced, "I believe I shall spend some time reading as well."

"But we were going to go angling today with a few of my friends," Bennett said.

"That sounds dreadfully dull," Miles responded. "You can go without me."

Bennett considered him for a moment before saying, "Of course it is dull. It is angling. There is only so much you can do when trying to catch fish. But it is fun to be around the other men. Are you sure that you would rather stay back and read?"

Miles reached for his glass, taking a sip before answering, "I would."

"I hadn't taken you much for a reader," Bennett said. "You didn't seem to have much time for books during our university days."

"I read all the time," Miles defended.

"That may be true, but they were books that we were required to read for the course," Bennett stated.

Lord Dallington chimed in, coming to Miles' defense. "Leave Miles be. If he wants to spend the day reading, so be it. Our library is well stocked with books."

Bennett tapped his fingers on the table, as if he were trying to sort out a puzzle. "All right, I will drop it… for now," he conceded with a small grin.

Miles began eating his food as Lord Dallington announced, "I have meetings all day today that will keep me away. But I shall return for supper."

Lady Dallington acknowledged his words with a smile. "I do appreciate you making time so we may dine as a family."

"I know it makes you happy," Lord Dallington responded, returning her smile. "Besides, a man has to eat."

"That he does, and I shall see that your favorite dishes are prepared," Lady Dallington said before she shifted her gaze towards Edwina. "How was the basket received by the Warrens?"

"They were most grateful," Edwina replied.

Lord Dallington let out a disapproving huff. "I do not know why you insist on spending time with the Warrens. They were merely servants in your father's household."

Edwina tilted her chin defiantly. "They have, and always will be, more than just servants to me. When I am with them, I feel a part of me is at home."

"Nonsense," Lord Dallington said. "You should be using your time for more worthwhile pursuits- like finding a suitable husband."

Lady Dallington shot her husband a sharp look. "Lionel…" she started, her voice holding a warning.

"Are we not allowed to discuss such serious matters?" Lord Dallington asked, his tone defensive.

"There is a time and place for such discussions and the

breakfast table is not one of them," Lady Dallington stated firmly.

Lord Dallington pursed his lips. "Edwina cannot live off our generosity forever. She needs to find a husband, and quickly. I will not have her be a drain on our finances."

Miles glanced over at Edwina and noticed the fire burning in her eyes. She seemed ready to fight back, but instead, she abruptly rose from her seat. "Excuse me, I just need a moment," she said, before swiftly exiting the room.

After Edwina departed, Lady Dallington let out a weary sigh and shook her head. "Why must you insist on putting undue pressure on Edwina?"

"Undue pressure?" Lord Dallington asked. "You were married to me at this very age."

"But those were different circumstances," Lady Dallington countered.

Lord Dallington pushed aside his plate and leaned forward. "We mustn't coddle Edwina forever. It is not good for her, or anyone else for that matter."

Bennett dabbed at the corners of his mouth with a napkin and placed it neatly beside his plate. "I think I should go speak with Edwina."

"Allow me," Miles offered, pushing back his chair and standing up.

Bennett's expression turned to one of skepticism. "You? Dare I ask why?" he questioned.

Miles met his friend's gaze steadily. "I can sympathize with what Lady Edwina is going through," he explained.

Bennett eyed him for a moment before he conceded. "Very well," he said with a wave of his hand. "But you better not upset her further."

Miles didn't need to be told twice. As he departed from the dining room, he heard Bennett inquire of his father, "Why must you be so critical towards Edwina?" A smile came to his lips, knowing that his friend was doing all he could to protect Edwina in his own way.

He quickly made his way down the corridors of the grand manor in search of Edwina. As he reached the entry hall, he saw the butler standing watch by the door.

"Have you seen Lady Edwina?" Miles asked.

The butler tipped his head. "Yes, my lord," he replied. "She was heading towards the gardens."

Miles wasted no time in making his way towards the gardens, eager to find Edwina. He stepped outside and saw Edwina sitting on a bench, a goat nestled contentedly in her lap.

Edwina looked up as he approached. "I see that you got the short straw," she quipped.

"No, quite the opposite, in fact," Miles said, coming to a stop by the bench. There wasn't much room for him to sit down, as the goat took up most of the space. "May I ask where the goat came from?"

A smile came to Edwina's face. "This is Matilda," she announced proudly. "She is one of the Warrens' goats and is constantly causing mischief."

"You two seem quite close," Miles observed.

"Looks can be deceiving," Edwina said. "Matilda has claimed this bench as her own and anyone who sits here must be prepared to give her attention."

Not wanting to stand any longer, Miles gently shifted the goat's backside and squeezed onto the far end of the bench.

The goat let out a loud bleat in response.

Edwina's eyes sparkled with mirth. "You have upset Matilda now."

"Matilda needs to learn how to share," Miles chided playfully.

"Well, she is just a goat after all."

"That may be true, but it is no excuse," Miles retorted.

Edwina ran her hand down the goat's neck as she posed

the question, "Do you think it is time for me to find a husband?"

Miles gave her a look that he hoped was filled with compassion. "What do you truly want, Edwina?"

"I want to marry, but I haven't even had my first Season," Edwina replied, her voice tinged with hesitation. "Besides, it is not as if this village is overflowing with eligible suitors."

"I understand your concerns. Marriage is not a decision to be made lightly," Miles counseled. "When I met Arabella, my whole life changed, and for the better."

Edwina grew silent. "Do you ever intend to remarry?"

"No, I do not," he admitted truthfully. "My first marriage brought me great love and happiness, and I doubt that I would find something like that again."

"That is fair." Edwina lowered her gaze to the goat, her thoughts clearly troubled.

Sensing her unease, Miles gently prodded, "What is it?"

A line between Edwina's brow appeared. "How did you know you were in love with Arabella?"

"That is easy," Miles replied. "It was her smile. The first time I saw it, I knew I wanted to see it every day for the rest of my life."

Doubt clouded Edwina's eyes as she took a deep breath. "But what if… what if I do not find a love like yours? What if I am forced to settle for less?"

"You won't be," Miles asserted.

Edwina raised her gaze again, the vulnerability evident in her expression. "How can you be so sure?"

With gentle sincerity, Miles responded, "Because it is no less than you deserve."

"It seems as if my uncle would have me marry anyone, just for the sake of marrying," Edwina said with a touch of bitterness in her voice.

Miles held her gaze, hoping his next words would bring

her some comfort. "You are a beautiful young woman with much to offer. Any gentleman would be lucky to have you."

Edwina's eyes widened in surprise. "You think I am beautiful?"

"I do," he replied, not sure why he had just admitted that so freely. He may care for Edwina, but he had no intention of pursuing her. He couldn't. His love for Arabella was still strong and he wouldn't betray her memory.

"No one has called me beautiful before," Edwina said, her voice barely above a whisper.

"Well, you better start getting used to it because the marriage mart is not for the faint of heart," Miles teased.

Edwina smiled, and it was as if the day had gotten brighter because of it. "Thank you, Miles," she said with genuine gratitude in her voice.

"That is what any good friend is for," he responded. "Shall we return to breakfast?"

"No, I think I would like to stay here," Edwina replied.

Miles settled back into his seat, content to sit in the peaceful gardens with Edwina by his side. "If you have no objections, I believe I shall remain with you."

"I have none."

"Good, because I doubt Matilda would have let me leave anyway," Miles joked.

As he basked in the warm sun and the gentle breeze, Miles knew that he was in trouble. He had little doubt that Edwina's large dowry and connection would make her well received by the *ton*. But the mere thought of Edwina being pursued by anyone did not settle well with him.

Chapter Ten

Edwina sifted through the gowns in her wardrobe, her fingers lingering on the soft silk and intricate lace. She needed a gown for a specific purpose- sneaking into her uncle's study. She was wearing a lavender gown, but she wasn't sure if it would attract any unwanted attention. Did any of her gowns cause unwanted attention, she wondered.

This was ridiculous.

With a sigh, she chided herself on overthinking this and just walked out to meet Miles in the entry hall. But even as she made her way down the corridor, her heart raced with nervous anticipation. It wasn't like her to partake in such underhanded actions, but she couldn't bring herself to ask her uncle for answers. If he was indeed lying to her, she would confront him about it. Until then, she would unravel the truth on her own terms.

As she descended the grand staircase, her eyes settled upon Miles. He looked dashing in his fitted blue jacket and buff trousers. Where had that thought even come from, she wondered. She needed to stay focused on the important matter at hand instead of getting lost in thoughts about his handsomeness.

Miles smiled as she approached. "Are you ready?" he asked, his voice low.

Edwina hesitated before answering. "Yes... no," she admitted, fidgeting with the folds of her lavender gown. "Am I dressed appropriately?"

"Yes, you are."

"But what if my gown attracts too much attention?" Edwina asked. "Or is it sneaky enough?"

"Lavender is indeed a very sneaky color," Miles teased, his smile widening.

Edwina lowered her hands to her sides. "Perhaps I should have worn my dark green gown instead. No one would have suspected me then."

Miles cocked his head. "I do not think it would have made a difference."

"But it does," Edwina insisted. "Everyone knows that yellow is the sneakiest of all colors. It is too bright, too suspicious. What could that color be hiding?"

"I do not think yellow is hiding anything," Miles responded.

Edwina arched an eyebrow. "What color do you think would be best for espionage?"

"Black," came his simple reply.

With a bob of her head, Edwina said, "You are right. Can I change my answer?"

Miles glanced over his shoulder before lowering his voice. "You are overthinking this," he assured her. "You are just going to step into your uncle's office for a book and no one will be the wiser."

"What if someone asks me which book I am looking for?" Edwina asked.

"No one will," Miles said.

"But what if they do?" Her brow furrowed in worry and she nervously wrung her hands together.

Miles placed a hand on her sleeve, his touch warm and comforting. "All right. What is your favorite book?"

Edwina pressed her lips together as she debated over his question. "I suppose at this time my favorite book is *Sense and Sensibility*."

"That is the book written by A Lady, is it not?"

"It is," Edwina replied. "Have you read it?"

He shook his head. "I have not."

"Is it because it is written by A Lady?" she asked, almost accusatorily.

Miles' face grew solemn. "No, it was Arabella's favorite book as well. She devoured it the moment she acquired it."

"Oh, I am sorry," Edwina acknowledged. "I shouldn't have assumed you were opposed to a woman writer."

"Some of the greatest books are written by women."

Edwina lowered her voice. "Do not let my uncle hear you say that," she warned jokingly. "He might even engage in fisticuffs over that remark."

Miles tipped his head. "I shall make note of that." He gave her an expectant look. "You can do this."

Her heart started racing at the mere thought of the task ahead. Could she really accomplish such a thing? "Can I?" she asked, trying to mask her nervousness.

"You can," Miles replied. "Besides, I will stand guard while you search through the files in your uncle's desk, looking for anything that might arouse your suspicion."

"And if I find nothing?"

Miles shrugged. "Then there is your answer."

Determined not to let her doubts consume her, Edwina squared her shoulders and forced herself to exude confidence. "I can do this," she murmured under her breath.

"We just get in and get out. It is that simple," Miles said.

Edwina eyed him curiously. "How is it that you are so comfortable with espionage?" she asked.

Miles smirked, a mischievous glint in his eyes. "This is not espionage," he replied. "You are simply searching for your father's will among your uncle's files."

"That doesn't answer my question."

"You never did ask what I did during the war," Miles said. "I may have dabbled in espionage a time or two."

"You may have?"

A cocky grin spread across his face, causing her to question what secrets he was keeping from her. "The less you know, the better," he remarked.

Edwina couldn't resist pressing for more information. "Is that all you intend to tell me?"

"For now," Miles replied. "I do not want you to be distracted."

"What if someone catches us?" Edwina asked, returning to the matter at hand.

Miles looked amused. "That is why you are searching your uncle's desk and not me. You are not the least bit suspicious."

She frowned. "Should I take that as a compliment?"

"I would take it more as a fact," Miles replied. "You being in your uncle's study is perfectly acceptable."

"You are right."

Miles offered his arm. "Shall I escort you to the study, my lady?"

Edwina placed her hand on his sleeve. "Thank you, kind sir."

As they made their way to her uncle's study, Edwina gathered her strength. Miles was right. There was no reason why anyone would suspect what she was truly doing. She had visited the study on numerous occasions before without any suspicion being raised.

They stopped outside the open door and Miles dropped his arm. "Remember, I will keep watch and alert you if anyone approaches."

"Will you signal me with a bird call?"

Miles looked baffled. "A bird call? Whatever for?"

"If someone is approaching, just mimic a nightingale's song and I will know to stop," Edwina explained.

He looked at her like she was mad. "How in the blazes am I supposed to mimic a nightingale?"

"It is not too difficult," she replied. "But if you prefer, just mimic a robin's song. Surely, you can do that."

Miles opened his mouth and closed it before saying, "Can you make those bird calls yourself?"

Edwina brought her hand up to her mouth, creating a seal with her fingers to avoid any air escaping, and let out a clear whistle that echoed down the corridor, a perfect mimicry of a robin's song.

While she dropped her hands, Miles said, "I still can't do that. What if I tell you if someone is approaching in words? Not bird calls?"

"Very well, but that isn't very spy-like," Edwina remarked.

"Trust me, neither is a bird call," Miles said. "Now go inside before our conversation attracts any unwanted attention."

Edwina took a quick glance at the study and noted the large wooden desk positioned by the long windows, filled with papers and books. "Can you come with me?"

"Then who would stand watch?" he asked. "Besides, it wouldn't be wise for us to be caught in the same room together."

Edwina reluctantly admitted that he had a point and began to step towards the study when her aunt suddenly appeared around the corner, spotting them immediately. "Whatever are you two doing?" she inquired.

Panicked, Edwina stumbled over her own words. "Nothing… why would we be doing anything?" she asked, turning her gaze towards Miles. "We are just standing here, minding our own business." Drats. Why couldn't she stop rambling?

Her aunt came to a stop in front of them. "Are you all right, Edwina?" she asked with concern in her voice.

Trying to cover up her discomfort, Edwina forced a bright smile to her face. "I am more than all right! I am so happy, in fact, that I feel like changing into my yellow gown." She resisted the urge to groan at her clumsy attempt at a diversion.

Her aunt perused the length of her. "What is wrong with the one you are wearing now?" she questioned.

"Nothing is wrong with this gown. Nothing at all," Edwina replied.

Miles cleared his throat. "Lady Edwina was hoping to collect a book from Lord Dallington's library. She is rather eager for me to read it."

"Oh, which book?" her aunt asked.

"*Sense and Sensibility*," Miles replied. "My late wife, Arabella, loved that book but I lost my copy when I left the Continent."

Sympathy filled her aunt's eyes as she offered words of comfort. "Reading can be a wonderful way to occupy one's mind during difficult times."

"Yes, it is," Miles agreed.

With questions in her eyes, her aunt turned towards Edwina. "Shall I retrieve the book for Lord Hilgrove, then?"

Edwina shook her head. "No, there is no need for you to go through any trouble," she replied. "I thought you had plans to have tea with Mrs. Walker."

"I was just about to depart when I saw the two of you loitering outside of Lionel's study," her aunt said.

Edwina let out a nervous chuckle. "We were not loitering. We have a purpose for being here."

"Perhaps you should rest after retrieving the book," her aunt suggested. "You seem rather out of sorts."

"That is an excellent idea. I will do just that," Edwina stated.

Her aunt paused for a moment before continuing down the corridor. "If you need me, send one of the servants to collect me," she said over her shoulder.

"I will, Aunt Catherine. And thank you," Edwina assured her.

As her aunt disappeared around the corner, Edwina let out a sigh of relief, grateful that was over and done with.

The corners of Miles' lips twitched as he joked, "I must say, that was quite an impressive performance. Have you ever considered a career in the theater?"

"I tend to get a little flustered when I'm caught doing something I'm not supposed to do," Edwina admitted.

"I can see that," Miles said with amusement in his voice. "It was almost painful to witness."

With a roll of her eyes, Edwina couldn't help but smile at his teasing. "Well, thank you for your honest critique," she remarked.

Miles gestured towards the study door. "The sooner you get in there, the sooner it will be over."

"That is some good advice."

"Stop stalling Edwina," Miles encouraged. "You are more than capable of engaging in subterfuge. In fact, I might even put in a good word to Wellington for you. He is always looking for a few good spies."

Edwina couldn't help but laugh at his absurd remark. "Please don't," she said. "Wish me luck."

Miles leaned closer, his warm breath tickling her ear. "You don't need luck," he whispered reassuringly. "I won't let anything bad happen to you."

And she believed him.

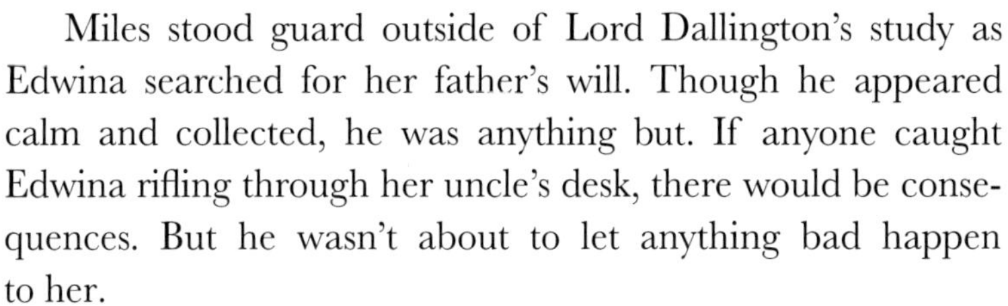

Miles stood guard outside of Lord Dallington's study as Edwina searched for her father's will. Though he appeared calm and collected, he was anything but. If anyone caught Edwina rifling through her uncle's desk, there would be consequences. But he wasn't about to let anything bad happen to her.

He would protect her, at all costs. It didn't quite make sense why he felt so protective of her, but he did. It may have had something to do with the feelings that he had developed for her. But those feelings were in no way reciprocated. Which was good. Edwina was a friend and he didn't want to hurt her.

He glanced in the study and saw Edwina searching her uncle's desk. She was moving fast, and he hoped she was giving the attention that was required. He didn't want her to miss anything.

A smile came to his lips as he thought about how Edwina wanted him to do a bird call as a warning sign of someone approaching. She was something special. That was for sure. She could make him smile even when he was determined to wallow in his own misery.

A gasp came from within the study. He watched as she read a paper on her uncle's desk, her expression changing from shock to anger. Without a word, she met his gaze, and he knew that she had found the will. Her uncle had indeed deceived her.

In a hushed voice, Miles instructed, "Keep the will but put everything back just the way you found it."

He could see the panic in her eyes, but she quickly composed herself and did as he had instructed. Once she stepped away from the desk, she hurried over to him and opened her mouth.

Miles held up a hand to stop her words. "Not here," he whispered. "Let's take a tour of the gardens."

Edwina nodded her understanding and followed him towards the rear of the manor. A footman opened the door and they stepped outside into the warm sunshine.

The gardens were alive with vibrant colors and sweet scents. Once they were walking down a path, Miles asked, "How much did your father leave you?"

Edwina looked surprised by his question. "Ten thousand pounds," she replied. "How did you know?"

Miles grinned. "You are truly terrible at hiding your emotions."

A soft blush spread across Edwina's cheeks and she murmured, "Oh, I hadn't realized."

"To be honest, I find it rather refreshing," Miles said. "Although, you must learn to place a mask on when dealing with the *ton*. One mustn't give too much away when you enter high Society."

Edwina grew quiet as she looked into his eyes, searching for answers that he knew he couldn't provide. "What am I to do?" she asked.

Miles held his hand out. "May I see the will?"

She extended it towards him and he made quick work of reading it. Edwina had been right. The late Lord Dallington had left her ten thousand pounds, in addition to her dowry. So why had her uncle kept this from her?

As he tried to make sense of the situation, he asked, "Did you ever meet with your father's solicitor after he passed away?"

"No, I did not. I didn't think there was a need," Edwina said, her voice laced with regret. "My uncle told me that he would take care of everything and I believed him." Her gaze drew downcast. "But now I see how wrong I was."

Miles could hear the sadness in her voice and it tugged at his heart. "You did nothing wrong, Edwina."

"Didn't I?" she asked, meeting his gaze once more. "I trusted my uncle and he deceived me. What else has he been lying to me about?"

Coming to a stop on the path, Miles turned to face her. "I think we should tell Bennett about this," he suggested.

Edwina shook her head firmly. "No, not yet."

"He can help us when we confront your uncle," Miles pressed.

"Before we bring Bennett into our confidence, I need to know if my uncle is lying about anything else," Edwina declared with determination in her voice.

Miles gave her a pointed look as he inquired, "Did you find anything else in your uncle's desk that aroused suspicion?"

"No, but if my uncle is lying about my inheritance, he must be lying about other things, too," Edwina asserted.

"That is not always the case, and Bennett is in the perfect position to help you," Miles said.

Edwina's eyes grew guarded. "What if Bennett knew about my inheritance, and kept it quiet for his father's sake?"

Miles knew his friend well, and he was confident that was not the case. "No, Bennett is a good man and he loves you. He would never have kept something like this from you."

"You are right. I guess I am just afraid of not knowing who to trust."

Miles held her gaze as he said, "You can trust me."

A small smile came to Edwina's lips. "I do," she said.

Pride swelled within Miles' chest as he heard those words. He had worked hard to earn her trust and he would never betray it. He would die first.

In a hushed, almost conspiratorial tone, Edwina asked, "Where do we go from here?"

"Well, if you don't want to tell Bennett, I suggest speaking to your father's solicitor," Miles proposed.

"That won't be easy. He is now my uncle's solicitor since he inherited my father's title," Edwina said.

"Ah, that does complicate matters some," Miles remarked.

Edwina's eyes lit up. "What if we follow my uncle into the village and see how he spends his time?" she suggested.

Miles raised an eyebrow skeptically. "And what would that prove?"

She shrugged. "I'm not sure. But it is a start."

Miles couldn't bring himself to dampen her enthusiasm, even though he knew it was likely a futile endeavor since Lord Dallington was probably in meetings all day. "Well, then, let's take a trip to the village and see what secrets it holds."

In response, a bright, infectious smile lit up Edwina's face and Miles couldn't help but grin in return, despite his best efforts not to. How was it that her smile seemed to penetrate the barriers around his heart? It was rather troublesome.

Bennett's voice came from down the path, his boots grinding on the gravel as he approached. "What, pray tell, are you two discussing?" he asked with a tilt of his head.

Miles exchanged a quick glance with Edwina before responding, "Nothing of importance."

But Bennett wasn't easily fooled. His piercing blue eyes narrowed as he observed them both. "Then why were you both smiling at one another?"

"Were we?" Miles asked, feigning innocence.

Edwina spoke up. "We were talking about the plants that needed to be tended to before we depart for London."

Bennett had seen through their charade. Not that it was overly difficult to do so. "Plants? You expect me to believe that?"

Edwina bobbed her head. "Yes, I do."

With a resigned sigh, Bennett relented. "Fine, do not tell me. But I will be keeping an eye on you two."

Miles interjected, "I thought you were angling with your friends."

"I am," Bennett replied. "I was making my way down to the stream when I saw you two taking a stroll in the gardens."

"We are about to take a trip into the village," Edwina revealed.

Bennett gave her a curious look. "For what purpose?"

"I wanted to show Lord Hilgrove around the village," Edwina replied.

"The village isn't that big, or interesting, for that matter," Bennett remarked with suspicion in his eyes.

Edwina's eyes darted towards Miles and he could see the hesitancy in them. He decided it was best if he spoke up. "I was hoping to buy a gift for my sister and Lady Edwina graciously offered to help me."

Bennett glanced between them before giving a curt nod. "Well, then, carry on," he said before he continued down the path towards the stream.

As they watched Bennett's retreating figure, Edwina turned to face him with relief on her face. "That was rather difficult," she expressed. "I didn't think he was ever going to leave."

Miles couldn't agree more but they had a bigger problem. "Bennett is many things, but he isn't a fool. We will have to be more careful if we wish to keep this from him."

"You make a good point," Edwina said. "Shall we depart for the village?"

"Let us," he replied, offering his arm.

Edwina placed her hand on his sleeve. "I can't quite believe my father left me ten thousand pounds and a generous dowry."

"You are truly an heiress now," Miles remarked.

"I am," she agreed. "Which poses a new conundrum."

"Whatever do you mean?"

Edwina pressed her lips together before asking, "How do I know if a suitor is genuinely interested in me, or simply my wealth?"

"It is certainly a challenge, but do not fear. I will be there to help you navigate through your hordes of potential suitors," Miles reassured her.

"You will?" Edwina asked.

Miles' lips quirked as he asked, "Did you think you could get rid of me so easily?" His tone carried a flirtatious edge.

Edwina ducked her head but not before he noticed the adorable blush on her cheeks. "You are too kind but let us not be hasty. I do not think I will have hordes of suitors vying for my hand."

Miles couldn't help but shake his head in disagreement. "I

do think you vastly underestimate yourself," he argued.

"Or perhaps you are *over*estimating me," Edwina countered. "Although, I will admit that I am relieved you shall be there for my first Season."

Miles was curious about one thing. "How is it that you haven't had your first Season yet?"

"My father grew sick and tarried for quite some time," Edwina replied solemnly. "I could not fathom leaving his side for a frivolous Season among high Society."

"And rightfully so," Miles agreed.

Edwina offered him a grateful smile before she continued. "You are kind to say so, but now I am debuting with my two cousins. I daresay it will be a competition to see which one of them will be the diamond of the first water."

"They don't strike me as the type of young women to care about such things," Miles stated.

"Indeed, they are not," Edwina replied. "Elodie and Melody would be content living as spinsters in a quaint cottage by a stream."

Miles chuckled at that thought. "I would love to overhear some of their conversations."

"It would certainly be entertaining," Edwina said. "They have a unique perspective as twins, but they don't realize how much attention they garner from their looks. Or they simply don't care."

Edwina glanced up at the sky and continued. "I will need to retrieve my bonnet for the ride to the village, and I might change into another gown."

He perused the length of her. "What is wrong with what you are wearing?"

"Do you think it is too lively?"

Miles furrowed his brow. "I do not think I would consider lavender to be a lively color."

Turning her attention away from him, she confessed, "It will be the first time in months that I have visited the village without wearing my mourning gowns."

Now he understood. "And you are worried about what people might think," he stated.

She winced. "I just don't want them to think I have forgotten about my father."

"Trust me, no one will think that," Miles reassured her. "But you can't live your life wondering what other people will think of you."

"I try not to, but doubt always seems to creep in," Edwina shared.

As they entered through the back door of the manor, Miles asked, "Do you think of your father every moment of every day?"

"I do."

"Then what else matters?" Miles asked as they walked down the corridor.

Edwina considered his words for a moment before she inquired, "When did you stop wearing your black armband?"

"I took it off before I departed to come here," he admitted.

Her surprise was evident in her slightly parted lips. "You wore it for a long time."

"I did, and I do not regret doing so."

Edwina came to a stop by the grand staircase and dropped her arm from his sleeve. "I think it is admirable."

"My sister thought I was foolish," Miles shared. "She wondered how I would ever get married again if I continued wearing it."

"I am sure your sister was just worried about you."

Miles let out a huff of air. "You could say that. You could also use the words overbearing and stubborn."

The corners of Edwina's mouth turned upwards in amusement. "Isn't that what sisters are for?" she teased.

"I suppose so," he replied. "She writes me all the time and I have yet to write her back."

Edwina tilted her head. "May I ask why?"

Miles ran a hand through his hair as he worked to keep the pained expression off his face. "She is blissfully happy with her husband and children and I am…" His words trailed off, unable to finish the sentence.

"Envious?" Edwina asked, finishing his thought.

"Yes, you could say that," Miles responded. "I also didn't want her to know how much I was struggling with Arabella and John's deaths."

Edwina placed a comforting hand on his sleeve. "You do not need to explain yourself to me."

"Thank you," Miles said.

Dropping her hand, she took a step back. "I will be down shortly. Will you ask White to prepare the carriage for our journey?"

"I will."

As Edwina headed up the stairs, she paused on the top step, turning to face him. She offered him a smile, one that he would no doubt remember in his dreams.

Chapter Eleven

Edwina sat across from Miles in the open-air carriage, her eyes fixated on the countryside passing by. She couldn't help but feel a sense of unease as they traveled towards the village. Would they discover anything else about her uncle? She hoped not. But it was rather obvious that he was not the man she had believed him to be.

For the past four months, Edwina had been plagued by questions and doubts surrounding her relationship with her uncle. What had she done to earn his ire? But she had been doing nothing wrong. It was him. All him. She wondered if he even felt a shred of guilt for lying to her.

Miles' voice broke through her musings. "It will be all right."

Edwina met his gaze, searching for reassurance. "Will it?" she asked. "My uncle has been lying to me. Once the truth is revealed, will he hate me even more than he already does?"

"He doesn't hate you."

Edwina lifted her brow. "He hardly can be in the same room as me."

"It might just be guilt," Miles proposed.

"Or perhaps he believes I don't deserve my inheritance," Edwina said.

Miles shook his head. "It doesn't matter what he thinks, you are legally entitled to that money."

"But I am his ward," Edwina pointed out. "He has complete control over my finances until I reach my majority, including how that money is spent."

"Regardless, he should have told you about the inheritance."

"Even so, I am at my uncle's mercy until I am twenty-one," Edwina sighed.

Miles leaned forward and held her gaze. "Bennett will ensure that nothing bad will happen to you. I can promise you that."

She had to acknowledge that Miles did make a good argument. Bennett had been fiercely protective of her since she was little. "You are right," she said.

Settling back into his seat, Miles smiled. "I like the sound of that."

A laugh escaped from Edwina's lips. "You must not hear that very often."

"Oh, I do indeed," Miles joked. "It is almost a curse, really."

"What a burden you must bear, my lord," Edwina teased, feeling herself relaxing against the bench. "We should be reaching the village soon."

Miles adjusted the top hat on his head. "But I must say, I am rather enjoying myself. The sun is shining down upon us, the birds are singing their songs, and the company is quite pleasant."

"Are you truly resorting to flattery?" she asked.

"I am, but only if it is working," Miles replied with a wink.

Edwina grinned. "I do not know whether to be flattered or insulted," she said.

With a dramatic flourish, Miles placed his hand over his heart. "Flattered, I assure you."

"All right, if you say so," Edwina responded. She had to admit that she rather enjoyed this playful side of Miles.

As they continued down the road towards the village, Edwina's eyes widened in surprise as she saw their crested coach parked outside a modest cottage, just set off the path.

She pointed towards the coach. "That is my uncle's coach," she revealed. "But what is he doing here?"

"Are you certain this is not the home of his solicitor or man of business?" Miles asked.

Edwina fixed him with a pointed look, challenging his thoughts. "Why would he visit one of their homes when they have offices set up in the village?" she asked. "Besides, this cottage is where Mrs. Wallington raised her children. She recently passed away, leaving it vacant. I hadn't realized anyone else moved in."

"Clearly someone has." Turning towards the driver, he ordered, "Stop here. We shall continue on foot to the village."

The driver reined in the team before asking, "Are you sure, my lord?"

"I am, but I will expect you to wait for us in the village," Miles replied firmly.

A footman stepped off his perch and came around to open the door. He offered his hand in assisting Edwina down the step.

Once she was standing on solid ground, she released the footman's hand and clasped her own in front of her. "What do we do now?" she asked as Miles came to stand next to her.

Miles gestured towards the woodlands, thick with towering trees that seemed to stretch on for miles. "We can position ourselves in the cover of those trees and wait for your uncle's appearance. With any luck, we may discover why he has come here."

"I think that is a fine plan," Edwina agreed.

As they made their way towards the edge of the woodlands, Miles said, "I do hope we do not soil your gown."

"The gown is the least of my concerns," she admitted. "My uncle is a liar, a cheat, and who knows what else."

Miles offered her a sympathetic smile. "I am sorry for what you are going through. I can't imagine how hard this is for you."

"Nothing is as difficult as losing my father," Edwina shared, her voice filled with emotion. "Everything else seems to pale in comparison."

With a nod of understanding, Miles said, "Yes, death has a way of putting things in perspective."

They stepped into the woodlands and the rustling leaves and melodic birdsong surrounded them. The canopy of trees covered their heads, creating a sense of sanctuary from the outside world. A nearby stream added to the calming ambiance.

"It is peaceful here," Edwina acknowledged.

Miles turned his attention towards the birds that flitted around them. "Perhaps I should learn how to mimic a bird call."

"It truly is not hard."

"It is for someone who can't whistle."

Edwina's mouth dropped. "You can't whistle?"

Miles simply shrugged. "It is not uncommon for someone to not know how to whistle," he defended.

"But it is so simple," Edwina insisted, demonstrating with a low whistle from her lips.

Miles' expression was a mixture of wry amusement and resignation. "Do you think I haven't tried doing just that at least a hundred times?"

"I have never met someone who couldn't whistle," Edwina remarked.

"It is not exactly a topic that comes up in conversation," Miles said dryly.

"Maybe it should be," she joked. "After one is introduced, they should follow up with whether or not they can whistle."

Miles let out a slight huff. "For what purpose?"

"Merely conversational," she responded. "It is fascinating."

"It is hardly fascinating. I am sure I can do things that you can't."

Edwina tilted her chin. "Name one."

"Well, to begin, I have attended university and participated in fisticuffs on occasion," Miles said.

"I could engage in fisticuffs if I wanted to," Edwina countered. "But I prefer to solve my problems without using my fists."

Miles chuckled. "You could never hit someone, even if you wanted to."

"I could, given the right reasons," she asserted.

"No, you couldn't," he insisted. "Your kind heart would never allow you to intentionally inflict pain on another person."

Edwina had to admit that Miles had a point, albeit reluctantly. She had never seen a reason to hit someone before.

As she opened her mouth to respond, Miles placed his finger against his lips and tilted his head towards the cottage. Her uncle emerged from the door, his top hat perched perfectly on his head, while a tall, slender woman appeared behind him, dressed in a simple gown. A young boy clung to her side.

With an affectionate smile, her uncle crouched down and opened his arms to the child who eagerly leapt into them. He released the child and embraced the woman.

Edwina felt a pang of anger as she watched from afar. It was evident what her uncle was doing at the cottage.

Miles placed his hand on her arm. "I'm sorry," he whispered.

"My uncle has a whole other family, hidden away right

under our noses," Edwina said through clenched teeth, her hands balling into tight fists. "I can't believe this. My poor aunt. My poor cousins. What this will do to them."

"We don't know for certain that was his mistress," Miles admitted.

Edwina's lips pursed in disbelief. "Surely you cannot be serious?" she asked. "Who else could that woman possibly be?"

Miles remained calm, his eyes warm and understanding as he spoke. "I understand your frustration but let's not make assumptions until we have all the facts. Perhaps I could go speak to this woman and gather more information."

"And say what?" Edwina asked. "Besides, if you do such a thing, then my uncle would surely find out."

"You are right," Miles conceded.

She took a deep breath, her chest rising and falling with the weight of her anger. "I think I could punch my uncle," she declared.

"I wouldn't blame you if you did," Miles said. "But let's not resort to violence just yet."

Edwina unclenched her fists and took a step back, trying to calm herself. "Should we tell Bennett?"

"Hold on," Miles replied. "If we are wrong about this, we could cause unnecessary pain to your family."

"But if we are right?" Edwina pressed.

Miles sighed deeply. "I don't know, but I think we should keep this between us for now. Just until we can gather more proof."

"If you think that is best."

"I do," Miles affirmed. "But it won't be easy for you. You will have to pretend that all is well, despite knowing what you know."

Edwina nodded resolutely. "I can do that."

Miles dropped his arm to his side but remained close. "We

can do this… together," he said, his eyes never leaving hers. "But you will need to trust me."

"I thought we already established that I did," Edwina replied lightly.

"Yes, we did, but now you *really* need to trust me," Miles said, his lips curling into a tight smile.

Despite her anger towards her uncle, Edwina couldn't help but feel a flicker of amusement at Miles' persistence.

Miles turned his head towards the direction of the village, his gaze searching the horizon. "How far off is the village?"

"Not too far," she replied, following his gaze. "We should be able to walk there in under twenty minutes or so."

"Are you up for a walk?"

Edwina felt her lips twitch. "Do we have a choice, considering you sent the carriage up ahead?"

"It was so Lord Dallington wouldn't see us," Miles explained, his tone slightly defensive.

"I never said it was wrong," Edwina said. "It is a good thing that I wore my boots today."

Miles held out his hand towards the road, gesturing that she should go first. "After you, my lady," he encouraged.

"Thank you," Edwina said as she brushed past him.

Once they started walking down the road, Miles asked, "Shall we play a game to pass the time?"

"We could, or you could practice your whistling skills," she teased.

Miles let out an exasperated sigh as he glanced heavenward. "Not this again," he muttered.

The sound of a carriage approaching from behind caught their attention and they quickly moved to the side of the road to let it pass. It came to an abrupt stop a short distance ahead and the door swung open, revealing Miss Bawden.

With a smile on her face, Miss Bawden asked, "Would you care for a ride into the village?"

"We would greatly appreciate one," Edwina replied.

"I can't help but wonder why you were walking in the first place," Miss Bawden remarked.

As they approached the coach, Edwina explained, "We sent our own carriage ahead of us to the village."

"Well, that certainly explains it," Miss Bawden joked before settling back into her seat.

Miles offered his hand and assisted Edwina into the coach. She sat next to Miss Bawden while Miles took a seat across from them.

With a jolt, the coach began its journey and Miss Bawden shifted in her seat to face Edwina. "I suppose you have no intention of enlightening me on your reasons for walking."

"You are correct in that assumption," Edwina confirmed.

Miss Bawden regarded her with a curious look, and Edwina worried she might persist with the matter. Fortunately, to Edwina's relief, Miss Bawden tilted her head and remarked, "I can accept that… for now."

Edwina exchanged a glance with Miles before she turned her attention towards the window. She would eventually tell her friend why they had been forced to abandon their carriage and continue on foot, but now was not the time. She needed more answers before she would be comfortable telling anyone.

One thing was certain, she was grateful for Miles. His strength had comforted her, leaving her feeling stronger than she was before. She did have a problem, though. Her feelings for him had started to deepen the more time they spent together.

She was setting herself up for heartache when he left, but, for now, she was just going to cherish every moment she had with Miles.

Miles adjusted his cravat as his valet removed a speck of

lint from his jacket. A distant chime echoed through the manor, beckoning everyone to gather in the drawing room for dinner.

Bailey took a step back. "Will there be anything else, my lord?"

"No, but thank you," Miles replied.

He walked towards the door and pulled it open, revealing Bennett leaning casually against the opposite wall.

Miles raised an eyebrow at his friend's unexpected presence. "Dare I ask why you are lurking outside of my bedchamber?"

"It isn't lurking when it is my home," Bennett replied as he straightened himself. "I thought we could make our way down to dinner together."

Miles worked to keep the disappointment off his face since he had been eager to escort Edwina down to dinner.

Bennett gave him a knowing look, as though he could read his thoughts. "My cousin has already made her way downstairs and is most likely waiting for us."

"That is good," Miles said, attempting to appear uninterested in what he had just revealed.

As they walked down the corridor, Bennett asked in a firm voice, "What are your intentions towards Edwina?"

Miles was caught off guard, not by the question itself, considering the amount of time he had spent with Edwina, but more so by the timing of it. How could he answer this question in such a short period of time? He cared for Edwina, but he had no intention of pursuing her. He couldn't. How could he when he still loved his wife?

Stumbling over his words, he said, "I… um… have none."

Bennett came to an abrupt stop and turned to face Miles, his nostrils flaring in a sign of anger. "You mean to have a dalliance with her then?"

Miles was taken aback by the accusation. "No! How could you even think such a thing?"

"What am I supposed to think?" Bennett asked. "You have been spending quite a lot of time together and growing rather close."

"We are simply friends," Miles insisted.

Bennett's expression was stern as he countered, "Your actions in the gardens this morning suggested otherwise."

"I assure you, my behavior towards Lady Edwina is entirely honorable," Miles said.

Bennett studied him for a long moment before saying, "I believe you, but that does not mean I have to like it. I do not want to see my cousin get hurt."

"I do not wish for that either," Miles replied earnestly.

With a heavy sigh, Bennett continued down the corridor as Miles matched his stride. "I worry about my cousin in the marriage mart," he confessed.

"As do I," Miles said.

Bennett ran a hand through his perfectly styled hair. "I don't know how I can possibly watch over both my sisters and Edwina this Season. It all seems too overwhelming."

"I can help you," Miles reassured him.

"You are attending the Season?" Bennett asked.

Miles nodded. "It is time for me to take up my seat in the House of Lords."

"That is commendable, but I did not think you would make time for the frivolousness of social events," Bennett commented.

"I am dreading those social events, but I made a promise to Lady Edwina that I would be there to help guide her," Miles shared.

Bennett regarded him with a curious gaze. "You? But you detest social events."

"I do, but, as I said before, Lady Edwina and I are friends," Miles replied.

"That is…" Bennett's words trailed off. "Intriguing."

Miles shook his head. "There is nothing 'intriguing' about it. I am merely helping a friend."

Bennett's lips quirked into a wry smile. "Men and women cannot truly be friends," he declared. "One always cares for the other more than they should. It is a disaster waiting to happen."

"You must not have very many friends, then," Miles quipped.

Bennett chuckled. "Says a man that pushes all his friends away," he countered.

Try as he might, Miles couldn't deny the truth in those words. "It is easier that way," he admitted with resignation.

The humor faded from Bennett's expression as he looked at Miles with concern. "It may be easier, but it is lonely to be alone."

"Loneliness is a constant friend, I'm afraid. It is what I am familiar with and, quite frankly, it is what I deserve," Miles said.

Bennett stopped at the top of the stairs and turned to face him. "You are more than your past. You have a future. You just need to know where to look for it."

Miles remained rooted in his spot as Bennett descended the stairs. His friend's words sounded simple, but they were anything but. How could he move on and forget about Arabella? He couldn't do that. Not to her. And not to himself.

Edwina emerged from the drawing room and looked up at him with a questioning look. Her dark green gown hugged her curves perfectly. She truly was a beautiful woman, radiating beauty from within. For when she smiled, his soul seemed to come alive.

He descended the stairs, his eyes never leaving Edwina's as he came to a stop in front of her. "Hello," he greeted softly.

She offered him a shy smile. "Hello."

"I missed escorting you down to the drawing room this

evening," he admitted. "Instead, I was forced to walk with Bennett."

"How awful for you," she teased, a twinkle in her eyes.

"It was," Miles replied with mock seriousness. "Thank you for acknowledging that."

With a glance over her shoulder, Edwina shared, "Bennett has been rather inquisitive of me regarding how much time we are spending together."

Miles gave her an understanding look. "I experienced the same thing on our walk here."

"We can't tell him the truth, not yet at least," Edwina said. "But he does suspect something is going on between us."

"He said that to you?" Miles asked.

"Not in so many words," Edwina replied. "I may just be a woman, but I am not entirely *un*clever."

Miles grinned. "You enjoy making up your own words, don't you?"

"Unclever is a word," she protested.

"No, it is not," Miles insisted.

Edwina tilted her chin defensively. "I read the word unclever in the writings of John Ash."

"The Baptist?" Miles asked, lowering his voice. "You read one of his books?"

"Do not look so surprised, considering he wrote many grammar books," Edwina replied. "My father had a penchant for grammar."

A smile tugged at Miles' lips at the thought of a young Edwina eagerly devouring a grammar book. "Well, I stand corrected on 'unclever' but you still made up the word 'earlish.'"

"It will catch on," she insisted.

"No, it won't," he said with a chuckle.

Lady Dallington's voice came from the doorway to the drawing room. "Lord Hilgrove, please join us in here as we wait for my husband."

"Very well," Miles said, offering his arm to Edwina.

As they walked into the drawing room, Edwina commented, "Thank you for being so 'earlish' by escorting me."

Miles let out a long sigh. "Now you are trying too hard. It is pathetic, really," he said, his words tinged with mirth.

Edwina laughed. "At least I can whistle," she stated.

Bennett looked between them curiously as he stood by the mantel. "Who cannot whistle?" he asked.

"Lord Hilgrove," Edwina said as she removed her arm from his. "I just discovered this today and it *shocketh* me."

"There is no shame in not knowing how to whistle," Lady Dallington remarked, "but there is shame in saying the word 'shocketh.'"

"It is a word," Edwina said.

"An archaic word that has no place in the vocabulary of a genteel woman," Lady Dallington remarked.

Miles smirked at Edwina. "Your aunt is a wise woman. You would do well to heed her words."

Rolling her eyes, Edwina retorted, "You just think she is wise because she agreed with you."

"Most wise people do," Miles responded.

Bennett interjected, "I recall that Miles used to *spuddle* away his time when he was at Eton."

"Perhaps when we first started, but by the time we went to university, I had grown out of that phase," Miles defended.

Edwina raised her hand.

Lady Dallington gave her a baffled look. "What is it, Edwina?"

"Why did no one criticize Bennett for using the word 'spuddle'? That is also an archaic word," Edwina pointed out.

"'Spuddle' implies inefficiency in the way one works," Lady Dallington replied. "It is still a perfectly acceptable word in our Society today."

"If you accept 'spuddle,' then I think you should accept

'shocketh,'" Edwina argued with amusement in her eyes. "At least in our home."

Miles let out a deep chuckle. "You are relentless, my lady."

"Yes, she is," Bennett remarked. "Quite frankly, I haven't seen Edwina this passionate about anything for far too long."

Lord Dallington stepped into the room and Miles watched as Edwina grew visibly tense. "I am sorry I am late," he said as he went to kiss his wife's cheek. "I assure you that it couldn't be helped."

"I know, Dear," Lady Dallington said. "We were just waiting for you to join us before we adjourned to the dining room."

"Well, let us not wait any longer," Lord Dallington responded, offering his arm to his wife.

Miles stepped forward and offered his arm to Edwina. "You need to breathe," he whispered.

"My uncle is a liar, and I can't believe that he would treat my aunt so distastefully," Edwina whispered back with determination in her voice.

"I warned you that this would be difficult, but we must gather all the facts before confronting him," Miles reminded her.

Edwina took a deep breath before saying, "You are right."

"Can you say that again, and perhaps a bit louder so others can hear you?" Miles quipped.

"Now who is trying too hard?" Edwina bantered back.

Miles led Edwina into the elegant dining room, pulling out her chair before taking the seat next to her.

Lord Dallington spoke up from the head of the table. "How was your day of angling?" he asked, glancing between Miles and Bennett.

"Oh, Miles didn't go angling," Bennett informed his father. "He decided a visit to the village with Edwina would be much more enjoyable."

"Is that so?" Lord Dallington asked.

"Yes, my lord," Miles responded. "I asked Lady Edwina to help me pick out a gift for my sister and we found some exquisite ribbon that will work quite nicely."

Lord Dallington let out a bored sigh. "Women do love their ribbons."

Miles bobbed his head in agreement. "Indeed, they do."

Bennett leaned forward in his seat. "Shall we finally play that game of pall-mall tomorrow morning?" he asked.

"I have no objections," Miles replied before he shifted his gaze to Edwina. "What do you say?"

As Edwina reached for her glass of water, she remarked, "I think that sounds like great fun. I shall send word to Miss Bawden."

"Wonderful," Bennett said, clasping his hands together. "And in the afternoon, we shall go shooting and make a competition out of it."

The footman placed a bowl of soup in front of Miles as he leaned to the side to reach for his spoon. "That hardly seems fair, considering I was a sharpshooter in the war."

"But have you picked up a pistol since the war?" Bennett asked knowingly.

Miles grew solemn and he worked hard to keep the anguish out of his expression. "No, because I have seen enough death to last a lifetime."

Bennett's face softened with understanding. "If you would prefer, we could do something else instead."

"It is all right," Miles responded, forcing a small, strained smile to his lips. "It is something that needs to be done sooner rather than later."

Miles turned his attention towards his bowl of soup and began to eat, retreating to his own thoughts. To some, it may have seemed silly that he had avoided guns for all this time, but it was a constant reminder of the lives he had taken. Each gunshot echoed in his mind, each life lost weighing heavily on his conscience.

Moreover, and no less significant, he had lost his brother in a duel. One single shot irrevocably altered his life forever. The mere thought of holding another pistol made his stomach churn.

Edwina's voice broke through his thoughts. "Are you all right, my lord?"

Miles turned his head towards her. "I will be."

And that was the truth.

Edwina's presence seemed to calm his racing mind and bring him a sense of comfort and solace that he so desperately craved.

Chapter Twelve

Edwina sat in the drawing room, her fingers delicately pulling the needle out of the fabric as she waited for Miss Bawden to arrive. Although her mind was far from being focused on her needlework. Instead, it was consumed by thoughts of Miles. But it was pointless to even think of him. He was so deeply in love with his late wife that she doubted his heart would ever recover.

One day, she hoped to have a love such as his, one that extended far after death. Her parents had shared a love like that.

Frustrated by her wandering thoughts, Edwina lowered the fabric to her lap. Why was she even thinking about this? She may have some inconvenient feelings for Miles, but they were not reciprocated. So what was the point of even dwelling on them? She had other more pressing matters. Her uncle had a whole other family and was trying to cheat her out of her inheritance. Yes. She should focus on that.

And yet, despite all logic telling her otherwise, her heart refused to let go of the image of Miles, his warm smile and kind eyes haunting her every thought.

White stepped into the room and announced, "Miss Bawden has arrived, my lady."

Edwina perked up, grateful for a reprieve from her thoughts. "Please send her in."

With a tip of his head, White spun on his heel to do her bidding.

It was only a moment before Miss Bawden entered the room with a bright smile on her face. "Good morning," she greeted. "I trust that you slept well."

"I did," Edwina replied.

Miss Bawden came to sit across from her. "Are you ready for a rousing game of pall-mall?" she asked, excitement evident in her voice.

Edwina leaned forward and placed her needlework onto the table. "I am," she replied.

With a glance at the empty doorway, Miss Bawden lowered her voice and asked, "Where do you stand with Lord Hilgrove?"

Edwina was taken aback by the sudden change in topic. "Pardon?"

Miss Bawden's eyes twinkled mischievously. "Do we like him or should I accidently hit him with my mallet in passing?"

"You should never hit someone with a mallet," Edwina chided lightly.

"That is why it would be an 'accident,'" Miss Bawden said with a sly grin.

A laugh escaped Edwina's lips. "You are truly awful."

Miss Bawden settled back into her seat, her expression softening. "You are one of my dearest friends, and I don't want to see you get hurt," she said. "An accidental mallet attack is the least I can do for you."

"There is no need to hit Lord Hilgrove with a mallet. We have come to an understanding," Edwina remarked.

Miss Bawden's brow flew up. "Oh?"

Edwina quickly clarified before any misunderstanding

could arise. "Not that type of understanding. We are simply friends, and he is helping me with a delicate matter."

Leaning forward in her seat, Miss Bawden's voice was laced with curiosity as she asked, "Which is?"

"I'm sorry, but I can't tell you just yet," Edwina replied. "But I promise to tell you soon enough."

Miss Bawden let out a dramatic sigh. "I am not quite sure if I should be insulted or not. You are putting your trust into a man that you hardly know instead of your favorite friend."

"Please do not take offense," Edwina said. "There are some things that are at play that will hurt my family when the truth comes out."

Miss Bawden's lips quirked. "You didn't deny that I am your favorite friend."

"That is what you took away from all of this?" Edwina asked incredulously.

"I trust that you know what you are doing, and I am glad that Lord Hilgrove is helping you," Miss Bawden said. "Besides, I saw the way you looked at him in the coach yesterday."

Edwina gave her a baffled look. "Whatever do you mean?"

"You clearly have feelings for Lord Hilgrove," Miss Bawden said matter-of-factly.

With a shake of her head, she replied, "You are mistaken. We are just friends."

A playful gleam shone in Miss Bawden's eyes. "If you say so."

"I do," Edwina insisted. "Can we drop this now?"

"As you wish," Miss Bawden conceded.

Having an immense desire to change the subject, Edwina gestured towards the teapot on the table. "Would you care for a cup of tea?"

"No, thank you," Miss Bawden replied. "The last time I indulged in tea before a game of pall-mall, I ended up losing."

"And you believe it was because of the tea?" Edwina asked skeptically.

"I cannot take any chances," Miss Bawden replied. "After all, I am here to win."

Edwina gave her an amused look. "I daresay that you are the most competitive person I know when it comes to pall-mall."

"More so than Lord Winston?"

She hesitated. "Well… perhaps not."

As she said her words, Bennett entered the room and informed them, "Everything has been set up and it is time to play that game of pall-mall."

Miss Bawden jumped up from her seat. "I call the blue mallet."

Bennett chuckled. "I assumed as much, considering you think it holds some kind of magic power."

"All I know is that whenever I play with the blue mallet, I win," Miss Bawden said. "It is too much of a coincidence to ignore."

Miles appeared in the doorway, his gaze seeking out Edwina's. "Are we to be partners again?" he asked.

"I am not opposed to it," Edwina replied.

Miss Bawden bobbed her head in approval. "And I shall partner with Lord Dunsby."

Edwina looked at her friend knowingly. "I can tell that you are already formulating a plan in your head," she said.

"I am," Miss Bawden confirmed. "One must not go into a game of pall-mall without a victory strategy."

Miles approached Edwina and offered his arm. "Shall we come up with a strategy as I escort you to the lawn?"

"I think we have no choice in the matter," Edwina replied, her gloved hand fitting perfectly into the crook of his elbow.

As they made their way out towards the lawn, Miles asked, "Did you go riding this morning?"

"I did, but it was rather early when I left the stables," she replied. "I'm afraid I had a lot on my mind this morning."

"Is that why you missed breakfast?"

"It was," Edwina admitted. "To be honest, I couldn't bring myself to face my uncle. He is not the man that I thought he was."

Miles' eyes held compassion. "We will figure everything out together. You need not worry."

"How can I not?" Edwina asked in a hushed voice. "My aunt will be devastated when she finds out. She adores my uncle."

"Do not be so quick to jump to conclusions," Miles attempted.

Edwina frowned. "I do not understand why you are trying to defend him. That little boy from the cottage looked very much like my uncle."

Miles patted her hand. "Whatever happens, it will be all right. I promise."

"Please don't make promises that you can't keep," Edwina said.

"Who says that I can't keep that promise?"

Edwina's lips tightened in a slight grimace. "When the truth comes out, our lives are going to change and not for the better."

Miles grew silent. "You are allowed to be hurt, angry, and even resentful, but for how long? At some point, you must accept what you cannot change and move forward."

They walked the rest of the way together in silence as Edwina considered Miles' words. She was angry. She was angry on behalf of her aunt. Her cousins. And for anyone else her uncle had deceived. But Miles was right. Her anger could only take her so far. If it consumed her, she was no better than her uncle.

Miles stopped on the lawn and dropped his arm. His eyes

strayed towards Miss Bawden, who was in the process of gracefully stretching with her blue mallet in hand.

"I do not understand why Miss Bawden needs to stretch before a game of pall-mall," Miles said.

"No one does, but it is a part of her process," Edwina joked.

Miles walked over and retrieved two mallets. He extended one towards Edwina. "We forgot to discuss our strategy."

"We did, but let's play to win. That could be our strategy."

Miles' eyes crinkled with amusement. "'Thou art as wise as thou art beautiful'," he said, quoting Shakespeare.

"You have read *A Midsummer Night's Dream*?"

"I do not know why you are surprised," Miles said. "I attended university, where we read most of Shakespeare's works in great detail."

Edwina practiced swinging the mallet. "You do not strike me as a man that enjoys Shakespeare."

"I never said I enjoyed Shakespeare, just that I read his works. There is a difference," he pointed out.

Turning to face him, Edwina said, "Yes, I suppose there is. What else do I not know about you?"

"That is a long and very intriguing list," Miles remarked.

Edwina smiled. "I have time, especially since Miss Bawden's stretching routine goes on for quite some time."

Miles swung the mallet over his shoulder. "You should know that pall-mall happens to be one of my talents. Arabella may have been dreadful at it, but I am quite skilled."

Bennett approached them with a confident stride. "Shall we make this game more interesting?" he asked eagerly. Almost too eagerly.

"What do you have in mind?" Miles asked.

"A wager, perhaps," Bennett suggested.

Edwina eyed him skeptically. "What kind of wager?"

"Something simple," Bennett replied. "Whoever wins this

match will have the honor of dancing with Edwina first at the soiree."

"What soiree?" Edwina inquired.

With a smirk, Bennett replied, "The one that my mother has been planning for the past few days. You didn't think she would pass on the opportunity to honor our esteemed house guest, did you?"

Edwina gave her cousin a blank stare. "Why hasn't she asked me for help in planning such an event?"

"You have been rather occupied as of late," Bennett remarked.

"When is it?" Edwina asked.

"In three days' time," her cousin informed her.

Edwina turned towards Miles. "Did you know about this?"

Miles shrugged. "This is the first I am hearing about it, as well."

"So we are in agreement, then?" Bennett asked. "The winner will have the privilege of dancing with Edwina for the first set."

Edwina hesitated, unsure if she wanted to be part of this bet. "I don't know, Cousin. What about Miss Bawden? Will she not feel left out?" she asked.

Miss Bawden spoke up from where she stood, adjusting the mallet behind her neck as she continued her stretching routine. "Do not concern yourself with me. I want no part of this wager."

"I accept your wager," Miles abruptly declared.

Bennett smiled triumphantly. "Then let us play pall-mall," he exclaimed, beckoning towards the lawn with a flourish of his hand.

Miles crouched down next to his ball as he tried to decide

how to play his next shot. Should he send the ball through the arch or should he hit Bennett's ball off course? He couldn't quite decide what he should do. But he wanted to win this game of pall-mall. Not just so he could claim the first dance with Edwina at the soiree, but so he could knock that smug look off Bennett's face.

At least that is what he kept telling himself.

He did want to dance with Edwina and hold her in his arms, even if it was just for a moment. He had longed to hold her again since they had embraced, an embrace that was merely an act of kindness for Edwina. But it had meant something to him. With every moment they spent together, he found himself becoming more bewitched by her beauty and her kindness.

As if sensing his inner turmoil, Edwina crouched down next to him, her delicate features illuminated by a halo of sunlight. "What is your play?" she asked softly.

Miles tore his gaze away from her and focused on the alley once more. But it was proving difficult when she was so close. "I'm not quite sure," he replied. "At this angle, I could hit my ball through the arch, or I could knock Bennett's ball out of the way, making his next shot much more difficult."

"Whatever you think is best," she encouraged.

"We are one point ahead, and I want to keep the lead," Miles said.

Edwina nodded her understanding. "I want to win, as well, but it doesn't seem like you are enjoying yourself."

Miles forced a smile onto his lips. "I am," he responded, but even he could hear the lack of genuine enthusiasm in his voice.

She didn't look convinced by his lackluster effort. "If you say so…" Her words trailed off.

"I do," he insisted.

Leaning closer, Edwina lowered her voice and said, "If this is about the dance…"

He spoke over her. "No, it is about beating Bennett," he lied. It was so much more than just beating Bennett. He wanted that first dance with her.

"Oh," Edwina responded, the hurt evident in her tone.

Miles felt like a muttonhead for treating Edwina so poorly. But he couldn't risk revealing his true feelings and potentially ruining everything between them.

"Well, I wish you luck," Edwina said before rising.

Miles rose with her. "Pall-mall is not purely a game of chance, but one of skill as well," he stated.

"It is also meant to be enjoyable," she pointed out with a teasing smile.

Bennett cleared his throat from where he stood back with Miss Bawden. "You two are doing an enormous amount of talking, but not enough playing," he called out to them.

Miles nodded in acknowledgement and adjusted his grip on the mallet as he took his position by his ball. He focused on lining up his shot, blocking out all other distractions. With a steady swing, he hit the ball and watched it knock Bennett's ball out of the way before going through the arch.

A smirk tugged at Miles' lips as he turned to face Bennett. "Good luck winning now," he declared.

As his words left his mouth, Edwina shouted, "Winston!"

Miles turned his head and saw Lord Winston approaching. His dark hair was brushed forward and there was a warm smile on his face as he held out his arms for Edwina.

Keeping hold of his mallet, Miles made his way over to Winston and greeted him. "It is good to see you. It has been far too long."

Winston's smile widened. "Yes, it has," he agreed. "Last I heard you were off saving the world on the Continent."

Miles chuckled wryly. "I didn't do much saving, but I was on the Continent," he corrected.

"Yes, but now you can enact real change in the House of Lords," Winston said. "Those stuffy lords would be fools if they didn't take advantage of your youth and unique perspective."

As soon as Bennett and Miss Bawden joined him, Winston's smile faltered. His expression turned stoic as he addressed Miss Bawden. "It is good to see you again, Miss Bawden," he said curtly.

Miss Bawden responded with a graceful curtsy, her voice matching the same tone as Winston's. "My lord," she murmured.

Edwina chimed in, drawing Winston's attention. "Did you hear your mother plans to throw a soiree?"

"I had not heard that, but Mother does love any excuse for a social event," Winston replied.

"It is to honor our esteemed guest," Bennett added.

Winston grinned. "Ah, yes. Times have certainly changed. Last time I saw Miles, he was running shirtless across the lawn at Oxford, which was quite out of character for him."

Miles let out a hearty laugh. "I may have had a bit too much to drink that night and Bennett dared me to do it."

"And naturally, you couldn't resist Bennett's dare," Winston joked.

"I am afraid not," Miles replied good-naturedly. "It was a matter of honor."

Winston let out his own laugh before saying, "Well, it is good to see that you haven't changed too much."

Miles' smile slowly faded as Winston's words reminded him of the past year's struggles. He had gone to hell and back, but with Edwina's unwavering support and friendship, he had emerged from his anger and pain. It still lingered in the corners of his mind, but it was now tolerable.

"Have you seen Mother yet?" Bennett asked.

Winston shook his head. "Not yet. I saw you were playing pall-mall on the lawn and I came out here first."

"Mother will want to see you at once," Bennett remarked. "Come, I will take you to her."

With a glance at the pall-mall alley on the lawn, Winston asked, "What of your game of pall-mall?"

"We can continue our game later this afternoon," Bennett said.

Miles interjected, "Bennett is just trying to delay the inevitable. He knows he is going to lose the bet."

Winston raised an eyebrow in curiosity. "What bet?"

"The honor of dancing the first set with Edwina at the soiree," Bennett replied.

Turning towards Edwina, Winston perused the length of her. "Last time I saw you, you were dressed in deep mourning for your father. But now you are attending soirees and dancing?"

Edwina bobbed her head. "It is more of a recent development."

"I'm glad, Cousin," Winston said, his words genuine. "Dare I ask what brought about this change?"

Edwina's green eyes flickered towards Miles, her lips curving into a small smile. "Lord Hilgrove helped me to look past my grief, allowing me to see the good in the world again."

"Interesting," Winston muttered, shifting his gaze towards Miles. "For what it is worth, thank you for helping my cousin."

Miles inclined his head graciously. "It was my pleasure, but she has helped me far more than I have helped her," he admitted.

After he uttered his words, Winston and Bennett exchanged a knowing look that Miles couldn't quite decipher.

Bennett gestured towards the manor behind them. "Shall we go see Mother now?"

Miss Bawden took a step back. "I should be going," she said. "But I shall return for the rest of our game."

"We shall send word," Edwina informed her.

"Thank you," Miss Bawden responded. "Although, I fear that my lucky blue mallet will not help us win this game."

Winston gave Miss Bawden a disbelieving look. "You are

resorting to a lucky mallet to win pall-mall now?" he asked with a hint of amusement.

"I've had quite the winning streak," Miss Bawden defended.

"Yes, well, that is because you have not played with me lately," Winston boasted with a smug smile. "I have beaten you more times than you have won."

"Many of those wins are contested," Miss Bawden remarked.

Miles lifted his brow. "Contested wins?" he asked.

"You shouldn't have asked," Winston muttered.

Miss Bawden tilted her chin. "Lord Winston has been known to move his ball to line up a better shot."

Winston scoffed. "That was one time, and it was just a practice game," he defended with a slight rise in his voice.

"So you say, but no one else moved their balls. Just you," Miss Bawden remarked.

Looking heavenward, Winston insisted, "It was a practice game."

Miss Bawden shrugged. "I suppose everyone else wanted a challenge by keeping their balls where they landed."

Winston narrowed his eyes at Miss Bawden, but before he could respond, Bennett interrupted, "As fun as this conversation is, we should probably go find Mother now."

"Yes, let's," Edwina said in agreement, no doubt sensing the tension between Winston and Miss Bawden.

Miss Bawden offered a polite smile to the rest of the group. "I look forward to finishing the game." Her smile disappeared when it landed on Winston. "Lord Winston, as always, a pleasure." Her words lacked any sincerity.

As Miss Bawden walked towards her coach, Winston placed his hand on Edwina's shoulder and said, "I don't know why you insist on spending your time with Miss Bawden."

Edwina laughed. "You are the only one that seems to have an issue with her. Everyone else seems to adore Miss Bawden."

"I find that hard to believe," Winston said.

Bennett chimed in "It is true. I find Miss Bawden to be quite delightful."

Winston dropped his hand from Edwina's shoulder and turned to Miles. "What say you?" he asked. "Is Miss Bawden diabolical or a delight?"

Miles put his hand up. "I take no issue with Miss Bawden since she has been nothing but kind to me."

"Traitors," Winston muttered.

Edwina linked her arm with Winston and led him towards the manor. "Your mother will be thrilled to see you since we don't see very much of you now that you are a barrister."

As the group made their way inside, Miles trailed behind and saw how Edwina's face lit up as she talked to her cousins. Did she smile that way when she was with him? He hoped so. Her happiness was starting to become very important to him.

Winston glanced back at Miles and asked, "How long do you intend on staying here?"

"About another week or so. I need to return to my estate to ensure everything is in order before I travel to London for the Season," Miles replied.

"Well, it seems that wonders never cease," Winston remarked. "I didn't think we would see you participate in the Season."

"It is time I take up my seat in the House of Lords," Miles explained.

Winston arched an eyebrow. "And you will be attending all the social events that come with it?"

"I intend to," Miles responded.

Edwina came to a stop in the entry hall and dropped her arm. "Lord Hilgrove has even offered to help ease me into Society."

"Did he now?" Winston's critical gaze swept over Miles, his lips pursed in disapproval. "How thoughtful of him."

"Isn't it, though?" Edwina responded.

Winston directed his attention towards Miles, his jaw set and his words taking on a sharp tone. "It would appear that you have been rather attentive to my cousin."

"No more than any friend would," Miles said, attempting to ward off Winston's anger.

"Winston!" Lady Dallington exclaimed as she appeared in the doorway of the drawing room. "You have finally arrived."

Leaning towards Miles, Winston spoke in a hushed voice, "We will continue this conversation later." With that, he rushed over to his mother's awaiting arms. "Mother!"

Lady Dallington embraced her son warmly. "How I have missed you! Your visits are far too infrequent."

"I'm afraid I have responsibilities in London that I must see to," Winston shared.

Taking a step back, Lady Dallington said, "You work too hard. You must learn to have fun. Perhaps even take a wife."

Winston let out an exasperated huff. "Bennett first."

"I fear that Bennett is a lost cause, at least in the marriage department," Lady Dallington sighed.

Bennett frowned. "You do realize I can hear you, Mother."

Lady Dallington's eyes twinkled mischievously. "Of course, Dear. I made sure to say it loud enough for you to hear," she said before turning her attention back to Winston. "Are you hungry? Tired?"

Winston brought a hand to his stomach. "Actually, now that you mention it, I am rather famished. The food at the boarding house was rather lacking this morning."

"Then let us go to the kitchen and have the cook prepare your favorites," Lady Dallington suggested.

"Before we go, is Father in his study?" Winston asked. "I should greet him."

Lady Dallington's smile faltered. "I'm afraid not. He had some business to attend to in the village, but he should be returning shortly."

Miles noticed Edwina's back had grown rigid at the mention of her uncle's absence. Seeking out her gaze, he saw a profound sadness in her eyes that made his heart ache for her. If only he could make everything better for Edwina, but he knew he was fighting an uphill battle.

Still, he was determined to try… for her sake.

Chapter Thirteen

Miles stood by his bedchamber door, fidgeting with the sleeves of his jacket as he waited for the dinner bell to ring. He was hoping to escort Edwina down to dinner. Ever since Winston had returned home, he hadn't been able to spend much time with her, and he missed her.

Botheration.

He shouldn't be so excited to see Edwina. But they were friends. That should count for something. Even though that line was starting to blur as his feelings grew deeper for her.

Bailey's voice broke through his thoughts. "May I ask what you are waiting for?"

Miles turned towards Bailey and explained, "The dinner bell to be rung."

"I assure you that there is nothing wrong with being first to dinner, my lord," Bailey responded with amusement in his voice.

Miles chuckled. "I am aware of that, but I am hoping to escort Lady Edwina down to dinner."

As if on cue, the distant sound of the dinner bell echoed throughout the manor, signaling the start of their evening meal.

"I do hope you have an enjoyable evening," Bailey remarked.

Miles eagerly went to open the door, his heart fluttering with the anticipation of seeing Edwina. But his excitement was short-lived as he saw Winston and Bennett leaning against the wall, waiting for him in the corridor.

Stepping out of his bedchamber, Miles asked, "What is this?"

Bennett straightened from the wall, a smile playing on his lips. "We have come to escort you to dinner."

"Why?" Miles questioned.

Placing a hand over his heart in mock sincerity, Bennett replied, "It is a time that I have grown to cherish."

"Spare me the theatrics," Miles grumbled.

Winston took a step towards him and replied, "We just want a moment of your time. That is all."

"Well, you have it," Miles said curtly, crossing his arms over his chest. "What is it that you want?"

With a knowing smirk, Winston remarked, "You are much less agreeable with Edwina not around."

Bennett nodded in agreement. "I told you as much."

"That you did," Winston agreed. "Which makes me wonder why that is.

Miles frowned, feeling like he was being interrogated by his friends. "You are reading too much into this."

"Am I?" Winston asked.

"Yes, Lady Edwina and I are just friends," Miles asserted firmly.

With a curious glint in his eyes, Winston studied Miles intently. "Is that what you truly want? Or Edwina?"

Miles held his friend's gaze and responded, "It is what we both want."

"Have you discussed this with her?" Winston pressed.

"There is no need," Miles said. "We have an understanding of friendship."

Winston exchanged a glance with Bennett before asking, "You clearly hold my cousin in high regard, why do you not wish to pursue her?"

Miles felt his back grow rigid, growing more frustrated with each passing moment. "I do not know what you speak of. Again, we are just friends."

Bennett let out a sigh. "You are in denial, I see."

"No, I am simply living in reality," Miles said. "In a week or so, I will go my way and Lady Edwina will go hers."

"And yet you offered to help her during the Season," Winston pointed out.

Miles pressed his lips together before saying, "This conversation is over. I have told you what you wanted to know, and now I am going down to dinner."

As Miles started down the dimly lit corridor, he hoped that his friends would drop it and they could move on from this.

Unfortunately, that was not the case.

Winston matched his stride and his voice was gentle yet persistent. "Is this about Arabella? Because she would want you to find happiness again."

Miles came to an abrupt halt and turned to face his friend, annoyance growing inside of him. "You do not get to presume what my wife would want," he said firmly.

"You seem to forget that I was friends with Arabella long before you came along," Winston responded.

"I would proceed very cautiously," Miles warned.

Winston's eyes held compassion. "There is no shame in moving on, Miles."

"I love my wife," Miles declared.

"I know, but she is no longer with us," Winston said. "You can't live in the past and expect a brighter future."

Miles narrowed his eyes. "You do not get to preach to me about my past. You have no idea what I have gone through. What depths of pain I have had to endure."

Winston bobbed his head. "You are right, I don't. But I

want you to be happy and I think that path begins with my cousin."

"You are wrong," Miles stated. "I love Arabella, and I always will."

"Arabella is gone, and you deserve to find love again," Winston insisted.

Miles scoffed. "Love?" he asked. "No, I am too broken to ever hope to find love again."

Bennett interjected, "You are not broken."

"I am," Miles declared, tossing up his hands. "And you two do not get to stand here and preach to me about how I should be feeling."

"That was not our intention," Winston assured him, his words calm and measured.

"Then what was?" Miles demanded, his voice rising with each word. "To remind me of everything that I have lost? But why stop there? Why not mention John, as well?"

Winston offered him a weak smile. "We are just trying to help."

"Help?" Miles repeated incredulously. "There is no helping me. I am incapable of moving on and marrying another. That would not be fair to them, or to me."

Winston's expression softened, turning into something akin to pity. Miles refused to stand here and be pitied by his friends. In one swift motion, he turned and headed towards the drawing room. There was only one person in the manor that could help him, and it was Edwina. She offered hope when he felt like all was lost.

As he entered the drawing room, he saw Edwina was standing by Lord and Lady Dallington. Her eyes met his as he entered the room, and he could see the questions in her eyes.

She moved closer to him and asked in a hushed tone, "What is troubling you?"

He could lie to her. Tell her everything was all right. But

he didn't want to do that. He wanted to be honest with her. She deserved that much.

Matching her tone, he replied, "Winston and Bennett are impossible."

A small smile tugged at her lips. "Yes, they can be quite insufferable at times. What did they do this time?"

"They are trying to convince me to move on and get remarried." Miles huffed in frustration. "As if I could do such a thing."

Edwina grew quiet. "I don't entirely disagree with them."

"Pardon?" he asked, taking a step back.

In a reassuring voice, she said, "You are a good man, and you deserve to be happy."

"I am happy," he lied.

Edwina didn't look convinced. "We both know that you are struggling, as am I," she replied. "Everyone struggles with their own battles, but that doesn't mean we give up on finding happiness."

Miles shook his head. "I don't think I am capable of loving another, not after I loved Arabella so deeply."

"The right woman will understand that your love for your first wife will never diminish," Edwina said. "But you must first open your heart before that can ever happen."

"What you are asking of me is impossible," he murmured.

Edwina held his gaze, her eyes sparkling with determination. "Nothing is impossible if you follow your heart."

As soon as the words left her lips, Lady Dallington appeared by their side. "I do hope I am not intruding but dinner has been announced."

Miles cleared his throat, grateful for the reprieve. "Thank you," he said.

Lady Dallington studied him for a moment before asking, "Is everything all right, Miles?" The concern in her voice was palpable, touching him deeply.

He forced a smile on his lips. "Yes, everything is fine."

Lady Dallington didn't quite look convinced, but thankfully she let it drop. "Shall we adjourn to the dining room?" she suggested.

"Yes, let us," Miles replied, offering his arm to Edwina.

While they followed the group out of the drawing room, Edwina leaned in and whispered, "My uncle only just returned from the village."

"Did he say what he was doing there?" Miles asked.

"Just that he had some meetings," Edwina replied. "But I do not trust him farther than I could throw him."

A burst of laughter unexpectedly escaped Miles' lips, echoing through the marble floors of the entry hall. "You couldn't even pick your uncle up, much less throw him."

"It is an expression," Edwina defended.

"In your case, it is a terrible one," Miles joked.

Edwina rolled her eyes. "I had not taken you for being so literal."

"At least I don't make up words," Miles retorted with a playful grin.

"Careful," Edwina said with mirth in her eyes. "I might take back all the nice things I have said about you."

"You wouldn't do that," Miles responded.

"And why not?"

Miles smiled. "You are too kindhearted to do such a thing."

They entered the dining room and Miles pulled out a chair for Edwina. Once she was situated, all the men in the room sat down. Bennett and Winston sat across from them and Lord and Lady Dallington were on either end of the long table.

The footmen promptly placed bowls of soup in front of them and Miles reached for his spoon to begin eating.

Lord Dallington spoke up, drawing everyone's attention. "It is wonderful to have Winston back home where he belongs," he said proudly.

Winston raised his glass in acknowledgement. "Thank you, Father."

Turning towards him with a hopeful expression, Lord Dallington asked, "Have you considered my offer?"

"Yes, Father, I have, and I must decline it… again," Winston replied. "I am content working as a barrister in London."

Lord Dallington's face fell into a frown. "But this village could use a barrister such as you."

"I would be of no use here," Winston insisted. "Besides, this will all be Bennett's one day. I need to forge my own path."

Lady Dallington suggested, "Perhaps you two could discuss this later over a glass of port?"

"Very well," Lord Dallington reluctantly agreed.

After she smoothed her napkin over her lap, Lady Dallington asked, "May I inquire as to who emerged victorious in the pall-mall match?"

A low groan escaped Bennett's lips. "Why must you bring that up?"

"I am simply curious," Lady Dallington replied.

Miles took the opportunity to proudly announce, "Lady Edwina and I won the match. We soundly defeated Bennett and Miss Bawden."

"You only beat us by one point," Bennett argued.

Miles shrugged off his comment with a smug smile. "A win is a win, regardless of the margin."

Lady Dallington let out a soft chuckle. "Well, I must admit that I am not surprised that Miles won."

Miles shifted in his seat to face Lady Dallington. "Why is that?"

"Oh, no reason," Lady Dallington responded with a warm smile. "Now, let us eat."

The sun was low in the sky as Edwina made her way towards the Warrens' cottage. She was smiling, something she was doing far more often now. It had taken her some time to find her way here, but she was finally happy, a feeling she thought she would never experience again after the passing of her father.

Despite all of this, she still had important matters that needed to be resolved. Her uncle had deceived her by withholding her inheritance, and he had a whole other family in the village.

As she approached the cottage, Edwina noticed Mrs. Warren crouched down on her knees, tending to her garden. Mr. Warren stood dutifully by her side, holding a set of gardening tools, engaged in conversation with his wife without noticing Edwina's arrival.

With a friendly greeting called out from a short distance away, Edwina announced her presence. "Good morning."

"Good morning," came the harmonious reply from both Mr. and Mrs. Warren.

Mrs. Warren rose from her kneeling position and removed the gloves from her hand. "What a lovely surprise. How are you faring this morning?"

Coming to a stop next to the couple, Edwina responded with equal cheerfulness. "I am well. And you?"

Mr. Warren slipped his hand over his wife's shoulders. "We have survived another day so that must count for something."

"I came to see how your ankle is healing," Edwina said.

With a weary sigh, Mr. Warren replied, "It is healing rather slowly."

Mrs. Warren gave her husband a chiding look. "That is because you are doing too much too soon. You need to rest more."

"I will rest when I die," Mr. Warren joked.

Edwina laughed. "You should listen to your wife more."

"I should have known that you womenfolk would stick together," Mr. Warren said lightly.

Mrs. Warren tucked her gloves into the pocket of her apron. "Are you hungry?" she asked. "We were just about to sit down for breakfast. You are more than welcome to join us."

"You are most kind, but I should have breakfast with my family," Edwina said. "Afterwards, I intend to go to the village with Lord Hilgrove and Winston."

"Is that so?" Mrs. Warren asked.

"Yes, when Lord Hilgrove proposed the idea of a carriage ride into the village, Winston was adamant that he should join us," Edwina shared.

Mrs. Warren's expression became worried, and she exchanged a glance with her husband.

Edwina noticed the unease between them and asked, "Is something wrong?"

"We should tell her," Mrs. Warren said to her husband, pursing her lips.

Now Edwina felt a twinge of worry, too. "Tell me what?" she asked, turning her gaze from Mrs. Warren to Mr. Warren.

Mr. Warren frowned as he removed his hand from his wife's shoulder. "I suppose it is time." He paused. "The villagers are not happy with your uncle's actions," he said slowly.

"What do you mean?" Edwina asked.

"Lord Dallington has withdrawn most of his funding for the village, causing suffering amongst the people," Mr. Warren explained.

Edwina couldn't understand it. "But why would he do such a thing? If people are suffering, shouldn't he be helping them?"

"Your father was generous to a fault, but your uncle

appears to have a different approach when it comes to assisting the village," Mr. Warren said.

Edwina furrowed her brow. "But it sounds like he is not helping them at all."

"There are some funds that are coming in, but it is minimal compared to what your father contributed," Mr. Warren clarified. "Furthermore, many tenants have complained about necessary repairs that are being ignored by Mr. Stanley."

"That doesn't sound like Mr. Stanley," Edwina said.

"Yes, but there are rumors that your uncle is driving his estate into bankruptcy, which will greatly impact the village," Mr. Warren remarked.

Edwina was taken aback. She didn't know much about the financial state of her father's estate, but she knew it had always prospered under his care. The thought of her uncle's actions causing harm to the villagers and the estate itself made her heart ache with worry.

Mrs. Warren stepped forward and placed a comforting hand on Edwina's sleeve. "I just worry that the villagers won't be as kind to you as they should be," she said, her voice filled with concern.

Not wanting to believe that to be true, Edwina remarked, "They have always shown me such kindness."

Mr. Warren grimaced. "Times are changing, and Lord Dallington doesn't seem to care what repairs the village needs."

Edwina's heart sank at those words. She didn't think her opinion of her uncle could get any worse. But she was determined not to stand by while the villagers suffered. "That is awful. There must be something that I can do to help them."

Mr. Warren's face softened slightly, but his answer was disheartening. "I don't know what you can do."

She tilted her chin, refusing to believe there was no hope.

"I could speak to Mr. Stanley," she suggested. "He is a good man and I am sure he will listen to what I have to say."

Mr. Warren nodded, but added a note of caution. "He will, but he still answers to Lord Dallington."

Undeterred, Edwina squared her shoulders and prepared herself for the challenge ahead. She wasn't about to give up on the villagers, not when they needed her the most. "I will find a way to help the villagers."

"I know you want to help, but I would be cautious around Lord Dallington," Mr. Warren advised. "He is nothing like the great man your father was."

"No, he isn't," Edwina agreed.

Mrs. Warren offered her a warm smile. "Enough of this serious talk, you should head back and join your family for breakfast."

Edwina bobbed her head. "Perhaps that would be for the best. I wouldn't wish to have my uncle chide me for being late... again."

"Maybe next time you come visit you can bring your Lord Hilgrove," Mrs. Warren proposed.

With a shake of her head, Edwina corrected, "Lord Hilgrove is not mine."

"My apologies, it was just a slip of the tongue," Mrs. Warren said, her smile broadening.

Mr. Warren chuckled. "You should leave before Mrs. Warren starts planning your wedding," he teased.

With a heavy heart, Edwina murmured her goodbyes before she headed back towards the manor. She racked her brain for a solution to help the struggling villagers, but she couldn't think of any real options. The cook could only make so many baskets of food for them.

The sound of her boots echoed through the opulent entry hall as she made her way inside. The polished marble floor shone under the warm light streaming in from the windows. A lesson from her father came to her mind- what was the point of acquiring wealth if it couldn't be used to better others' lives? Her father had always lived by that philosophy.

She sighed as she headed towards the dining room. She felt helpless, and that was not a good feeling to have.

As she stepped into the dining room, she saw her uncle seated at the head of the table and he was reading the newssheets. Beside him sat Winston and Bennett, while Miles occupied the seat across from them with his back to her.

The gentlemen rose as soon as they caught sight of her, but she waved them back down and took a seat next to Miles. Her eyes fell on her napkin as she reached for it, trying to mask the turmoil brewing inside her.

"Good morning," Miles greeted.

She forced a smile onto her lips. "Good morning."

Miles studied her with concern. "Is everything all right?"

"It is," Edwina rushed to assure him, though it was far from true. But this was not the time or place to confide in Miles about her worries.

Her uncle spoke up. "You are late, Edwina," he chided. "Either strive to be on time or take your breakfast in your bedchamber, like your aunt."

"My apologies, Uncle. I went to visit the Warrens this morning," Edwina shared.

Her uncle huffed disapprovingly. "A colossal waste of time, in my opinion," he said, returning his attention to the newssheets.

Miles shifted in his seat to face her. "How are the Warrens?"

"They are well," she replied.

"And Mr. Warren's ankle? Is it healing properly?" Miles inquired with a genuineness to his words.

Edwina was touched by his concern. "Yes, it seems to be healing nicely."

"Good, good," Miles murmured as he resumed eating his breakfast.

A footman placed a plate in front of her with one egg and a slice of toast. She picked up her fork and knife and began to eat, savoring each bite.

After a long moment of silence, Winston said, "I am eager for our carriage ride so I may see the village."

"It hasn't changed much since you were last here," Edwina responded nonchalantly, taking another bite of her toast.

"Does that quaint little shop on the corner still sell sponge cake?" Winston inquired eagerly.

Edwina brushed the crumbs off her hands as she replied, "It does, but I am not quite feeling well. I think it would be best if I passed on the carriage ride."

Winston gave her a baffled look. "What ails you?"

Bringing a hand to her forehead, Edwina replied, "I feel a headache coming on and I think I might have a fever. Yes, a fever. And I don't dare go out and get other people sick. That wouldn't be fair of me." Why couldn't she stop rattling on?

"If you are sure…" Winston said, his words trailing off.

"I am," Edwina responded firmly, pushing her plate away.

Miles glanced over at her, his brow arched in question. "Should we send for a doctor?" he asked.

She waved her hand dismissively. "No need for a doctor. I am sure this will pass shortly and I do not wish to waste his time."

"All right, then I shall stay behind as well," Miles said. "Just in case you change your mind about the doctor. I could fetch one for you."

Bennett smirked from across the table. "Or we could simply ask one of our servants to fetch the doctor without any trouble."

Edwina pushed back her chair and rose, causing all the men to stand. "I think it would be best if I go lie down. I wouldn't wish to get any of you sick."

Without waiting for any of their responses, she hurried out

the door and down the corridor. She had just reached the entry hall when she heard Miles calling her name.

She turned around and faced him. "I wouldn't get too close," she warned. "I am sick, after all."

Miles grinned in response, undeterred by her warning. "We both know you aren't sick. You always ramble when you lie. It is a trait that I find rather endearing."

With a quick glance over her shoulder to ensure they were alone, Edwina lowered her voice and shared, "The Warrens informed me that the villagers might not be very accommodating to my family since my uncle has reduced the funds given to them and is neglecting his tenants."

Miles nodded somberly. "Bennett and I have experienced that firsthand when he was confronted by one of your uncle's angry tenants."

"You didn't say anything to me," Edwina said.

"Quite frankly, I didn't think it was important. Bennett and I spoke to Mr. Stanley about it and assumed that it had been taken care of," Miles replied.

Edwina let out a sigh of frustration. "What do we do?" she asked. "If the rumors are to be believed, my uncle is bankrupting this estate."

"Perhaps that is why he never told you about your inheritance," Miles suggested. "There is no money to give."

"I don't understand how this could happen. When my father died, he passed a thriving estate on to my uncle," Edwina said.

Miles gave her a meaningful look. "Or perhaps your father protected you from the harsh realities of the state of his estate."

"My father wouldn't do that," Edwina insisted. "He always valued honesty above all else."

"Be that as it may, I think it might be best if we brought Bennett into our confidence," Miles suggested.

Edwina considered his words before asking, "Do you truly think that is wise?"

"It was only a matter of time before we did," Miles reminded her gently. "Why not now?"

Clasping her hands in front of her, Edwina held Miles' gaze and knew that he was right. She trusted him, more so than she had ever trusted anyone before. "All right, we can tell him."

Miles took a step closer to her, causing her to tilt her head back to meet his eyes. "I do believe it is the right call."

"I trust you," Edwina said.

As she said her words, Winston's booming voice came from behind them. "Miles!" he exclaimed, striding towards them. "There you are."

Miles jumped back, creating distance between them.

Winston came to stand beside them and addressed Miles. "Since our trip to the village has been delayed, I was hoping you would want to practice fencing on the back lawn with me."

Clearing his throat, Miles responded, "I would greatly enjoy that."

"Wonderful," Winston said with a satisfied nod. "Shall we go now?"

Miles hesitated, his gaze flickering towards Edwina with a look that she couldn't quite decipher. "Now?" he repeated, his tone uncertain.

Winston quirked an eyebrow, challenging him silently. "Unless there is a reason why you can't do it now?"

"No… no… I can do it now," Miles said. "I just wanted to ensure that Lady Edwina was well."

Turning towards Edwina, Winston remarked, "I think some rest would do Edwina some good."

Edwina took a small step back. "I agree," she said. "Enjoy your fencing, gentlemen."

She spun on her heel and headed towards her bedchamber, her thoughts swirling with a growing realization about Miles. Before she knew it, before she was even aware of it, she had gotten her heart involved.

Chapter Fourteen

Miles headed towards the library, assuming that is where he would find Edwina. He had spent the past few hours fencing with Winston and he needed a respite. And for him, that meant being in the presence of Edwina. Just the thought of her brought a smile to his lips.

As he entered the library, Miles caught sight of Edwina sitting by the window, her attention fully absorbed in a book. The afternoon sun streamed through the window and illuminated her delicate features. How was it possible for someone to become more beautiful with each passing day?

Miles decided to make his presence known. "Edwina," he said gently, not wanting to startle her from her reading.

Edwina brought her head up and met his gaze. "Miles." The way she said his name caused his heart to soar.

He took a step closer to her. "How are you feeling?" he asked with a teasing smile on his lips.

"I am much better, thank you," Edwina replied.

"I assumed that you would grow tired of pretending to be resting and you would eventually end up in the library," Miles said.

Edwina smiled. "You know me so well."

"Perhaps I do," he replied.

"I am not sure if I should be flattered or insulted by how easily you can read me," she remarked.

"Flattered, I assure you."

Lowering the book to her lap, Edwina said, "I assume you sought me out for a reason."

Miles closed the distance between them and sat on a chair facing Edwina. "I asked Bennett to meet us here."

A deep furrow formed between Edwina's brows. "This is going to be a very difficult conversation," she mused.

"It will be, but we can do it together," Miles said with determination.

In a hesitant voice, Edwina asked, "Do you think he will believe us?"

"I don't see why he wouldn't," Miles replied. "Besides, I can be rather convincing when I want to be."

Edwina shifted her gaze towards the window. "What we will reveal to Bennett will no doubt shatter his idyllic life."

Miles leaned forward in his chair, drawing back Edwina's attention. "No life is idyllic. Everyone has their own struggles and hardships. Some just hide it better than others."

A wistful sigh escaped Edwina's lips as she admitted softly, "My life was pretty idyllic when my father was still alive."

Miles heard the sadness in her voice and he wished he had the power to wipe away the lingering pain in her heart. He wanted nothing more than for her to be happy- no, he *needed* it.

Edwina lowered her gaze to her lap. "I'm sorry," she murmured, almost too quiet for him to hear.

"There is no need to apologize," Miles said. "I want you to be honest with me about how you are feeling."

"Sometimes I feel like I take five steps forward but then I take ten steps backward," Edwina sighed, her voice filled with frustration. "I can't seem to ever get ahead."

Miles chuckled. "That is called life," he stated. "We stumble and fall, but we get back up."

Edwina regarded him with a curious expression. "How is it that you have become so optimistic all of a sudden?"

"If I am, it is because of you and your tutelage."

"I do not deserve such praise."

Miles moved closer, sitting on the edge of his seat and holding her gaze. "You have no idea what you do to me, do you?"

"What is it that I do to you?" she asked.

"You have forever altered my course, for the better," Miles declared earnestly.

Edwina shook her head. "You would have gotten there eventually."

"I am not sure if that is true," he said. "I was content in my misery, convinced that it was what I deserved and that there was no way out. But then you came along and showed me a different path, one filled with hope."

"You are too kind, but it was *you* that had to decide to change. No one else could do that for you," Edwina said.

Miles couldn't seem to stop staring at Edwina. Her green eyes held some kind of unspoken power over him, drawing him in with an irresistible force. It was as if every moment in his life had been leading him up to this precise moment.

He knew he should look away and end whatever hold Edwina had over him. Instead, he found himself inching closer to her, his breath mingling with hers. His eyes flickered down to her lips. Her perfectly shaped lips.

A small part of him hoped she would push him away, ending this strange dance between them. But a larger part of him wanted to kiss her. Desperately.

Edwina didn't shy away, making him wonder if perhaps she wanted this, too. He looked for any signs of hesitation that his advances were unwelcome, but he saw none.

As he was about to give in to the temptation, Bennett's

thunderous voice came from next to them. "What in the blazes is going on here?" he demanded.

Miles jumped back and rose. "I… uh… nothing."

"Nothing?" Bennett asked. "You almost kissed my cousin."

Rising, Edwina said, "But he didn't."

Bennett narrowed his eyes at Miles. "This is how you act as a guest in my home?" he asked, his voice rising. "You take advantage of my cousin? Have you no shame?"

Realizing he had been caught in a scandalous position, Miles knew there was only one honorable thing he could do. "I will marry Lady Edwina."

"What?" Edwina asked, turning her gaze towards him. "Surely you cannot be serious."

"I am," Miles replied.

Edwina placed a hand on her hip. "Am I not to have a say in this?"

Bennett took a commanding step forward. "No. You will marry Miles."

"I will not!" Edwina exclaimed. "You are making a big deal out of nothing, Bennett. We didn't even kiss."

"But you would have if I hadn't walked in when I did," Bennett remarked.

"You don't know that for certain," Edwina challenged.

Miles grimaced. "We would have," he admitted. "I'm sorry, my lady. But to save your honor, I must marry you."

"My honor? Is that what you are concerned about?" Edwina asked.

Reaching out, Miles placed a hand on her sleeve. "I know this is not what you wanted, but it is the only way."

Edwina tilted her chin defiantly, yanking back her arm. "No."

"No?" Miles asked.

"You told me yourself that you don't want to get married ever again," Edwina said. "I refuse to trap you in an unwanted marriage."

With a glance at Bennett, Miles admitted, "It isn't entirely unwanted."

Edwina gave him a knowing look. "But it isn't a love match," she argued. "Do I not deserve to fall in love?"

"You do, but—" Miles started.

She spoke over him. "There is no 'but' about it," she stated. "I will only marry for love. That is what I deserve."

"Edwina, be reasonable," Bennett attempted.

Turning to face her cousin, Edwina's expression was set in firm determination. "You are the only one that knows about what almost happened here. You must promise not to say a thing and this talk of marriage nonsense goes away."

Bennett frowned. "And why should I promise such a thing?"

"Because you will want my discretion as well," Edwina replied.

"With what?" Bennett asked.

Edwina pressed her lips together before saying, "Uncle Lionel is not the man that he claims to be."

Bennett eyed her warily. "What is that supposed to mean?"

"It means…" Edwina's voice trailed off and she looked over at Miles with uncertainty in her eyes.

Miles knew Edwina would probably chide him on his familiarity but he knew she could use his help at the moment. He placed his hand on the small of her back and murmured, "You can do this."

Edwina gave him a grateful look. "Where should I even begin?"

"At the beginning," Miles replied.

Bennett tossed his hands up in the air. "What are you two even going on about?" he demanded.

With a decisive nod, Edwina replied, "Uncle Lionel lied about me not receiving an inheritance. My father specified in the will that I was to receive ten thousand pounds."

"Why would he do such a thing?" Bennett asked.

"I don't know, but I have seen the will," Edwina replied. "Furthermore, if the rumors from the villagers are true, your father is bankrupting this estate."

Bennett let out a wry chuckle. "You know not what you speak of."

"Then enlighten me," Edwina said.

"Our estate is profitable. Father has told me as much," Bennett responded.

Miles gave Bennett a questioning look. "Have you seen the ledgers to confirm that?"

Bennett scoffed. "No, but my father is very particular about who gets to see the ledgers. He wants to prove that he can do it himself," he explained.

"But you are the heir," Miles remarked.

"Regardless, there is no proof to what you are saying," Bennett said. "You are asking me to trust the word of villagers over my own father."

Edwina arched an eyebrow. "What about my inheritance?"

Bennett paused. "I will admit that is disconcerting, but I am sure my father has a perfectly rational explanation to it all."

Miles turned towards Edwina and said, "You need to tell him the worst part."

"I don't know if he is ready," Edwina whispered.

"It is the only way," Miles assured her.

Bennett glanced between them, an irate look on his face. "Will someone explain to me what is going on?"

Edwina met her cousin's gaze and revealed, "Your father has a mistress."

Bennett's mouth dropped. "You cannot be in earnest," he claimed.

"I… *we*… saw them on the way to the village," Edwina said. "Uncle Lionel's coach was parked out front of a cottage and we saw them embrace warmly."

"How do you know it was his mistress?" Bennett asked.

Miles' voice was calm as he shared, "The boy that was by his mother's side looked a lot like Lord Dallington."

Bennett ran a hand through his hair, making it terribly disheveled. "I don't believe you. Either of you."

"Why would we lie?" Edwina asked.

"I don't know, but this is all impossible," Bennett declared. "You must have been mistaken on what you saw."

Compassion echoed in every word that Miles spoke as he tried to convince his friend of what they had witnessed. "I'm sorry, but we know what we saw. And it was far from innocent."

"You are wrong!" Bennett shouted.

Edwina's face softened. "I wish we were," she said.

Bennett started pacing the small room as he retreated to his own thoughts. Miles dropped his hand and created more distance between him and Edwina.

After a long, tense moment, Bennett stopped pacing and turned to face them. "I know you believe what you are saying to be true, but my father can't be who you claim he is. He is not a liar or a cheater."

Miles opened his mouth to reply, but Bennett continued. "And I will prove it to you. We shall confront my father and he will tell you this is all one big misunderstanding."

"Do you think that is wise?" Miles inquired.

Bennett's jaw clenched. His voice was gruff as he spoke, the strain of emotions evident in every word. "What choice do we have?" he asked. "You two seem to believe the worst of my father."

Edwina approached her cousin and slipped her arms around his waist. "I'm sorry, Cousin. I truly am," she said before she turned and quickly left the room.

Once Edwina had departed from the library, Bennett pointed his finger at Miles. "This changes nothing," he declared. "You will marry my cousin!"

Miles met Bennett's gaze with a calm determination. "If she will have me," he replied.

"Oh, she will!" Bennett exclaimed. "Her actions have consequences. She must accept that."

With that, Bennett stormed out of the room, slamming the door behind him.

Miles dropped down onto the nearest chair, finally feeling as if he could breathe. The conversation with Bennett had gotten away from them, but he could understand his friend's hesitation. They were asking him to believe his father was capable of despicable things.

As bad as that was, he now had the terrible misfortune of trying to convince Edwina to marry him. He had vowed never to get married again, but he couldn't risk leaving Edwina's reputation in shambles. Not for his mistake. He should never have tried to kiss her. But a part of him didn't regret his actions.

A marriage to Edwina wouldn't be so bad, he thought, and that is when he realized he was smiling.

Edwina made her way over to the Warrens' cottage, each step becoming more irate. She was furious at Miles for even proposing the ludicrous idea of a union between them. She refused to enter an arranged marriage, knowing Miles would never truly love her. He was too in love with his late wife to ever open his heart again.

She wanted more out of a marriage. She deserved that. Yet Miles and Bennett were so keen on her throwing away her life on a kiss that never happened. Yes, she wanted to kiss Miles. In that moment, nothing else had mattered. All she wanted was to feel his lips on her own. But they had been interrupted. Which was for the best.

So why did she hope Miles would try kissing her again?

Edwina arrived on the Warrens' doorstep and pounded on the door. The door promptly opened and Mr. Warren greeted her with a kind smile.

"Good afternoon, my lady…" His words trailed off. "What is wrong?"

"Bennett is trying to force me into an arranged marriage," she informed him.

Mr. Warren put his finger up, indicating he needed a moment. He turned his head and shouted, "Betsy!"

A moment later, Mrs. Warren appeared in the doorway as she rubbed her hands on an apron that was tied around her neck. "Whatever is the matter, Dear?"

Mr. Warren tilted his head towards Edwina. "Lord Dunsby is trying to force Lady Edwina into an arranged marriage."

Mrs. Warren gasped. "Dear heavens, no!"

Edwina bobbed her head. "Yes, and he is being entirely unfair about it."

Ushering her inside, Mrs. Warren asked, "Can I get you a cup of tea?"

"No, thank you," Edwina said.

"Are you sure? It has been my experience that a cup of tea can help even the most difficult situations seem a little bit more tolerable," Mrs. Warren encouraged.

Edwina frowned. "Not this situation."

Mrs. Warren led her into the room off the entry hall and said, "Now tell us what happened and do not leave anything out."

With a sigh, Edwina shared, "Lord Hilgrove and I were having a discussion and one thing led to another and we almost kissed."

"You did?" Mrs. Warren asked, exchanging a worried glance with her husband.

"Yes, and Bennett caught us," Edwina said. "Next thing I

know, Lord Hilgrove has offered to marry me, and Bennett accepted on my behalf."

Mr. Warren furrowed his brow. "You do realize that people have married for much less," he said, the concern evident in his frown.

"Yes, but we didn't kiss," Edwina said. "We *almost* kissed. There is a difference."

"That may be true, but you were caught in a scandalous position by your cousin," Mr. Warren pressed. "It is only right that you marry Lord Hilgrove."

Tossing up her hands, Edwina asked, "Whose side are you on?"

"Yours, and always yours," Mr. Warren replied. "But I am trying to have you look at this objectively."

Edwina turned her attention towards Mrs. Warren, who had been unusually silent. "What do you think?"

Mrs. Warren offered her a weak smile. "We would be happy to hide you away until this passes, but I do not think that is the right thing to do."

"You don't?"

"No, Lord Hilgrove seems to be a fine man," Mrs. Warren said. "Why do you take issue with marrying him?"

Edwina felt her shoulders slump. "Because he could never love me. He is still in love with his late wife."

Mrs. Warren approached her and placed a comforting hand on her sleeve. "There is only one reason why I see you objecting to this marriage, then."

"What is that?" Edwina asked.

In a calm voice, Mrs. Warren said, "You love him, don't you?"

Edwina reared back, not wanting to believe it was true. "No, that is impossible. We are friends, nothing more."

"Yet your eyes betray your emotions," Mrs. Warren said. "You care for him far more than just a friend."

"I may care for him, but that is a far cry from loving him,"

Edwina defended. "Besides, it doesn't matter. Lord Hilgrove is marrying me only out of honor."

Mrs. Warren dropped her arm but remained close. "I think there is more there, for both of you."

"You would be wrong," Edwina asserted. "I can't… I won't… marry a man that doesn't love me."

"Then what shall you do?" Mrs. Warren asked.

A thought occurred to Edwina. "I can run away and play golf. It is all the rage in Scotland and I am sure I can learn to love it."

"That is an interesting option, but let's put it aside for now," Mrs. Warren suggested.

A knock came at the door of the cottage, interrupting their conversation.

Mrs. Warren departed from the room to open the door and a moment later she returned with Miles by her side.

Edwina huffed, dispensing with the pleasantries. "What are you doing here?"

Miles smiled, as if he found her blunt question to be humorous. "Hello, my lady," he replied. "It is good to see you, too."

"We just saw one another in the library, or have you forgotten?" Edwina asked, her voice taking on an edge.

"I remember perfectly, but Bennett was hoping we could speak to his father soon about the important matter we discussed earlier," Miles replied.

Edwina tensed. "Already?"

"Yes, Bennett is rather eager to get the issue resolved," Miles explained. "May I escort you back to the manor?"

With a wave of her hand, Edwina said, "That is not necessary. I can find my way back on my own."

"It would be no bother, my lady, seeing as I am already here," Miles pressed.

Edwina had been raised to be a lady, but she didn't feel like it. Not here. Not now. Her emotions were too discombobulated for her to even attempt to make sense of them. All she was certain of was that she cared too much for Miles to marry him and pine after him for the rest of her days.

Miles took a step closer to her and lowered his voice. "Nothing has changed between us, my lady. We are still friends."

Her eyes widened. "How can you say that?" she asked. "You want me to marry you."

"Yes, and I hope to convince you of that. But first, we have more important issues to discuss with Lord Dallington," Miles insisted.

Edwina knew that Miles was right and it irked her. She needed to be rational about all of this. One thing at a time.

"Very well," she conceded. "You may walk me back to the manor."

"Thank you," Miles said, offering his arm.

She glanced down at his arm, desperately wanting to refuse his assistance, but propriety won out. She placed her hand on his arm and forced a smile to her lips. "Thank you, my lord."

Mrs. Warren walked with them to the door. "It was a pleasure to see both of you today," she said as she opened the door. "You are always welcome in our home."

As they walked out onto the path that led back to the manor, Edwina asked, "Did you truly have to offer for me?"

"Are we doing this now?" he asked with a smirk.

"Yes!" she exclaimed. "What were you thinking?"

He stopped and turned to face her. "We were caught in a compromising situation. It was the only thing I could think of to save your reputation."

"That is ridiculous," she said. "I could have threatened Bennett to not say anything."

"You, threaten someone?" Miles asked, amused.

Edwina nodded. "I can be quite scary when I want to be."

"I'm afraid I haven't seen it," Miles responded. "Regardless, do you truly think that Bennett won't tell your aunt, or your uncle?"

"So what if my family knows?" she asked.

"It has been my experience that servants love nothing more than to gossip and word will eventually get out." Miles reached out and placed a hand on her sleeve. "Bennett was right that we should marry, and quickly."

"Why?" she asked.

With a devilish grin, Miles said, "Because I want to kiss you and it is only a matter of time before I do so."

Edwina felt a blush forming on her cheeks, knowing she felt the same, but she didn't dare admit that. Not to him. "But that doesn't mean we should have to get married."

"Does this mean you wish to kiss me, too?" Miles asked, his grin widening.

"No, you flatter yourself, my lord," she said as she worked to keep her voice steady.

Miles winked at her. "I understand."

Edwina pursed her lips together before asking, "Did you just wink at me?"

"Yes, I did," Miles replied. "I suspect you wish to kiss me, just as much as I wish to kiss you."

Her mouth dropped, feeling a spark of outrage. "I am a lady, and you are supposed to be a gentleman."

Miles took a step closer to her. "I know precisely who you are, Edwina, and that is why I wish to marry you."

How she wished his words were in earnest. He only wanted to do the honorable thing by marrying her. She could feel tears prick in the back of her eyes and she blinked them away. "But could you ever love me?"

"I don't know," Miles replied with a look of regret on his features. "I do know that I care for you. Greatly."

"And I care for you, but that isn't enough for me," Edwina said, brushing past him.

Miles quickly caught up to her and matched her stride. "I am not going to give up that easily," he responded.

"I wish you would."

"What if your cousin challenges me to a duel?" Miles asked.

Edwina glanced over at him and said, "Then I will be your second."

Miles chuckled. "You, my second?"

"Yes, I know how to shoot a pistol," she replied. "I am quite good at it, actually."

"That may be true, but women are not seconds."

Coming to a stop on the path, Edwina turned to face Miles, feeling her chest heave with anger. "Women are not some defenseless creatures that need protecting."

"I never said that," Miles said. "But women are more rational, and duels stem more from passion and misplaced honor. I daresay you would spend most of your time trying to talk us out of the duel."

"Of course I would. Duels are stupid," Edwina declared.

"I won't disagree with you there."

Edwina let out a deep breath as she tried to contain her emotions. "I am sure that we can speak rationally to Bennett about our circumstance, and he will come to the same agreement as we have."

"That we should marry," he said.

She rolled her eyes. "No, that we part as friends since it was an unfortunate misunderstanding."

Miles gave her a knowing look. "But it wasn't a misunderstanding."

"I thought you didn't want to ever get married again."

"That is true. But I am not as opposed to it as I once was," Miles said.

Edwina crossed her arms over her chest. "Don't you want to marry the girl of your choosing and not someone you were forced to marry?"

"Who says I am not?"

"Be serious."

Miles' lips twitched. "I am," he replied. "I know our circumstances are not ideal, but we could make this marriage work."

She dropped her arms to her sides. "I'm sorry, Miles, but I want more out of a marriage than mutual toleration."

"Is that what you think I am offering?"

Edwina stepped forward and placed her hand over his heart. "If we did marry, I would want all of you, including all the spaces of your heart."

Miles grew somber. "I can't give you that, at least right now."

"Would you be ready in the future?"

His face fell. "I don't know," he said, his words sounding pained.

Edwina took a step back. "Thank you for trying to do the honorable thing. You are a good man, perhaps the best that I know. But I would rather remain a spinster than marry a man that couldn't love me."

And with that, she turned and hurried down the path, not bothering to wait for Miles. She then realized that she had made a terrible mistake. She had fallen in love with him.

Chapter Fifteen

Miles watched as Edwina walked away and he let out a sigh. It was a matter of honor for him to marry her, at least that is what he kept telling himself. He knew that she wanted love, but he couldn't give that to her. How could he? He loved his late wife and she had died, leaving him broken.

He couldn't risk that, not again. It was better to marry Edwina and keep his emotions tucked away. It was the only way he could think of that he could protect himself from the heartache that would eventually come.

Edwina may be against this marriage for now, but she would come around. She had to. And he would be good to her.

He hurried to catch up with Edwina and remarked, "You are a remarkably fast walker when you are angry."

She glanced over at him. "I'm not angry."

"You aren't?"

"No, I am sad."

Miles furrowed his brow. He had anticipated her anger, but not sadness. "May I ask why that is?" he asked.

Edwina bit her lower lip, a sure sign that she was upset.

"You are right. Once my uncle finds out about our *almost* kiss, he will force me to marry you."

"And that makes you sad?"

"No, what makes me sad is that you could never love me," Edwina said. "I understand why that is, but I had wanted more out of this life."

Miles felt his heart ache for Edwina, knowing she deserved more. "If that is the case, I rescind my offer of marriage."

"You rescind it?"

"Yes, I take it back," Miles said. "You don't have to marry me unless you choose to."

Edwina winced. "It isn't that easy. My uncle may disown me if I don't marry you."

Miles stopped on the path, his boots grinding on the gravel as he turned to face her. "I just want you to be happy, Edwina. Whatever you decide, I will support your decision," he said. "And I would never let you suffer because of my thoughtless actions."

"I could always run away to Scotland and play golf," Edwina said with a wistful look.

Miles eyed her curiously. "Do you play golf?"

"No, but women have been playing for two years now," Edwina remarked. "I have read about it in the newssheets."

A smile tugged at the corners of his lips. "Your plan is flawless, my dear, but perhaps we should think of one that would keep you in England."

Edwina's eyes lit up. "I could be a falconer."

"Yes, you could, but do you truly wish to train falcons?" he asked.

"I love birds."

Miles chuckled. "I love eating food, but I would not make a career out of that."

Edwina rolled her eyes. "I would be a falconer to just earn some extra money until I can access my dowry at twenty-five."

"I am trying to be supportive, but surely there is something else you could do," Miles insisted.

"This is hard," Edwina remarked, blowing out a puff of air. "Not everyone can be an earl."

Miles shook his head. "It is not as if I asked for this responsibility. I was content serving in the Army."

"I know, and I am sorry for making light of it," Edwina said. "I just don't know what to do. I feel lost."

Taking a step towards her, Miles responded, "I am here, and I will help you in any way I can. I promise you that."

Edwina smiled. "I know. Thank you."

"Just so you know, I would marry you today, tomorrow or in a week," Miles said. "We can marry in name only, if that is what you would prefer."

Her smile dimmed. "Do you not require an heir?"

Miles' gaze became distant, tinged with a sense of anguish. "I would never ask you to risk your life over that."

"Not everyone dies in childbirth," Edwina said.

"I can't risk it… I won't," Miles insisted, his jaw clenching.

Edwina's eyes held compassion as she remarked, "I know you want to protect me, but even you can't predict the future."

Miles shifted his gaze away from Edwina. "No, but I won't tempt fate," he said. "My title will be passed to a cousin."

"Just to clarify, you are now offering me a loveless marriage that is in name only," Edwina remarked.

Shifting uncomfortably in his stance, Miles responded, "Yes, but I will buy you whatever you want."

"What I want is not something you can buy, Miles," Edwina said. "I daresay your offer is getting worse and worse."

Miles held her gaze. "Tell me what to say, and I will say it."

Edwina offered him a weak smile. "For the longest time, it felt like I was trying to make sense of my life, but now I see there is no sense to be made. I just need to live my life and embrace my journey."

Bennett's irate voice came from behind them. "Dear heavens, you two are taking far too long to return to the manor."

Miles turned to see his friend approaching them with purposeful strides. "I'm afraid we got caught up in our conversation."

"You were supposed to retrieve Edwina, not lollygag," Bennett said, coming to a stop next to them. "Dare I ask what you two were discussing?"

Edwina spoke up. "I am thinking about becoming a falconer."

Bennett's brow shot up. "You expect me to believe that?"

"No, it is true," Miles confirmed. "Lady Edwina has decided to either become a falconer or a golfer."

"What nonsense are you spewing?" Bennett asked.

With a tilt of her chin, Edwina replied, "I am not going to marry Lord Hilgrove and I thought becoming a falconer would be rather lucrative."

Bennett huffed, looking clearly unimpressed by Edwina's declaration. "Have you tried to train a bird before?"

"No, but surely it can't be that difficult," Edwina replied.

Looking heavenward, Bennett muttered a few words under his breath before returning his gaze to Edwina. "You are being impossible."

Edwina visibly tensed. "Says the man that is trying to force me to marry Lord Hilgrove."

"Did you already forget that I caught you in a compromising position?" Bennett asked, his voice taking on an edge. "What choice do I have?"

"You do not have to be a jackanapes!" Edwina exclaimed before she continued down the path.

Together, they watched Edwina's retreating figure. After a long moment, Bennett's voice broke through the silence. "My cousin is stubborn, but surely- in due time- she will realize this is the only way."

Miles was sure that Edwina was his future, but now he had to convince her of that. Why couldn't she see that he was trying to protect her by wanting a marriage in name only?

In a hesitant voice, Miles shared, "She wants love."

Bennett turned to face him. "And you can't give that to her?"

"No, I'm afraid I can't," Miles admitted. "I have loved once and it did not go well for me. I can't risk it… not again."

"That was a tragic circumstance, but that doesn't mean you should give up on love," Bennett said.

"What choice do I have?" Miles asked.

Bennett ran a hand through his hair. "Love is a choice. You must make it every single day."

Miles scoffed. "Pardon me for not wishing to take advice from someone that has never been in love."

A pained look came into Bennett's eyes. "I have loved before, but my affection was not returned," he shared.

Feeling contrite, Miles said, "I'm sorry. I didn't know."

"How could you?" Bennett asked. "I never told you or anyone for that matter. It is not something I wish to dwell on."

Miles watched as Edwina disappeared within the manor as he asked, "How do you propose I can convince your cousin to marry me?"

Bennett shrugged. "You could always buy her a falcon," he joked.

"I would prefer not to," Miles said.

Growing serious, Bennett remarked, "Regardless, we need to deal with the issues that you have brought up about my father." He paused. "My father is a good man. I do not believe what you are claiming he is capable of."

"It isn't uncommon for a man of Lord Dallington's position to have a mistress," Miles attempted.

Bennett narrowed his eyes. "My parents love each other, and I resent the accusation."

"I know what I saw, and it did not look good for your father," Miles asserted.

"You were mistaken," Bennett declared with a swipe of his hand. "It is preposterous to even think that my father has another family."

Miles gave his friend an understanding look. "Perhaps you should come see for yourself the next time your father says he is departing for the village."

"Fine. Then I can prove to you that it was just a misunderstanding," Bennett said. "But first we need to speak to my father about the state of the estate."

"What of Lady Edwina's inheritance?" Miles asked.

Bennett looked displeased by his question. "I will take a look at my uncle's will, but I am sure there is a perfectly plausible reason for why my father didn't say anything."

Miles nodded. "If you say so."

"I do," Bennett stated. "I know my father and he is not a bad man."

"I am not insinuating that he is," Miles said.

Bennett gestured towards the manor. "Come along," he encouraged. "My father is in his study, and he has agreed to see us before he departs for the village."

Miles arched an eyebrow but thought it would be prudent if he didn't say anything.

"I know what you are going to say," Bennett started, "but he has a meeting with his man of business."

"What if we followed him, just to be sure?" Miles asked.

Bennett pursed his lips. "I shall agree to that but just so I can prove you wrong."

Miles winced. "I wish I was wrong," he said.

They both seemed to retreat to their own thoughts as they made their way back to the manor. Once they stepped inside, he watched Edwina pace back and forth in the entry hall, a frown creasing her brow.

Bennett leaned closer to him and whispered, "I would proceed with caution with Edwina. I haven't seen her this upset in quite some time."

Miles approached Edwina and waited until she came to a stop in front of him. He smiled, hoping to disarm her. "May I get you some chocolate, my lady?"

Edwina stared at him like he was mad. "Why?"

"I recall that Arabella would always ask for chocolate when she was upset," Miles replied. "It seemed to help her calm down."

Apparently, that was the wrong thing to say because Edwina placed her hand on her hip. "I am only upset because of you and Bennett. And, no, chocolate would not help this."

Bennett moved closer to them and said, "I apologize for interrupting, but we should go speak to my father."

Some of the anger dissipated from Edwina's expression and it was replaced by uncertainty. A feeling that he knew all too well.

Miles offered his arm. "Remember that we are in this together. Always."

His words had the desired effect on Edwina, and she placed her hand on his arm. "Thank you," she murmured.

As they walked towards Lord Dallington's study, Miles glanced over at Edwina and knew that she was nervous. But she could do this. He had never met a braver soul than her. He knew in his heart that he would do whatever it took to make her his own.

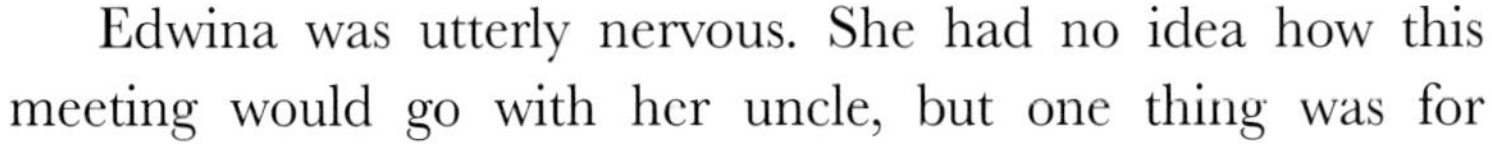

Edwina was utterly nervous. She had no idea how this meeting would go with her uncle, but one thing was for certain, she was grateful to have Miles by her side. He gave her the strength to continue on, despite knowing how difficult this conversation would be for her.

She quickly glanced at Miles and admired his handsome face. How she was growing to love this man, but it didn't matter. He would never reciprocate her feelings. Although, he had admitted that he cared for her. But that wasn't enough. She wanted more.

As they arrived at the study, Miles leaned in and whispered, "You can do this."

"*We* can do this," she corrected.

Miles smiled and she knew that everything would be all right. "We can do anything together," he said.

"Except whistle," Edwina quipped. "Only one of us can do that."

He chuckled. "You are right."

They followed Bennett into the study and Edwina saw her uncle was hunched over his large desk. Papers were neatly formed into piles and a ledger sat in front of him.

Bennett's voice broke through the silence. "Father, do you have a moment to talk?"

Her uncle closed the ledger in front of him and leaned back in his seat, a satisfied smile on his lips. "I have been expecting this," he said.

"You have?" Bennett asked, the confusion evident on his features.

"Yes, and it is about time," her uncle declared. "I must say that I couldn't be more pleased. It is not every day that one's niece marries an earl."

Edwina's brow shot up. "Pardon?"

Her uncle looked at her like she was a simpleton. "Is that not why you and Miles are here? To ask for my blessing."

"No, we are here for an entirely different matter," Edwina replied.

"Then you two aren't engaged?" her uncle asked.

Edwina exchanged a look with Miles before confirming, "We are not."

Her uncle frowned. "Whyever not?" he demanded. "I have seen the way you two look at one another and the hushed conversations."

"We are just friends," Edwina insisted.

With a huff, her uncle turned to Bennett. "What are your thoughts on this?"

Edwina held her breath, not knowing if Bennett would reveal that he had caught them in a compromising situation. If he did, she had no doubt that her uncle would demand that they should be married at once.

But to her pleasant- and rather unexpected- surprise, Bennett just shrugged. "I do believe the decision rests solely on them."

She released her breath, grateful for her cousin's discretion.

Her uncle shifted his gaze to Miles. "And what say you?" he asked. "Is my niece not good enough for you?"

Miles shook his head. "No, my lord, I would gladly marry Lady Edwina, assuming she would have me."

"She will have you," her uncle said.

"Uncle!" Edwina exclaimed. "I do believe I should have a choice in the matter."

Her uncle gave her an exasperated look. "Lord Hilgrove would make a fine husband for you. He is an earl, and I doubt you would fare much better in the marriage mart."

Miles interjected, "I agree with Lady Edwina. It is her decision and hers alone."

"But she is a woman," her uncle cried out. "They are prone to make irrational decisions based on their emotions and whatnot."

Her aunt's voice came from the doorway. "Lionel!" she exclaimed. "That was entirely unfair of you to say."

Her uncle had the decency to look ashamed. "My apologies, my love. I am just trying to make a point."

"A poorly worded point," her aunt said, walking further into the room. "Edwina has every right to make this decision on her own."

"But Miles is an earl," her uncle pointed out.

"Yes, he is, but you can't force these things," her aunt said. "You must trust Edwina is making the best choice for herself."

Her uncle looked displeased. "It would be far better if Edwina marries now than having her endure the Season."

"You just don't want to pay for her Season," her aunt remarked.

"Precisely," her uncle declared. "The purpose of having a Season is to make yourself as desirable as possible so you can attract a suitor. But Edwina has already attracted an earl. Is that not enough for her?"

Edwina lowered her gaze, not knowing what to say. Her uncle was adamant about her marrying Miles, not that she expected any different. But she didn't dare reveal the reasonings behind her decision not to marry him.

Miles leaned closer to her and whispered, "Your uncle is acting very 'marquess*ish*.'"

A laugh escaped her lips and she brought her hand up to cover her mouth.

"Did I say that right?" he asked.

She brought her gaze back up. "You did, and I am rather impressed by your ability to make up words as well," she joked.

"I learned from the best," Miles said with a smile.

Her uncle cleared his throat. "Are you two quite finished?" he asked.

"We are," Edwina replied.

With a sigh, her uncle rose from his seat and asked, "Why, pray tell, do you not wish to marry Lord Hilgrove?"

Edwina tilted her chin. "I have my reasons."

"Would you care to elaborate on those?" her uncle asked.

Her aunt stepped closer to Edwina and placed a hand on her sleeve. "It is all right, Child. You do not need to tell us. We trust that you are making the right decision for yourself."

Walking over to the drink cart, her uncle picked up a decanter and asked, "Do you like living here, Edwina?"

"I do," she responded hesitantly, not sure where this conversation was heading.

"And do you think I will let you remain here for the remainder of your days?" her uncle inquired as he poured himself a drink.

Edwina shook her head.

Her uncle placed down the decanter and picked up his drink. "You are right. My generosity has its limits. I will not allow you to become a drain on my finances."

"Lionel, can we discuss this in private?" her aunt asked, her words holding a warning.

Turning towards his wife, her uncle said, "We will not. It is time that Edwina understood that her time here will come to an end when she reaches her majority. If she is not married by then, she will be forced to seek out employment."

Bennett eyed his father trepidatiously. "What about Edwina's dowry?"

"Under her father's stipulations, Edwina cannot access her dowry until she is twenty-five years old," her uncle explained.

"Surely Edwina can remain with us until she is twenty-five," her aunt remarked. "That is what Richard would have wanted."

Her uncle stiffened. "Richard is not here, is he?" he demanded.

Edwina felt the tears burn in the back of her eyes at the mention of her father and blinked them back. However, one managed to escape and it slipped down her cheek. This was the moment to be brave, to inquire about her inheritance, but her words eluded her.

As she struggled to find her voice, Miles extended her a white handkerchief from his jacket pocket.

With a weak smile, she accepted it and swiped at her cheek. "Thank you," she murmured.

Miles' eyes held compassion as he held her gaze. "It will be all right," he whispered. "Trust me."

"I do," she responded.

Her uncle's voice broke through their conversation. "Is everyone truly this blind?" he asked. "It is obvious that Edwina and Miles care for one another."

"Perhaps, but you must let them find their own path," her aunt insisted.

Bennett shifted in his stance before saying, "As enjoyable as this conversation is, we did want to speak to you about something much more important."

Her uncle lifted his brow. "More important than my niece refusing to marry a wealthy earl?"

"Yes, it has to do with the funding you are providing to the village," Bennett replied.

With a scoff, her uncle placed his glass down onto the desk. "What do those ingrates want now?" he asked.

Bennett furrowed his brow. "Why do you suppose they want something?"

"Mr. Stanley has told me that they are complaining that I don't fund the repairs needed in the village." Coming around his desk, her uncle sat down and reached for the ledger. "I give those villagers enough of my money. I have paid for the clock tower and cobblestone road to be repaired. And I just put a new roof on the chapel. Is that not enough for them?"

"Father…" Bennett started.

Her uncle put his hand up, stilling his words. "I already have enough to do and I refuse to continue this conversation any longer."

"Well, you will have to make the time," Bennett said firmly.

"I beg your pardon?" her uncle growled.

Bennett walked closer to the desk. "How much are you giving to help the villagers?"

"Enough," came her uncle's response.

"Can you expand on that?" Bennett asked.

Her uncle tapped his finger on the ledger. "Why do you care so much?"

"Because we have heard the grumblings from the villagers and I even had an unfortunate altercation with one of your disgruntled tenants," Bennett responded.

Opening the ledger, her uncle made a show of turning it towards Bennett and pointed. "That is what I just gave to support the upkeep of the village this month."

Bennett approached the desk and studied the ledger. "That seems like a fair amount."

"It is more than fair," her uncle said. "Now do you see that the villagers are just complaining about their lots in life?"

Edwina was curious about one thing so she asked, "Did you reduce the funding to the village after my father died?"

"Not at first, but Mr. Stanley convinced me that I was being far too generous," her uncle replied. "And he did warn me that the villagers would respond this way. They are truly ungrateful."

Her uncle reached for the ledger and pulled it back towards him. "Now if you will excuse me, I have a meeting in the village."

"With Mr. Stanley?" Bennett questioned.

"Why does it matter to you with whom I am meeting?" her uncle demanded. "Last I checked, I don't answer to you."

Bennett put his hands up in surrender. "My apologies, Father," he responded, his words curt.

Picking up the ledger, her uncle placed it under his arm

and walked over to his wife. He kissed her cheek and said, "I shall return home for supper."

Her aunt smiled. "I do hope so."

After her uncle stepped out of the room, her aunt turned towards Bennett and asked, "What was that all about?"

Bennett gave her an innocent look. "Nothing. I was merely curious."

"Since when did you take an interest in your father's business dealings?" her aunt asked with a knowing look.

"I suppose since this will be all mine one day I should take a more vested interest in it all," Bennett said.

Her aunt didn't look convinced. "Very well, don't tell me. But I always manage to root out the truth on my own," she stated before departing from the study.

Bennett approached them and lowered his voice. "We need to see who my father is truly meeting."

"Shall we take our horses or the carriage?" Edwina asked.

"I would prefer if you remained at the manor while Miles and I go trail after my father," Bennett said.

Edwina pressed her lips together. "Why, exactly?"

"Because I think it is for the best," Bennett replied.

With a shake of her head, Edwina said, "You are acting very 'earlish.'"

"What does that even mean?" Bennett inquired.

Miles spoke up, his lips twitching. "It is not a good thing, I assure you."

Bennett dismissed his comment with a wave of his hand. "Regardless, we are in agreement. Edwina will stay home," he said.

"No," Edwina responded. "I am going with you."

Bennett opened his mouth to no doubt object, but Miles put a hand on his shoulder. "You might as well save your breath."

"Fine, we do not have time for this," Bennett muttered. "Let us depart."

Edwina resisted the urge to smile at her cousin's lackluster response, but she was glad that she was going. Perhaps she could even prove to her cousin that she was capable of so much more than what he gave her credit for.

Chapter Sixteen

Miles remained in a crouched position in the woodlands, hidden by the thick foliage and trees. He was flanked by Edwina on one side and Bennett on the other, their eyes fixed on the quaint cottage. Lord Dallington's coach sat idly in front of it, as if it had always belonged.

The three of them had been waiting for what seemed like hours, but Miles could see that Bennett was growing rather restless.

"What could my father possibly be doing in there?" Bennett grumbled.

Miles smirked. "I have an idea."

Bennett scowled, clearly not amused. "That is a terrible thing to suggest."

"I was only suggesting that they might be engaged in a game of chess," Miles responded innocently. "What did you think I was implying?"

Casting his eyes skyward, Bennett let out a deep sigh. "You are an idiot," he muttered.

Edwina chimed in with a mischievous grin. "We could always practice bird calls to pass the time."

"I would rather not," Bennett said.

"Then what would you suggest we do to pass the time?" Edwina asked.

Bennett's gaze returned to the cottage, his expression grave once more. "I do not know how you two can make light of this situation."

Miles placed a comforting hand on his friend's shoulder. "We are trying to distract you from the truth."

"It isn't working," Bennett admitted. "This is going to devastate my mother. My whole family, in fact. I never thought that my father would betray my mother."

As Bennett uttered his last word, Lord Dallington emerged from the cottage and the same tall woman stood in the doorway with her young son at her side. He kissed the woman on her cheek and ruffled the boy's hair affectionally before turning to enter the awaiting coach.

As the coach made its way down the road towards the village, Bennett jumped up from his crouched position. "I wouldn't have believed it if I hadn't seen it with my own eyes."

"I know, which is why we brought you here," Miles said.

"My father is a blackguard," Bennett declared. "How could he do this to us?"

Miles struggled to find words of reassurance but thankfully Edwina spoke up. "Uncle is not the man that I thought he was."

"No, you were right about my father," Bennett remarked. "I didn't want it to be true."

Edwina approached her cousin and wrapped her arms around his waist. "It will be all right," she said in a vain attempt to reassure him.

"How?" Bennett asked. "My father is hated by the villagers and now he has a whole other family."

"You can fix this," Edwina said, taking a step back. "I know you, and I know what you are capable of."

"I don't think I am capable of keeping our family together once the truth is revealed," Bennett admitted.

Edwina smiled at Bennett. "You will find a way."

Bennett sighed. "I think I preferred you when you were moping around the manor," he said lightly. "You are far too optimistic now."

"I am starting to see things differently now," Edwina remarked as she glanced over at Miles. "It took a friend to help me realize what is truly important."

Miles held her gaze. "You would have figured it out on your own soon enough."

"You give me far too much credit," Edwina said.

Bennett cleared his throat. "Can we discuss the matter at hand?" he asked. "I am of half a mind to go speak to the woman in the cottage."

"That is a terrible idea," Miles stated. "Then Lord Dallington will know you have discovered his secret."

"Well, what am I to do?" Bennett asked as his shoulders slumped slightly. "Do I dare confront my father or continue on as if nothing is amiss?"

Miles knew that holding on to a secret such as this would gnaw at his friend until it began to rob him of his joy. "No, that wouldn't be fair to you or your family."

Edwina bobbed her head. "Lord Hilgrove is right. Your family has a right to know the truth."

"But what is the truth?" Bennett asked. "We know nothing about that woman or her son. What if it was all perfectly innocent?"

Miles could see the turmoil in Bennett's eyes as he struggled to come to terms with what he had just witnessed. But pretending everything was well would not benefit anyone, especially his friend. "Is that what you think in your heart?" he asked gently, knowing that this question was difficult for Bennett to answer truthfully.

Bennett let out a sigh. "No," he responded.

"We can help you," Edwina reassured him.

With a pained look on his face, Bennett responded, "No

one can help me. This is something that I need to do on my own." He paused. "But it makes me wonder what else my father is hiding from me. From us."

Bennett continued. "I cannot imagine the enormous pressure that my father has endured since taking over his title, but that doesn't excuse his behavior."

"No, it doesn't," Miles agreed.

"It is time that I take a more active role in the estate," Bennett remarked firmly. "My father has brushed me aside for far too long."

Edwina's eyes held approval. "I believe in you. *We* believe in you." She turned towards Miles. "Don't we, my lord?"

Miles shrugged. "I am still on the fence," he joked.

Bennett walked over to where the horses were secured. "We should be heading back. I don't want Winston to start asking questions, questions that I do not want to answer."

"We could always go to the village and select some ribbon for Elodie and Melody," Edwina suggested.

"No, I do not want to risk having my father see us," Bennett said with a shake of his head.

Miles retrieved his horse and held the reins loosely in his hand. "For what it is worth, I am sorry."

Bennett offered him an appreciative smile. "You and Edwina tried to warn me. But I didn't believe you. Quite frankly, I didn't *want* to believe you. Now I am forced to question everything."

"Well, I am willing to help in any way that I can," Miles said.

Bennett grew pensive. "It is ironic, though. I brought you here so I could help you, and yet it seems that you ended up helping me in return."

Attempting to lighten the mood that had fallen over the group, Miles said, "I am a man of many talents, after all."

"No, that is most assuredly not true," Bennett responded

in a serious tone. "But you are returning to the man that you once were."

Miles furrowed his brow. "Meaning?"

Bennett gave him a knowing look. "You are smiling again, Miles."

Miles glanced at Edwina, knowing she was the true reason that his smile had returned. But he didn't dare admit that. Not to her. Not to anybody. If he did, then they would see through him and know that he held deep affection for Edwina.

Edwina led her horse over to a fallen log and, in a swift motion, mounted her horse with expert precision.

"Bennett or I could have assisted you," Miles pointed out.

"I know, but I prefer to do it on my own," Edwina responded.

Miles approached her horse and placed a hand on its neck. "You don't have to do everything on your own. Not anymore. I am here."

"But you will be going away, my lord," she said. A flicker of sadness crossed Edwina's green eyes before she blinked it away. Or did he just imagine that?

His lips twitched into a small smile. "Not for a while, my lady. There is something I must do first."

"Which is?"

Miles held her gaze firmly as he replied, "Convince a very stubborn young woman to marry me."

Her expression remained inscrutable, giving nothing away. "I wish you luck with that."

Taking a step back, Miles responded confidently, "I just have to show you that you cannot live without me."

"And, pray tell, how do you intend to do that?" Edwina asked.

Miles decided to do the last thing that she would expect him to do. He puckered his lips and let out a soft whistle.

With a line between her brow, Edwina asked, "Did you just attempt to whistle?"

"I did, albeit weakly," he admitted proudly. "I have been practicing in my bedchamber with my valet."

Edwina's eyes lit up. "Did you do that just for me?"

"Perhaps. Did it impress you?"

"Yes, very much so," Edwina replied.

Miles puffed out his chest. "Then I did it for you."

Edwina laughed, and the noise seemed to dance through the woodlands. "I may have underestimated you."

Bennett's voice came from behind them. "That was not a whistle. He just blew air through his lips."

"I heard a faint whistle," Edwina argued.

"I daresay you were hearing things," Bennett remarked as he mounted his horse. "Come along. We can race home."

A smug smile came to Edwina's face. "It is hardly fair. You always lose."

After Miles sat atop his horse, they exited the woodlands and headed down the path towards the manor.

"I'll see you two back at the manor," Edwina said before she kicked her horse into a run.

Miles was about to do the same when Bennett's voice stopped him. "Edwina is the happiest I have seen her in a long time."

"Is that so?" Miles asked.

"Yes, and I suspect it has to do with you," Bennett said with a pointed look. "You two have managed to help each other in ways that no one else could."

Miles kept his gaze straight ahead as he admitted, "I want to marry her."

"Do you love her?"

He winced at the question, his heart aching with conflict. "I love Arabella."

"There is no shame in moving on and opening your heart to another," Bennett said. "It is what makes us human."

Miles tightened the reins in his hand, feeling trapped by his own emotions. "I care for Edwina. Is that not enough?"

"No, she deserves more, and so do you," Bennett replied, his voice firm but understanding.

With a glance at Bennett, Miles said, "Thank you for not telling your father about the compromising position you found Edwina and me in."

"I didn't think it was prudent to do so, considering I know you are trying to do the honorable thing," Bennett responded.

"I am."

"But, perhaps, doing the honorable thing is letting my cousin go, if you can't love her," Bennett remarked.

Miles was taken aback at his friend's remark. "I thought you would challenge me to a duel if I didn't marry Edwina."

Bennett grew quiet for a long moment before responding. "Above all else, I want my cousin to be happy. And if she doesn't believe that you will bring her happiness, then I shall respect her decision."

As Miles mulled over Bennett's words, his friend kicked his horse into a run, leaving him with his conflicted thoughts. He wanted to be the one to make Edwina smile. But he couldn't give her the one thing that she wanted. He should let her go, but a part of him didn't want to. He wanted to fight for her. Because maybe, just maybe, he could come to love her.

But a wave of guilt washed over him at that thought. Could he forget Arabella so easily? No. It might be for the best if he let Edwina go so she could find someone who could give her everything she desired and more.

Edwina peeked out of her bedchamber door and down the corridor. She was waiting for Miles to make an appearance so they could walk down to dinner together.

Empty.

Just as it had been the last ten times that she had checked.

She closed the door and rested her back against the wall. Why was she so eager to spend time with Miles? But she already knew that answer. She loved him. He lifted her spirits and made her happy.

She knew that Miles would leave soon and they would both go their own ways. But she didn't want to waste one moment with him.

A knock came at the door.

Excitement coursed through her at the thought it might be Miles on the other side of the door. Edwina quickly smoothed back her hair and brought a smile to her face, as if it had been there all day.

She opened the door and saw Bennett. Her smile dimmed. "Oh, it is just you," she muttered.

Bennett grinned. "Were you expecting someone else?"

"No," she lied.

"You are a terrible liar, Cousin," Bennett said. "May I come in?"

Edwina took a step back. "Please do," she encouraged.

Bennett stepped into the bedchamber and closed the door behind him. "I think it is best if this conversation stays between us."

"As you wish," Edwina said, her curiosity piqued.

All humor left Bennett's face as he shared, "I read your father's will and confirmed that he left you ten thousand pounds. I'm sorry that I doubted you."

"I understand why you did," Edwina said.

"I didn't want it to be true," Bennett sighed.

Edwina placed a hand on his sleeve. "I'm sorry," she murmured, knowing her words were wholly inadequate at this moment.

Bennett's eyes looked tired as he said, "I will speak to my father at once and try to get this all sorted out."

An idea came to Edwina. "What if I spoke to Mr. Stanley first?" she asked.

"Why would you speak to my father's man of business?"

"I have known Mr. Stanley most of my life and he has always been kind to me," Edwina shared. "He might be able to give us some insight on your father's reasonings."

Bennett's next words hung heavy with regret. "I'm afraid I can't go with you tomorrow. I had planned to go angling with Winston."

"I can go with Lord Hilgrove," she said. She wanted to spend time with Miles but tried to hide her eagerness from Bennett.

Her cousin's brow furrowed in thought as he considered her suggestion. After a long moment, he spoke again. "I am not sure if that is wise."

"Whyever not?"

Bennett's expression grew even more concerned as he explained, "Miles is fighting a battle within himself right now."

With a knowing look, Edwina asked, "Aren't we all?"

"Yes, but I don't know what the outcome will be," Bennett replied. "However, I don't want you to give up on him. Not yet."

Unsure of his meaning, Edwina asked, "Whatever do you mean?"

A cocky grin came to Bennett's lips. "Why did you think I invited Miles to Brockhall Manor?" he asked. "I had a feeling the two of you could help each other through your struggles. Perhaps even find love along the way."

"You orchestrated this?"

"I did, and I am still hopeful," Bennett replied.

Edwina arched an eyebrow. "Now who is the optimistic one?" she teased.

Bennett chuckled. "I just want you to be happy, Cousin. No matter what path you choose. But I will say that Miles has been good for you."

"He has," she agreed. "He is a good man."

"Yes, he is."

The dinner bell chimed in the distance, beckoning them to come.

Glancing towards the door, Bennett asked, "Shall we take another look to see if Miles is approaching?"

Embarrassment washed over her and she responded with a slight wince, "You saw that?"

"I did indeed, but I find it rather encouraging."

Edwina went to open the door. "Why don't we just walk down together?"

"All right."

As they started walking down the corridor, Edwina remarked, "I haven't seen a lot of Winston."

"That is because he has been hiding away in his bedchamber working on a case that he has coming up," Bennett shared. "I was surprised when he agreed to go angling with me."

"He works too hard," Edwina said.

"Winston always has and he always will," Bennett remarked. "It is as if he is competing against himself."

As they descended the stairs, Edwina caught sight of Miles in the entry hall, causing her breath to hitch. He was finely dressed, and his dark hair was brushed forward. He was handsome, there was no denying that, but she had seen his heart. And it was kind. Loving. He was a man that she could spend forever with.

But he didn't love her.

That realization hit her and she grew somber.

Bennett glanced over at her. "Is everything all right?" he asked.

She mustered up a smile. "It is," she replied. "I was just thinking about… my book. Yes, I love reading. It is so much fun."

An amused look came to Bennett's face. "You really are a terrible liar. It is almost painful to witness," he joked.

As they stepped onto the last step, Miles strode forward and greeted her. "Good evening, my lady. You are looking lovely."

"Thank you," Edwina said.

Bennett spoke up, addressing Miles. "Are you sure you don't want to go angling with me and Winston tomorrow?"

"I am sure," Miles replied.

In a hushed voice, Edwina asked, "Would you be willing to escort me to the village so we can speak to Mr. Stanley?"

Miles smiled. "It would be my honor to do so."

Edwina found herself returning his smile. "Thank you, my lord."

Her words had just left her mouth when her aunt stepped out of the drawing room. "Shall we adjourn to the dining room?"

Miles offered his arm to Edwina. "May I escort you?"

She accepted his arm and they began to make their way to the dining room. She snuck a quick glance at him and wondered why he couldn't love her. But she stopped herself. This had nothing to do with her, and everything to do with him. His heart had been claimed long ago, and it was up to him to decide how to proceed.

Miles' voice broke through her musings. "I have been working on my whistling. I can now emit a sound loud enough that everyone knows it is a whistle."

"I'm impressed," she said.

"I thought that might please you."

They stepped into the dining room and Miles pulled out a chair for her. Then he claimed the seat next to her.

Winston sat across from her, as did Bennett, and her aunt and uncle sat at the ends of the table. The footmen promptly came around and started placing bowls of soup in front of them.

Edwina reached for her soup and started eating. No one

seemed to be in a talkative mood and a silence engulfed the table.

Her aunt glanced at the long clock in the corner. "I wonder what is taking the girls so long to arrive," she said.

"The roads might have been such that they might have stopped at a coaching inn for the evening," her uncle remarked. "There is no need to worry."

"I am a mother. Worrying comes with the title," her aunt said.

Her uncle gave his wife an understanding look. "I sent my best team to bring our girls home. Do try to enjoy dinner."

"I will try," her aunt murmured as she took a bite of her soup.

With a chuckle, her uncle asked, "You are still worrying, aren't you?"

"I am," her aunt replied.

Her uncle turned towards White. "Will you send out two riders to look for Lady Elodie and Lady Melody?"

"Yes, my lord," the butler replied with a tip of his head.

Bennett interrupted, "I could go look for them, as well."

"As could I," Miles offered.

Her uncle shook his head. "That won't be necessary."

"What if the coach has a broken wheel and they are on the side of the road, utterly helpless?" her aunt asked.

Winston chuckled. "Elodie... helpless? I think not," he said. "Most likely, she would have tried to replace the wheel herself."

The sound of a door slamming in the distance could be heard and it was followed by someone shouting, "Mother!"

Her aunt perked up in her seat. "They are home."

A moment later, a disheveled looking Elodie and Melody stepped into the dining room. Their blonde hair had escaped their chignons, dirt coated their gowns and Elodie even had dirt splattered on her face.

"What happened to you?" Edwina's aunt asked, rising.

Elodie blew out a puff of air. "I had to drive the coach when our driver grew ill."

"*You did what?!*" her father exclaimed.

With a slight shrug of her shoulder, Elodie responded, "It was either that or walk to the nearest village for help."

Melody clasped her hands in front of her. "I thought it was rather brave of Elodie," she declared.

Bennett rose from his chair and addressed Elodie. "How did you even know how to drive a coach?"

"It was difficult at first, but I got the hang of it." Elodie turned to one of the footmen. "Will you fetch the doctor for Alfred? I worry that he is more ill than he was letting on."

Edwina's uncle tossed his napkin onto the table. "A lady does not drive a coach, under any circumstances," he shouted.

"Well, this *lady* didn't want to walk miles to the next village," Elodie responded.

Melody nodded. "It really was our best option, Father."

"No, your best option was to wait in the coach until help arrived," their father countered.

Elodie reached up and removed a leaf from her hair. "I am not some helpless female," she stated. "Besides, I have always wanted to drive the coach and I succeeded. No one died."

Edwina's aunt approached her daughters and said, "What's done is done. Why don't you two go take a long soak and I will send dinner up to your bedchambers?"

Melody sighed. "That sounds delightful."

Elodie looked longingly at the table. "I do want a long soak but I am famished." She walked over to the table and retrieved a piece of bread. "This should hold me over until I have dinner."

"Allow me to escort you to your bedchambers," Lady Dallington said before leading them out of the dining room.

Edwina's uncle huffed. "What am I going to do with Elodie?"

Winston grinned. "I think she is fine the way she is."

"She acts more like a hoyden than a lady," her uncle remarked. "I wonder what bad habits she learned at that boarding school."

"Melody went to the same boarding school and she doesn't appear to have picked up any bad habits," Bennett stated.

Edwina's uncle waved his hand in front of him. "Yes, but Melody has always been much more reserved than her sister."

Edwina knew that no truer statement had ever been said. Elodie and Melody may look very much like one another, but that was where the similarities stopped. Elodie was outspoken, loud and opinionated, whereas Melody was more of an observer and tended to just follow her sister's lead.

Shoving back his seat, her uncle said, "Pardon me, but I have work that I need to see to. Will you inform Mother of this?"

Bennett nodded. "I will."

After her uncle departed from the dining room, Winston said, "I must admit that I am rather nervous about Elodie attending her first Season."

"You and me both," Bennett muttered. "I could see her challenging a gentleman to a duel for the slightest offense."

"What is worse is that she would probably win," Winston retorted.

Edwina laughed, knowing her cousins' words held some truth to them.

Bennett leaned to the side as a footman collected his soup bowl. "Regardless, we have our work cut out for us."

"Yes, we do," Winston agreed.

As the footmen brought out the next course, Edwina was happy to have Elodie and Melody home. She had always been close to them and she looked forward to learning more about the circumstances surrounding Elodie driving a coach.

Chapter Seventeen

As the sun climbed higher in the sky and streamed its warm light through the windows, Miles entered the dining room and saw Elodie and Melody sitting at the long, rectangular table.

"Good morning," he greeted with a smile as he pulled out a chair and took a seat across from them.

The sisters murmured their greetings in return, their voices gentle and refined.

At first glance, it was difficult to distinguish between Elodie and Melody, but upon closer inspection, subtle differences could be seen. Elodie's delicate features were adorned with a sprinkling of freckles along the bridge of her nose and cheeks. Meanwhile, Melody had a single dimple that appeared on her right cheek whenever she smiled.

Elodie reached for her teacup, her eyes meeting Miles' as she asked, "How are you enjoying your stay at Brockhall Manor, my lord?"

"I have enjoyed my time immensely," he replied honestly, taking a sip of his own tea.

"That is good to hear," Elodie said. "I understand Bennett and Winston are planning to go angling today. Will you be joining them?"

Miles shook his head. "No, I have agreed to escort Lady Edwina to the village instead."

"For what purpose?" Elodie inquired.

Melody quickly interjected, "That is not our concern, Sister. Remember what our headmistress said."

Elodie blew out a puff of air. "I do try to forget everything that Mrs. Taylor said."

"A genteel lady does not pry into the personal lives of others," Melody shared. "It is uncouth to do so."

"But it is imperative that I know why they are going to the village," Elodie argued.

Melody gave her a disbelieving look. "Why is that, exactly?"

"I need to know if I should accompany them," Elodie replied. "Or I might need to buy some more ribbons."

"You have plenty of ribbons," Melody pointed out.

Elodie grinned. "Can a lady ever have too many ribbons?"

"In your case, perhaps," Melody replied with a smile of her own.

Miles chuckled. "I would invite you along, my lady, but our purpose in going is for Lady Edwina to meet with Mr. Stanley."

The grin disappeared from Elodie's lips. "That does not sound the least bit enjoyable. I would rather stay here."

Lady Dallington glided through the doorway and announced, "Good, because we are meeting with the dressmaker soon. You will require a whole new wardrobe for the Season."

Elodie's shoulders slumped as she groaned in response. "That sounds awful."

Melody perked up. "I disagree. That sounds wonderful."

"I do not wish to be poked and prodded," Elodie complained.

With a slight shrug, Melody replied, "Then don't move

when the dressmaker is attempting to measure you. It is a simple process, really."

Elodie sat back in her seat, clearly unhappy with the situation. "What is wrong with the gowns that I have now?"

"They are far too simple for London," Lady Dallington replied matter-of-factly. "All eyes will be on you as you two make your debuts. You both must make quite the impression to set yourselves apart from the other debutantes."

Miles ate his food as he listened intently to the conversation, grateful that he didn't have to worry about such things. He had learned long ago that he cared little about what people thought about him. Except Edwina. Her opinion mattered greatly to him.

"What of Edwina?" Elodie asked. "Won't she need an entire new wardrobe as well?"

Lady Dallington nodded. "She does, indeed. But her appointment is scheduled for next week."

"Why not today, with us?" Elodie prodded.

Sitting down at the head of the table, Lady Dallington replied, "We shall discuss this later, Dear, since we are being terribly rude to our guest." Her voice was gentle but firm.

Miles wiped the corners of his mouth with his napkin. "Not at all. I was just enjoying the conversation around me."

Lady Dallington smiled warmly. "I do appreciate you taking Edwina into the village today."

"It is my pleasure," Miles responded. And it truly was. He found that he was greatly looking forward to spending time with Edwina again. He didn't think he would ever tire of being in her presence.

As if on cue, Edwina entered the dining room and Miles promptly rose to his feet. She looked radiant in a dark blue gown and her hair was pinned up in a loose chignon, with a few tendrils delicately framing her face. The bright smile she wore on her lips made it nearly impossible for him to look away.

"Good morning, my lord," Edwina greeted as she came to sit next to him.

Miles returned to his seat and said, "Good morning. I trust that you slept well."

"I did," Edwina replied. "And did you sleep well?"

He grinned. "I do not have any complaints."

Their eyes met for a brief moment and Miles had to forcefully turn his attention elsewhere to avoid being caught staring.

"I am pleased that you are out of mourning," Elodie said, addressing Edwina with curiosity in her voice.

Edwina placed her napkin on her lap. "I thought it was best, considering the Season is coming up shortly."

"And you intend to make your debut?" Elodie prodded.

"I do," Edwina replied. "Lord Hilgrove has graciously offered to help me."

Elodie exchanged a look with Melody before speaking again. "How kind of him."

"Indeed," Edwina agreed.

Lady Dallington spoke up. "I think that is enough talk about the Season. We should discuss the particulars of the soiree this evening."

"Why did you truly have to plan a soiree?" Elodie asked.

"To honor our esteemed guest, of course," Lady Dallington replied.

Elodie lifted her brow. "And who is our esteemed guest, again?" she inquired with a teasing lilt to her voice.

Miles chuckled. "I must agree with Lady Elodie. I do not feel very esteemed."

"You are a war hero, and the gentry will be eager to speak to you," Lady Dallington pointed out.

He sobered. "No, I simply fought in the war. I am no hero, nor would I pretend to be such," he argued, his voice much harsher than he had intended.

Edwina's smile was weak, but genuine. "Regardless, it is not every day that our village is honored to meet someone who fought valiantly in the war."

"I do not wish to give the illusion that I am something that I am not," Miles said.

"Nor should you. But I do not believe you are giving yourself enough credit, my lord," Edwina remarked as she held his gaze.

Miles let out a resigned sigh. "Very well. Then I will not turn away anyone who wishes to discuss the war with me."

"Wonderful," Lady Dallington said, clasping her hands together. "Lionel and I will be starting the dancing and Miles and Edwina will join in shortly thereafter."

At that moment, Bennett stepped into the dining room. "Thank heavens, I lost the bet. That sounds truly dreadful."

Edwina playfully narrowed her eyes at her cousin. "Are you in some way implying that dancing with me is dreadful?"

"Heavens, no, but dancing the first set when all eyes are upon you? It does sound quite terrible," Bennett replied.

Elodie chimed in, "What bet did you lose?"

Taking a seat next to his sisters, Bennett explained with a smirk, "The winner of our pall-mall game had the honor of dancing with Edwina for the first set."

"I consider it a privilege to dance with Lady Edwina," Miles said.

Bennett's smirk only grew wider as he replied, "Of course you do."

With a glance at Edwina's plate, Miles noticed that she had finished her breakfast. He stood and offered his hand to assist her in rising. "Shall we depart for the village?"

"Yes, please," Edwina replied.

As he moved Edwina's hand into the crook of his arm, Winston walked into the dining room and asked, "Where, pray tell, are you two going?"

"To the village," Edwina informed him.

A skeptical expression came to Winston's face as he asked, "Without a chaperone?"

"We shall be taking the open drawn carriage," Edwina said. "It is perfectly acceptable for us to venture to the village alone."

Winston turned to his mother for confirmation. "Are you allowing this?"

"I am," Lady Dallington confirmed. "The rules of polite Society are more relaxed in the countryside."

Winston didn't look convinced. "Perhaps I should accompany them."

"Or I could always go with them," Elodie suggested in a far too eager voice.

Lady Dallington gave her daughter a pointed look that left no room for argument. "Do I need to remind you that you are meeting with the dressmaker?"

"Drats," Elodie muttered under her breath.

"Language, Dear," Lady Dallington chided lightly.

Melody giggled. "You should have heard Elodie at the boarding school," she said, her words laced with amusement. "At times, she sounded like a drunken sailor."

Elodie's mouth dropped. "That is not the least bit true."

Lady Dallington gave Elodie a disapproving look. "I do hope that isn't true, young lady."

"Young lady?" Bennett repeated with a playful grin as he turned towards Elodie. "You are in trouble now."

Miles couldn't help but feel a pang of longing as he listened to the siblings banter back and forth. It reminded him of his own brother, who was always quick with a joke or a witty remark.

Edwina must have sensed his thoughts because she leaned closer and whispered, "This may seem amusing, but it gets old rather quickly."

"Not to me," Miles admitted. "It feels a little bit like home."

Winston stepped closer to them and spoke sternly, "Go to the village and come back straightaway. No dilly-dallying."

"Yes, sir," Edwina replied with a mock salute.

With a shake of his head, Winston responded, "I wish you would take this seriously."

"Why, Cousin?" Edwina asked. "Lord Hilgrove and I are just friends."

Friends.

There was that word again. It echoed in Miles' mind and for some reason, it left an unsettling feeling in his chest. He couldn't quite say why it bothered him so much. It was the truth. They were friends- good friends even- but he cared for her far more than any friend should.

Botheration.

What happened to staying away from Edwina?

Winston crossed his arms over his chest and there was a warning glint in his eyes. "I expect you to behave yourself," he said pointedly.

Miles nodded in agreement. "You need not worry," he assured him. "I shall treat Lady Edwina with the utmost respect that she deserves."

They stared at one another for a tense moment before Winston finally relented with a step to the side. "Very well," he said. "Enjoy your carriage ride."

As they made their way towards the entry hall, Miles didn't quite know what to do. He knew he should keep his distance from Edwina, but at the same time, he wanted nothing more than to be near her. What kind of torture was this?

Edwina sat in the carriage as it traveled towards the village. She used to love this journey, but now her heart was heavy with worry and uncertainty. She wasn't quite sure what reception they would receive. She hoped, and not for the first time, that Mr. Stanley would help her persuade her uncle to return the funding needed to sustain the upkeep of the village.

Miles eyed her with concern. "You have been rather quiet," he remarked.

"I have been," she admitted. "My father would have been so disappointed in my uncle. He loved the villagers."

"Perhaps this is just a big misunderstanding," Miles said.

Edwina frowned. "Do you honestly believe that?"

He shook his head. "No, I don't."

"My uncle has a duty to this village and he has destroyed their trust," she sighed.

Leaning forward in his seat, Miles proposed in a gentle voice, "I could take you far away from here, far away from all your troubles and worries. All you have to do is agree to marry me."

"What would that solve?" she asked. "I would think of these villagers often and worry about their plight."

"If you marry me, I am rich. I can provide some aid."

She smiled, touched by his thoughtfulness. "It is not your responsibility to care for this village. You have your own troubles to worry about."

"I do not like seeing you so upset."

"You are kind, but I have to try to make a difference," Edwina insisted. "With any luck, we can convince Mr. Stanley to encourage my uncle to do the right thing."

Miles settled back into his seat. "You, my dear, have far too much faith in other people."

"You don't know Mr. Stanley like I do," Edwina said. "He always offered me a kind smile and a thoughtful word. I do not think I ever heard him say one cross thing. He isn't that type of man."

"But he is your uncle's man of business now. His loyalty belongs to your uncle, not your father," Miles pointed out.

"True, but he couldn't have changed that much," Edwina asserted. "He will want to do the right thing. I am sure of that."

Miles put his hand up in surrender. "Very well. I believe you."

"Thank you."

"Regardless, I can help you secure a barrister to ensure your uncle is held accountable for your inheritance," Miles said.

"I do hope it won't come to that," she admitted.

Miles grew silent before asking, "Did you know that my library at my country estate is larger than your uncle's?"

"I did not."

"And there are far more paths in the woodlands for someone to explore," Miles continued.

Edwina eyed him curiously. "Your point being?"

"Marry me and it will be yours. The library. The woodlands. I will even throw in some diamonds. Loads of them," Miles said, his eyes full of mirth.

She laughed. "I have my mother's diamonds. That is all I need."

Miles waggled his eyebrows. "What about the library? There are so many books that you haven't read yet. Just waiting to be explored by you."

Her face softened. "I know you could give me everything I ever wanted, but it is not what I need," she said. "I need to be loved, and love in return."

"I am trying, Edwina," Miles responded, his voice pained.

She leaned forward and reached for his hand. "I know, and I am appreciative of it. But I will always wonder if you are thinking of Arabella when I'm with you."

Miles' eyes held a rawness that made her heart ache, a

vulnerability she hadn't seen from him before. "I can't forget about Arabella."

She squeezed his fingers gently, trying to convey her understanding. "I wouldn't expect you to. She was a part of your life and helped shape who you are today."

His voice was thick with emotion as he whispered, "I don't want to lose you."

"You won't. I promise," Edwina reassured him. "I will always be here for you, just as I know you will be there for me."

Miles winced. "I do not think I can stand by and watch you marry another."

"Who says I will be getting married anytime soon?"

He gave her an incredulous look. "Once the *ton* sees you for who you truly are, the suitors will line up to vie for your attention."

"I am nothing special."

Miles lifted her gloved hand and pressed a kiss to the back of it. "If I had to go through all of this, everything, just to meet you, I can most assuredly say that I would do it all over again."

Edwina felt the tears prick at the back of her eyes and she wondered if she could marry Miles, knowing he was quickly becoming her everything. But he didn't feel the same. She would always have to compete against the memory of Arabella.

The carriage rolled into the village and Edwina slipped her hand out of Miles'. Her resolve was weakening with each passing moment she spent with him.

Once the carriage came to a stop in front of a brick building where Mr. Stanley had an office, Miles stepped out and assisted her down. She promptly removed her hand from his and clasped her hands in front of her.

They started walking towards the door when she saw Miss Price pass by her.

"Miss Price," Edwina said, calling after her.

With a hesitant look, Miss Price turned around and said, "Hello, Lady Edwina." Her voice was timid and awkward.

Edwina offered her a warm smile. "How is your baby?"

That brought a smile, albeit small, to her face. "She is not quite so young anymore," Miss Price said. "Can you believe that she is almost six months old?"

"Time does certainly fly by when it is not your own child," Edwina remarked.

Miss Price's eyes darted around the pavement. "I should be going," she said. "But it was nice talking to you, my lady."

Without saying another word, Miss Price put her head down and walked swiftly down the pavement.

Edwina stared after Miss Price and she felt a weight on her shoulders. If her interaction with Miss Price was any indication, then the villagers had turned against her, as well. What was she going to do?

Miles placed a hand on her sleeve and encouraged, "Let us go speak to Mr. Stanley."

She let him lead her into the building until they arrived at Mr. Stanley's office. Miles removed his hand and rapped on the door.

"Enter," came a voice from within.

Miles opened the door and stood to the side to let her enter.

As she entered the room, Mr. Stanley stood and said, "Lady Edwina. Lord Hilgrove. What a pleasant surprise. To what do I owe this pleasure?"

Edwina waited for Miles to close the door, ensuring their conversation remained private, before saying, "I was hoping you could help."

"Oh, I would be happy to," Mr. Stanley said, gesturing towards a chair. "Please have a seat and tell me what troubles you."

After she was situated, she pressed her lips together as she tried to gather her courage to say what needed to be said.

Taking a deep breath, Edwina said, "I am concerned about my uncle's ill-treatment of the villagers."

Mr. Stanley's brow shot up. "Pardon?"

"My uncle informed me that he reduced the funding he gave the village and I understand that is causing some discontent here," Edwina replied.

With a heavy sigh, Mr. Stanley said, "I'm afraid not much can be done. It is up to Lord Dallington's discretion on how much he gives to the village and what those funds are allocated for."

"Perhaps you could speak to him and suggest he provide more aid…" Edwina attempted.

Mr. Stanley put his hand up, stilling her words. "I do understand your concern, but your uncle does things differently than your father. You must give him time to execute his vision."

"Does he even have one?" Edwina asked.

With a look that could only be construed as pity, Mr. Stanley inquired, "Have you spoken to your uncle about this?"

"In a way. He wasn't entirely forthcoming," Edwina shared.

Rising, Mr. Stanley said, "I'm afraid I can't be much help. I work for your uncle and I rather like being employed."

"Thank you, Mr. Stanley," Edwina responded as she rose. "I do apologize if I put you in an uncomfortable position."

"You did no such thing, and your father would be proud of you for attempting to help the villagers," Mr. Stanley remarked.

Edwina walked over to the door but stopped. "Would you know why my uncle would keep my inheritance from me?"

Mr. Stanley's face went slack. "Whatever do you mean?"

"My father left me ten thousand pounds but my uncle has failed to mention that," Edwina replied.

"How did you learn of your inheritance then?" Mr. Stanley questioned.

Edwina gave him a sheepish smile. "I may have gone looking through my uncle's desk."

Mr. Stanley pursed his lips, disapproval etched in his features. "What if your uncle would have caught you?"

"It wouldn't matter because Bennett is now involved," Edwina replied. "Together, we will convince my uncle to provide more aid."

"You told Lord Dunsby of this?" Mr. Stanley asked, his voice growing terse.

"I did," Edwina confirmed. "Bennett insists that he will start taking a more active role in running the estate."

Mr. Stanley brought his hand up and rubbed his jaw. "I think that is a fine idea. He is the heir, after all."

"Precisely, and he is proficient at balancing the ledger. With any luck, he will be able to come up with a way to acquire additional funds," Edwina said.

"Yes, well, if he needs any help understanding the books, please inform him that I would be happy to help," Mr. Stanley responded, coming around his desk.

Miles opened the door and offered his arm to Edwina. "Shall we, my lady?"

As they walked out of the building, Edwina leaned into Miles and said, "Thank you for coming with me."

"I didn't do much."

"Just you being there was enough for me," Edwina assured him. Which was the truth. His strong, steady presence gave her a sense of strength that she desperately needed at this time.

Miles smirked. "You are rather easy to please."

Edwina glanced over at him. "Do you think Bennett will be able to convince my uncle to allow him to review the books?"

"I sure hope so since you told Mr. Stanley as much," Miles replied as he assisted her into the carriage.

After she was situated on the bench, she said, "I think I have a plan."

"For what?"

In a hesitant voice, she asked, "What if I gave my inheritance to the village? It could help fund a girls' school, amongst other things."

Miles' brow shot up. "That is madness. That is your money to secure *your* future."

"I know, but…" Her voice trailed off. "I just want to help them."

The carriage jerked forward and Miles' eyes held sympathy. "I understand your concern, but ten thousand pounds is a fortune."

Edwina lowered her gaze. "It is," she said.

Miles moved to sit next to her on the bench, and his nearness provided her with immense comfort. "Before you make any rash decisions, let Bennett try to sort this out with Lord Dallington."

"And if he can't?" Edwina asked, bringing her gaze back up.

"Then I will give the village ten thousand pounds and you can decide how it is spent," Miles replied, his tone resolute.

Edwina's mouth dropped. "You cannot be in earnest!"

"I am," Miles replied, leaning in closer. "As I said before, your happiness is of great importance to me, Edwina. I will do anything to win your favor."

Overwhelmed by his kindness, Edwina's heart swelled with emotion. "I couldn't possibly ask you to do such a thing."

Miles reached out and gently took her hand in his own. "You didn't ask. I offered," he said. "And I would do it again, just to see you smile."

Edwina stared at Miles in astonishment. How could she

not love this man? He was the man of her dreams, the one she never thought she would have. But he wasn't hers.

However, that didn't mean she couldn't enjoy this moment. The way he was looking at her made her feel beautiful. Giving her hope that perhaps he might one day love her as much as she loved him.

It was sheer foolishness on her part, but why couldn't she pretend? Just for now.

Chapter Eighteen

The afternoon sun filtered through the windows, casting a warm glow over the music room where Miles sat with the ladies. Elodie's skilled fingers danced across the ivory keys of the pianoforte while Melody's voice soared in perfect harmony. Edwina sat on a camelback settee with her head bent over her needlework.

Miles held a book in his hand but it had long been forgotten. His thoughts were consumed by Edwina. He wanted to marry her, and he was doing a poor job of trying to convince her of such. He knew her reasons for turning down his offer, but he couldn't help but hope that she would change her mind.

The internal struggle between his desire for Edwina and his duty to Arabella weighed heavily on his heart. The familiar stab of guilt tugged at him once again, as it had been doing ever since he met Edwina.

Edwina lifted her head from her needlework and met his gaze. "You haven't even opened your book yet, my lord," she said.

Miles should have felt some embarrassment for being

caught staring at her, but he felt none. Instead, he smiled. "I'm afraid it hasn't caught my attention."

"You might try opening the book and reading before coming to that conclusion," Edwina remarked, a spark of mirth dancing in her eyes.

Miles chuckled. "Perhaps I shall." He rose from his seat and moved to sit next to her on the settee. "Do you play the pianoforte?"

"I do," Edwina replied, turning her gaze towards Elodie who was still playing. "But not quite as magnificently as my cousin."

"Can you sing?" Miles inquired.

Edwina made a face. "No, I possess the vocal prowess of a rusted wagon wheel."

Miles grinned at her unique comparison. "That is rather specific."

"It is true, I'm afraid," Edwina said.

Curiosity getting the better of him, Miles asked, "Then what are you good at?"

Edwina lowered the needlework she had been working on to her lap. "I enjoy painting and I have been told that I have some skill in it."

"Who told you that?"

Edwina's lips twitched. "My father."

"Only your father?"

With a graceful gesture towards a painting hanging on the far wall, Edwina replied, "You may decide for yourself. I painted that one last summer."

Miles rose and walked over to the painting. It was a scene of the woodlands where he had first truly spoken to Edwina. She had managed to capture the essence of the place perfectly and it invoked a sense of calm as he admired the painting.

Edwina came to stand next to him, her eyes watching his reaction intently. "It isn't awful, is it?" she asked, almost hesitant.

"No, it is far from that. It is… perfect." And he meant every word.

"You are very kind."

"It has nothing to do with kindness," Miles insisted. "When I look at this painting, I feel like I am there in the woodlands, sitting on that rock and listening to the gentle trickle of the stream."

Edwina turned her attention towards the painting. "It took me many days to capture the serenity and beauty of that spot."

"You succeeded," he praised.

Their conversation was interrupted by the end of the musical piece, and Miles looked over to see Bennett and Winston entering the room.

Elodie broke the silence as she removed her hands from the keys. "How was angling?"

"It was terrible," Winston sighed. "I hardly caught anything."

Bennett smiled at his brother. "But we did get to enjoy some brotherly bonding time instead. That is far more important than a few fish."

Winston shrugged. "I still would have preferred some fish though," he said in a teasing voice.

Meeting Miles' gaze, Bennett asked, "And how did your meeting in the village go?"

"It went quite well, but perhaps we could discuss it in private," Miles suggested.

Bennett nodded his understanding. "Of course. Shall we adjourn to the drawing room for a moment?"

Elodie rose gracefully from her seat. "I do not like this. It would appear that everyone has secrets but me."

"I don't have any secrets," Melody said.

Winston joined his sisters, placing a comforting hand on Elodie's shoulder. "Do not fret. They are keeping secrets from me as well."

A mischievous glint appeared in Elodie's eyes as she proposed, "Perhaps we should go around the room and spill our secrets."

Bennett gave his sister an amused look. "When the right time comes, I promise I will tell you all my secrets."

Elodie raised an eyebrow skeptically. "You have more than one?"

"I have many," Bennett admitted. "But let us focus on the matter at hand. We will return shortly."

Miles followed Bennett out of the music room with Edwina on his arm. Once they arrived in the drawing room, Bennett turned to face them with an uncharacteristic solemn look on his face and asked, "What did Mr. Stanley say?"

Edwina dropped her hand from Miles' sleeve and replied, "He didn't say much. Quite frankly, he couldn't say much. He is loyal to your father."

"That is what I feared would happen," Bennett said.

With a resigned sigh, Edwina remarked, "I just thought that Mr. Stanley would sympathize with the villagers' plight. But I was wrong."

"You have a good heart, Edwina," Bennett praised. "It is my turn to do something about this. I will speak to my father and encourage him to do the right thing."

"But we already tried that," Edwina pointed out.

Bennett placed a hand on her shoulder. "I can be rather persuasive when I want to be."

Miles interjected, "I do think it would be a good thing for you to become more involved in the running of the estate."

"As do I," Bennett responded. "I don't know why my father has been so insistent that he handles the accounts. It makes me wonder what else he is hiding."

Edwina kept her voice low as she asked, "Did you tell Winston about your father's mistress?"

"No," Bennett said with a shake of his head. "I want to speak to my father first."

"When do you intend to do that?" Miles asked.

Bennett's eyes held a sadness to them as he replied, "Tomorrow, after the soiree. I must admit that I am not looking forward to this difficult conversation, but it must be done."

Edwina gave her cousin an encouraging look. "Would you like me to accompany you?"

"I appreciate the offer, but this is something I have to do on my own," Bennett stated.

As he uttered his words, Lady Dallington stepped into the room and said, "Edwina, there you are. It is time for you to start getting ready for the soiree. I just sent Elodie and Melody up to their bedchambers."

Edwina tipped her head. "Yes, Aunt Catherine," she responded before giving Miles a private smile.

Once Edwina departed from the room, Lady Dallington met Miles' gaze and said, "I was hoping to speak to you in private."

Bennett performed an exaggerated bow. "I do believe that is my cue to leave," he declared before he stepped out, leaving them alone.

Lady Dallington gestured towards the settees and asked, "Shall we sit for a moment?"

Unsure of what Lady Dallington wished to speak to him about, Miles walked over to the settee and sat down with an expectant gaze.

A smile came to her lips, setting him at ease. "How are you faring?" she asked.

"I am well," came his honest reply.

Lady Dallington seemed to consider him for a moment before saying, "I can't help but notice the remarkable change that has come over you since you arrived at our doorstep." She paused. "And I do believe that Edwina had something to do with that."

Miles saw no reason to deny that fact. "It is true," he

replied. "She helped me to look past my grief and made me realize that I was living in the past."

"Yes, and you helped Edwina as well," Lady Dallington said.

"I do believe we helped each other."

Lady Dallington's smile grew. "Yes, you did, which is why I think you two would be perfect for one another."

Miles shifted uncomfortably in his seat. "As do I, but I can't convince Edwina to marry me."

"Do you know why that is?"

His jaw clenched as he admitted, "I can't give her the one thing that she so desperately wants- love."

"Interesting, and why is that?" Lady Dallington asked. "After all, you two are quite enamored with one another."

Miles decided it would be best just to be honest with Lady Dallington. "I love my wife, Arabella, and it is my duty to love her to the end of my days," he said in an unwavering voice.

Understanding crossed Lady Dallington's features. "Did you know that I was married before Lionel?"

Miles shook his head. "No, I did not."

"I, too, married the love of my life, and we set out to have a life together," Lady Dallington shared, her eyes growing reflective. "But he died shortly thereafter, leaving me alone. Rather than let me grieve, my father was insistent that I marry again and even arranged a marriage with Lionel."

Miles remained quiet, unsure of what to say.

Lady Dallington continued. "Lionel was persistent in his affection, just as I suspect you are, and I grew to love him."

"How was that possible?" he asked.

Her face softened. "Love doesn't always make sense. In fact, falling in love when you least expect it is the greatest kind of love."

"What about my love for Arabella?"

"You are always going to love Arabella, but opening your heart again is not betraying her. It is honoring her memory,"

Lady Dallington said. "Do you truly think that Arabella would have wanted you to stop living?"

Miles lowered his gaze. "No, she wouldn't have."

Leaning forward in her seat, Lady Dallington said, "I know this is not my place, but I can see it in your eyes. You love Edwina."

His gaze shot up. "That is impossible," he exclaimed. "I care for Edwina- greatly- but love…" His words trailed off as he searched for what to say to convince Lady Dallington that he didn't love Edwina.

Lady Dallington gave him a warm smile. "Are you attempting to convince me that you don't love Edwina or are you trying to convince yourself of that?"

Miles' shoulders slumped. "I don't know." And that was the truth. Did he love Edwina? He wasn't sure, but he couldn't deny that even though they had been together for only a short time, he couldn't imagine a life without her.

"Life is a journey. One never knows what unexpected surprises will be waiting around the corner," Lady Dallington said.

"And what if…" His voice hitched as he struggled to say his next words. It was the one fear that weighed heavily on his heart. "What if I lose Edwina, too?"

Lady Dallington's eyes held compassion as she replied, "Then you pick yourself back up and live another day."

"I don't know if I can take that chance," Miles admitted.

Rising, Lady Dallington said, "Then your journey will be a lonely one." She placed a comforting hand on his shoulder. "Trust your heart and choose to let go of fear."

As she departed from the room, Miles settled back into his seat. Lady Dallington made it sound so easy. But he was scared. If he didn't love Edwina, it wouldn't hurt as much when she inevitably would depart from his life.

But his heart was telling him a different story. A heart that was supposed to be impenetrable. Yet, it seemed to have started beating again- the moment he met Edwina.

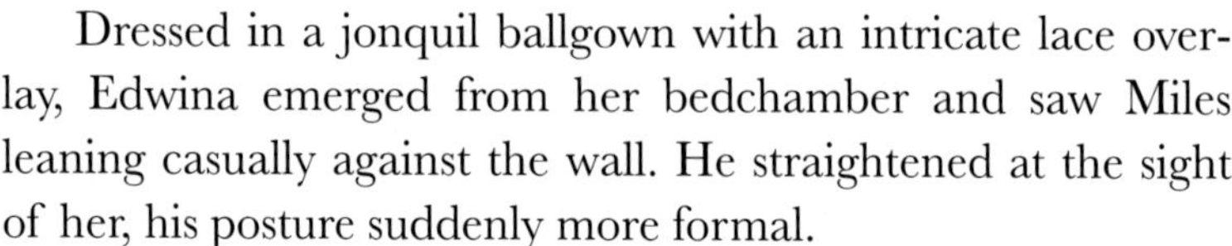

Dressed in a jonquil ballgown with an intricate lace overlay, Edwina emerged from her bedchamber and saw Miles leaning casually against the wall. He straightened at the sight of her, his posture suddenly more formal.

His eyes perused the length of her, and in them, she saw a glimmer of approval, making her feel beautiful. She had never felt more beautiful than when she was in Miles' presence. The way he looked at her made her feel appreciated. Cherished, even.

"Good evening, Edwina," he greeted with a charming smile, causing her heart to take flight.

She gave him a questioning look. "Do tell, why were you loitering outside of my bedchamber?" she asked, playfully.

"I was merely waiting for you," he replied. "I had hoped to accompany you to the library where your family is gathering before the soiree."

Edwina smiled, secretly pleased by his gesture. "I would greatly appreciate that, kind sir."

As Miles offered his arm, he said, "I must admit that I look forward to these moments alone with you."

"As do I," she admitted.

They started walking down the corridor and a comfortable silence descended over them. She wanted to say something clever, but she was at a loss for words.

Fortunately, Miles broke the silence. "Are you looking forward to the soiree?"

Edwina nodded. "Yes, it will be the first social event that I have attended since my father passed away."

"And how are you coping with that realization?" Miles asked gently.

"Better than I expected. It feels like the right time to move on and embrace Society," she answered.

Miles gave her a knowing look. "So you have no objections to dancing the first set with me?"

"I have many," Edwina replied. "Not that I object to dancing with you, but the fact that all eyes will surely be upon us when we join my aunt and uncle on the dance floor."

With a curious glance at her, Miles asked, "Dare I ask if you are a proficient dancer?"

"I am a much better dancer than I am a singer," she responded.

His lips curled into a smirk. "That doesn't give me much hope then."

"I would say my dancing is perfectly adequate," Edwina said.

"That is what every dance partner wishes to hear," he teased, his eyes sparking with amusement.

Edwina laughed. "I promise that I won't step on your boots or trip you," she said. "But it has been quite some time since I danced a set."

"Well, that makes two of us. My last dance was with Arabella…" His words trailed off as a pained look came into his eyes.

Unsure of how to respond, she gently asked, "Would you prefer if we didn't dance?"

After a moment, the pain seemed to dissipate from his eyes and the familiar light returned. "No, no," he said quickly, shaking his head. "I am glad that I am dancing a set with you." His words sounded genuine.

"I don't want to make you uncomfortable…" Edwina started.

Miles stopped and turned to face her, stilling her words. "I want to dance with you, Edwina. You must know that."

Holding his gaze, she asked softly, "But will it bring back painful memories?"

A determined look came over Miles' features as he spoke in a resolute voice. "I have decided it is time to create new memories."

A blush crept up Edwina's cheeks at his words. "That is good," she remarked, pleased that her voice remained steady.

A look of uncertainty flashed across Miles' expression- a stark contrast to his usual confident demeanor. "Actually, there is something I wanted to speak to you about," he said hesitantly.

"We are speaking," she joked.

"Yes, we are, but—"

The booming voice of Winston echoed down the corridor, interrupting their conversation. "Did you two get lost?" he called out.

Miles quickly took a step back from Edwina, creating more distance between them. "No, we were just conversing with one another."

Coming to stand next to them, Winston's eyes darted between them. "Dare I ask what you two were speaking of?"

Miles opened his mouth to speak, but Edwina spoke first. "The weather, Cousin," she said. "Was it not a lovely day today?"

A frown came to Winston's lips. "Fine. Do not tell me, but we should adjourn to the library before anyone comes looking for us."

They walked the short distance to the library in silence. Upon entering, she saw her aunt and uncle conversing with Bennett.

Her aunt turned towards her with a bright smile. "Oh, my. Edwina, you look positively stunning!" she exclaimed. "That ballgown is rather exquisite."

Edwina smoothed a hand over the delicate fabric of her

gown. "It was commissioned before my father passed," she shared.

"Well, you will shine among the other guests this evening," her aunt remarked.

Her uncle perused the length of her and said, "I must agree with my wife. That ballgown does suit you."

Surprised by her uncle's comment- despite how lackluster it was- Edwina found herself smiling. "Thank you, Uncle."

Her aunt's attention then turned to Melody and Elodie as they entered the room, both clad in identical pale blue gowns with their hair styled in a similar fashion.

Her aunt did not look pleased. "Pray tell, what do you think you two are doing?"

A mischievous glint sparkled in Elodie's eyes as she held out the skirts of her gown. "We both liked this ballgown so we had it commissioned… twice."

"I daresay that the guests will not be able to tell you apart," her aunt remarked in a disapproving tone.

Melody smiled. "That is our intention. It is much more fun that way."

Her aunt let out a sigh of disapproval. "This type of buffoonery will not be tolerated in London," she warned sternly.

Elodie's smile grew. "Where is the fun in that?" she quipped.

Her aunt glanced at the mantel clock. "It is too late for you two to change, but we shall discuss this later."

"I shall have something to look forward to then," Elodie remarked.

Bennett spoke up. "I think Father should marry Elodie off to the Duke of Devonshire. I have heard that he is looking for a young, vigorous wife to give him an heir," he suggested with a smirk.

Elodie narrowed her eyes. "Father wouldn't dare do such a thing," she stated.

Her uncle shrugged his shoulders. "It does sound like a feasible option, considering you two are not taking this soiree seriously," he said, giving his daughter a pointed look.

"Very well, I shall take the soiree seriously," Elodie remarked. "And I promise that I won't speak any hog Latin to Melody." She hesitated before adding, "Or any other guest."

Her uncle shook his head. "I'm beginning to wonder if I wasted my money on that prestigious boarding school of yours."

Placing her hand on her husband's sleeve, her aunt said, "Come now, it is time for us to arrive at the soiree." She turned to Edwina. "When we give you the signal, you and Miles will join us on the dance floor for the rest of the set."

Edwina nodded, placing a hand on her stomach to calm her nerves. "I understand."

As they filed out of the library, Miles offered his arm to her. "There is no reason to be nervous," he assured her.

"Is it so obvious?" she asked.

He grinned. "It is to me."

"I suppose this soiree serves as good practice for my upcoming Season," Edwina said.

Winston joined them, his arms clasped behind his back. "Out of curiosity, when do you plan on leaving Brockhall Manor, Miles?"

Miles seemed to consider Winston for a moment before answering, "I have yet to decide."

"Interesting," Winston muttered. "You would think with the Season approaching, you would need to tend to your estate."

Arching an eyebrow, Miles asked, "Are you eager to be rid of me already?"

Winston's hands unclasped from behind his back and dropped to his sides. "No, but I do think it is time for this game to end."

"What game?" Miles asked.

With a stern expression, Winston replied, "If you don't know, then it would be best for you to take your leave now."

As Winston walked away, leaving them behind, Edwina furrowed her brow. "Do you know what game my cousin was referring to?"

"I think I have a fairly good idea."

She glanced over at Miles. "Will you tell me?"

His jaw clenched. "Soon, I promise."

Edwina decided not to press Miles, knowing it was neither the time nor place to be having a serious discussion. They were about to walk into the ballroom and all eyes would be upon them.

She snuck a glance at Miles, wondering why he was so tense. What had transpired between Winston and Miles that caused such a reaction out of him?

Leaning closer, Edwina whispered to him, "You need to relax."

"I am relaxed," he said in a stern tone.

Despite his insistence, Edwina could see otherwise. A small smile came to her lips as she continued to observe him. "It doesn't appear that is the case," she responded. "Your body betrays your words."

Miles let out a deep sigh, finally releasing some of the tension in his body. "I apologize for retreating into my own thoughts."

"Is there anything you wish to share?"

"No," he responded quickly.

Edwina turned her head towards the ornate doors that the footmen were about to open, signaling their entrance into the ballroom. She didn't understand the change that had swept over Miles, but she didn't have time to dwell on it.

The doors opened and they stepped into the ballroom, all eyes turning towards them. Whispers filled the room as people took notice of their arrival.

Her aunt and uncle came to a stop in the center of the

dance floor and the orchestra started up. They began dancing to the music, their eyes fixated on one another.

After a long moment, her aunt met her gaze and signaled for them to join them. Miles must have seen the signal, as well, because he led her onto the dance floor.

As he placed his arm around her waist, Edwina sucked in a breath. She found being this close to Miles was rather unnerving. Miles must have sensed her discomfort because he silently waited for her to grant him permission to continue.

Edwina nodded and Miles brought up their arms before he started leading her around the dance floor.

At first, she counted her steps, ensuring that she was true to her word and not stepping on Miles' boots. But as they moved to the music, she felt herself relax in his arms, as if she had always belonged there. It was comfortable. Familiar. And she didn't want this dance to end.

Miles gazed deep into her eyes, searching for something she couldn't quite identify. She held his gaze confidently, hoping her eyes wouldn't betray the feelings she held for him. For how she loved this man. He was good. Kind. And everything she hoped to find in a suitor.

However, he didn't love her.

And no matter how much hoping she did on her part, it would not change that fact.

Edwina lowered her gaze to his chest, knowing it was time to let him go.

Miles' gentle voice could be heard over the music, "Edwina." She allowed herself to meet his gaze and she could see the questions in his eyes. Fortunately, the music came to an end and Edwina dropped her arms.

"Thank you for the dance, my lord," she said before dropping into a curtsy.

Knowing her heart could not take another moment of being around Miles, she headed towards the back doors and stepped out onto the veranda. She was met with the cool night air and she finally felt as if she could breathe again.

As she took a few deep breaths, she noticed a light was on in her uncle's study. That was odd. But as she turned to look away, she saw a shadow moving from within.

Who was in her uncle's study at this hour?

Without hesitation, she walked towards the door that led to her uncle's study. Perhaps she was making too much out of this, but she needed to see *who* was there. It was most definitely not her uncle since she had left him in the ballroom.

Chapter Nineteen

Miles watched Edwina's retreating figure and he didn't quite understand what had transpired. His mind raced, trying to understand what had caused Edwina to flee from him. But it only took a moment for him to realize that he needed to go after her.

He had to make this right.

As he headed towards the veranda, Winston stepped in his path with a stern expression. "I refuse to stand by and not say anything," he said firmly. "What are your intentions towards my cousin? And I want the truth this time."

Miles knew he owed Winston the truth. "I want to marry Edwina, but she has been rather hesitant to accept my proposal."

"Why is that?"

"Because she wants a love match," Miles admitted.

Winston raised an eyebrow inquisitively. "Yes, and…?"

Miles winced. "I cannot love her."

"Pardon?"

With a heavy heart, Miles confessed, "I love Arabella…"

Winston put his hand up, stilling his words. "I know this, but why do you believe you couldn't love Edwina?"

"I cannot betray Arabella's memory," Miles said.

Crossing his arms over his chest, Winston studied him intently for a long moment before saying, "I know you want to believe that, but it isn't true."

Now it was Miles' turn to ask, "Pardon?"

Winston's eyes held compassion as he replied, "You love Edwina. It is evident every time you lay eyes on her. It is rather revolting, if I must be honest."

"You must be mistaken."

Dropping his arms to his sides, Winston said, "As a barrister, I deal in facts, not emotions. And it is a simple fact that you love Edwina." He gave him a pointed look. "Tell me I am wrong."

Miles shifted his gaze towards the veranda, knowing that Edwina was still out there. Alone. And all he wanted was to be with her.

To love her.

He closed his eyes as the truth dawned on him. He did love Edwina. He had fought against it for so long, but he could deny it no longer. He loved her, and he always would.

Miles opened his eyes and confessed, "I love her."

Winston gave him a smug smile. "I know," he responded. "Now what are you going to do about it?"

Hope blossomed in his heart as he responded, "I am going to offer for her… again. But this time, I will tell her how much I love her."

"That is a good start, but you might have to grovel."

Miles nodded, knowing that Winston spoke true. "I am not opposed to groveling."

After he said his words, Miss Bawden joined them with a concerned look on her face. She leaned in and whispered, "Have either of you seen Edwina?"

"She is on the veranda," Miles replied.

Miss Bawden shook her head. "I looked outside and I saw no sign of her."

Miles eyed her with disbelief. "That is impossible. I just saw her go outside."

"As did I, which is why I decided to go after her," Miss Bawden said.

Winston turned his head towards the veranda. "Surely you must have missed her," he remarked dismissively.

Miss Bawden's eyes flashed with annoyance. "Yes, because I often manage to overlook a whole person." Her words were dry.

"I never said that, but Edwina might have ventured further into the gardens," Winston said.

"Why didn't I think of that?" Miss Bawden asked. "Oh, wait. I did. And I searched the gardens."

"The gardens are vast and you are just…" Winston started.

Miss Bawden spoke over him. "A woman?"

Undeterred, Winston met her gaze. "Yes, it would be difficult for anyone to do a thorough search in a ballgown."

Placing a hand on her hip, Miss Bawden said, "I went down several paths and I did not see Edwina. Although, I did stumble upon a couple engaged in a passionate embrace in the rear of the gardens."

Miles had heard enough. Edwina had to be out in the gardens and he would find her. He needed to tell her that he was wrong and he did love her.

"I will go look for her," Miles stated before he started to walk outside.

He stepped onto the veranda and saw a few couples enjoying the night air. But Edwina was not here- just as Miss Bawden had said.

As he went to step onto a path, Winston came to stand next to him. "We will find her. Edwina must be out here somewhere."

Miles had an uneasy feeling about this, but he didn't dare

express his thoughts. Not yet. He just needed to find Edwina, and quickly.

Taking one of the paths, Miles hurried down it, looking for any sign of Edwina. But when he couldn't find her, he headed towards another path. And then another. It felt like hours, but was probably only a short time, before he arrived back on the veranda.

Winston approached him with a worried look on his face. "Any sign of her?"

"No," Miles replied. "Where could she have gone?"

Miss Bawden spoke up from behind them. "I just spoke to a maid and Edwina is not in her bedchamber."

Miles was hesitant to ask his next question, but he had to ask it. "Do you think Edwina has been abducted?"

Winston's brow shot up. "By whom? Edwina is loved by the villagers."

"But your father isn't," Miles pointed out.

His friend frowned. "Why wouldn't the villagers love my father?"

Miss Bawden leaned closer and shared, "Because he isn't taking care of the village as he promised."

"Meaning?" Winston asked.

"My father is thinking of leaving this parish because your father isn't contributing as much as your uncle did," Miss Bawden replied. "The church has fallen into disrepair and there are no funds to fix it."

"Has your father spoken to mine about this?" Winston inquired.

With a shake of her head, Miss Bawden replied, "No, but he has spoken in length to Mr. Stanley about this."

"What does Mr. Stanley say about it?" Winston pressed.

Miss Bawden clasped her hands in front of her. "Mr. Stanley always listens but claims there are no additional funds available to help."

Winston reared back. "No funds? That is impossible."

Miles bobbed his head. "It is true. If the rumors are to be believed from the villagers, your father is bankrupting his estate."

"No, that cannot be," Winston asserted. "You are wrong."

"Regardless, one of the villagers might have abducted her to make a point," Miles suggested.

Winston's expression held skepticism. "I cannot believe that to be true."

Turning towards Miles, Miss Bawden asked, "What would you like me to do?"

"Go inform Lord Dunsby of what is going on. He can help aid in the search," Miles said.

Miss Bawden tipped her head in acknowledgement before she went to do his bidding.

Miles faced his friend. "I need a pistol."

With a concerned look, Winston asked, "Why?"

"I do not know what we are up against, and I do not want to be caught unprepared," Miles replied.

Winston glanced towards the manor. "My father keeps his dueling pistols on display in the parlor. Would that be sufficient?"

"It would," Miles said.

Without saying another word, Miles strode through the ballroom as he headed towards the parlor.

Bennett stepped up to walk next to him, matching his stride. In a hushed voice, he said, "Miss Bawden just informed me that Edwina is missing."

"It is true," Miles confirmed.

"You don't truly think she was abducted, do you?" Bennett asked.

Miles shrugged. "I don't know what to think at this point, but I do not wish to cause any undue panic to Lord and Lady Dallington until we know for sure."

"Where are you going now?" Bennett asked.

"To retrieve one of your father's dueling pistols," Miles responded.

As they exited the ballroom, Bennett said, "Do try to use some discretion. Edwina may be hiding in the corner of the library, lost in a book."

Miles understood his friend's concern. They couldn't risk tarnishing Edwina's reputation by spreading word that she might have been abducted.

Bennett reached out and grasped Miles' arm, halting their steps. "Have you stopped to consider that you might be acting irrationally?"

No.

Miles' jaw was clenched in determination as he replied, "Until I am sure that Edwina is safe, I will stop at nothing to find her."

"Just promise me that you will search the manor before going off half-cocked," Bennett said.

With a firm, unyielding voice, Miles responded, "I cannot promise that."

Bennett gave him a knowing smile. "You love Edwina." His words were more of a statement than a question.

"I do," Miles admitted, seeing no reason to deny it.

"Then I will join you in your search for Edwina," Bennett declared.

Miles swiftly turned on his heel and strode towards the parlor. His plan was simple- find Edwina and never let her go. He cursed himself for not realizing his true feelings sooner, but he had been too afraid to face them. He had convinced himself that loving Edwina would be a betrayal to Arabella, but he had been wrong. Fear had held him back. And it was time to let go of that fear.

Arabella wouldn't have wanted him to stop living life. But that didn't mean he wasn't scared. He didn't know what he would do if he ever lost Edwina. His heart would never recover. He was sure of that.

Arriving at the parlor, Miles walked up to the mantel and removed one of the dueling pistols. He felt the familiar weight in his hand and took a deep breath, steeling himself for what might come. He would do anything to protect Edwina, even if it meant taking a life again.

The pistol glinted in the dim light as memories flooded into his mind. Unpleasant memories. Ones that he wanted to remain buried forever. But now was not the time to worry about his past. All that mattered was his future.

Bennett retrieved the other pistol. "I am not saying that you are right, but it is better to be prepared."

"I agree, wholeheartedly," Miles said with a tight voice. "We will need to search each room, thoroughly, so as not to miss Edwina."

Bennett's eyes roamed over the room before meeting Miles' gaze. "I can safely say that Edwina is not here."

Miles resisted the urge to look heavenward. He didn't know if Bennett would be a help or a hindrance in this search.

But he didn't have time to wonder. His first, and only, concern was finding Edwina.

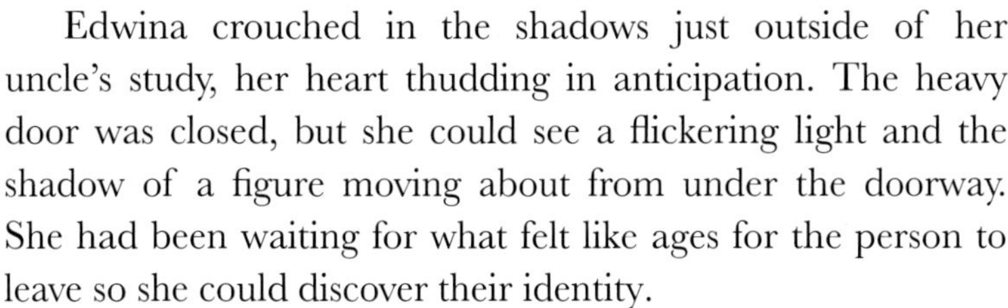

Edwina crouched in the shadows just outside of her uncle's study, her heart thudding in anticipation. The heavy door was closed, but she could see a flickering light and the shadow of a figure moving about from under the doorway. She had been waiting for what felt like ages for the person to leave so she could discover their identity.

What were they doing in there?

She considered going to find her uncle or a footman but couldn't risk missing the person's departure. No, she was on her own. Slowly, she stepped out of the shadows and approached the door. With a steady hand, she turned the handle and pushed it open just enough to slip inside before leaving it slightly ajar behind her.

The room was dimly lit with only one candle burning on the desk. Edwina saw a figure crouched down behind it and her heart leapt into her throat. Gathering her courage, she reached for the iron poker from the hearth and demanded, "Who is there?"

To her surprise, Mr. Stanley's head popped up from behind the desk. "Lady Edwina?" he exclaimed.

Edwina let out a sigh of relief. "Mr. Stanley," she said. "What are you doing here?"

With a sheepish smile, he rose to his feet and showed her a file in his hand. "I came to retrieve a file from Lord Dallington's desk that I had forgotten earlier."

"Oh," Edwina said, placing the poker back by the hearth. "I thought someone was breaking into my uncle's study."

Mr. Stanley chuckled. "No need to worry, my lady. It is just me."

Feeling foolish for suspecting foul play, Edwina allowed herself a small smile. "I find myself greatly relieved."

"Dare I ask how the soiree is going?" Mr. Stanley inquired.

Edwina's smile faltered. "I have had better days," she admitted.

Mr. Stanley's eyes crinkled around the edges. "We all have good days and bad days. It is how we make the most of each that truly matters."

"I just wish that my father was here," Edwina said wistfully.

"Your father was a good man," Mr. Stanley remarked. "We were lucky to have him for as long as we did."

Edwina nodded. "I agree."

Mr. Stanley reached down and retrieved the ledger on the desk. "Now if you will excuse me, I have work I need to see to."

Her eyes dropped to the ledger in his hand. "You are taking my uncle's ledger?" she asked.

"I am."

Edwina furrowed her brow. "But he doesn't like anyone to touch it, including Bennett at the moment."

Mr. Stanley tucked the book securely under his arm as he spoke. "I understand your concern. But this is important business that must be attended to. I shall return it shortly."

Her gaze flickered from the book to Mr. Stanley's face. "Does my uncle know that you are taking his ledger?"

"He does," Mr. Stanley replied. "Who do you think gave me the key to his desk where he keeps it locked up?"

As her eyes scanned the bookshelf, Edwina noticed a gap where a book should have been. It was the one that held the spare key to her uncle's desk.

"Did he give you the key or did you use the spare key?" she asked, trying to hide her growing suspicion.

Mr. Stanley smiled. "You are being rather inquisitive tonight, but I assure you that everything is aboveboard."

A sense of unease stirred within Edwina, though she couldn't say why. Mr. Stanley had never given her a reason before not to trust him, but his responses seemed too contrived.

"Perhaps we could ask my uncle together about the ledger," Edwina suggested, hoping to ease her worry.

"I do not wish to bother him during the soiree," Mr. Stanley said as he came around the desk. "And you shouldn't be here at all. You should be dancing with a plethora of suitors, including Lord Hilgrove, if the rumors are to be believed."

Edwina refused to back down, not when she felt such a pressing need to get to the bottom of this. "Do you mind waiting here while I go speak to my uncle?"

An annoyed expression crossed Mr. Stanley's face. "I am

simply trying to do my job. Do you truly wish to disturb your uncle over something as trivial as this?"

"I do."

"It's no wonder your uncle has been so disappointed in you lately," Mr. Stanley remarked with a hint of disdain. "Your persistence can be rather tiresome."

Edwina was taken aback by Mr. Stanley's stinging remark. "That is entirely uncalled for, and not the least bit true."

For a moment, Mr. Stanley had the decency to look ashamed before his demeanor shifted back to one of impatience. "I apologize, but you are keeping me from my work."

Knowing she risked her uncle's ire, Edwina stood her ground and held out her hand. "I think it would be best if you returned the ledger until we can discuss this further with my uncle."

Mr. Stanley's eyebrows shot up in disbelief. "You cannot be in earnest."

"I am," she declared, lifting her chin defiantly.

With a calm grace, Mr. Stanley placed the book back onto the desk and reached behind him, retrieving a pistol that had been hidden from sight. He aimed it directly at Edwina and said, "I didn't want it to come to this, but I need this ledger."

Stunned, Edwina lowered her hand to her side. "What are you doing?"

A flicker of regret passed over Mr. Stanley's eyes before he hardened them once more. "You had to make this difficult. Why couldn't you have just let me take the ledger and mind your own business?" he demanded.

"I don't understand," Edwina said, taking a step back.

Mr. Stanley scoffed, a sneer twisting his lips. "Clearly," he mocked. "You live in a world where everything is handed to you on a silver platter, but I do not have that luxury. I have had to fight for every penny given to me."

Edwina's frown deepened as she listened to his words. "But why do you truly need the ledger?"

"Ever since your father passed away, I have been skimming off the funds from what your uncle provides for the village," Mr. Stanley confessed. "Your father kept meticulous books but your uncle is a fool when it comes to estate management. He has no idea how to balance a ledger. Which bodes greatly in my favor."

"If that is the case, then why do you need my uncle's ledger?" Edwina asked.

Mr. Stanley held the worn book up. "If anyone were to compare this ledger to mine, it would reveal discrepancies and prove that I have been stealing the funds."

"Couldn't you just get rid of your ledger?" she inquired.

Mr. Stanley looked at her like she was a simpleton. "Do you think it wouldn't raise suspicion if the man in charge of finances suddenly lost his ledgers?"

Edwina shook her head. "How could you steal from the villagers?"

"They don't need their cobblestone streets and clock tower to be repaired," he replied.

"And what of the tenants?"

Mr. Stanley shrugged. "So their roofs leak? That is hardly a concern of mine."

Edwina looked at him incredulously. "How did you keep this from my uncle?" she asked.

"As I said, your uncle is a fool and believed that any discontent among the tenants and villagers was simply ungratefulness, just as I had convinced him of such," Mr. Stanley boasted with a smirk.

"You are not the man I thought you were," Edwina remarked.

Mr. Stanley's smirk widened into a malicious grin. "I thought my scheme would be uncovered when I stole from your inheritance," he admitted. "But your uncle bought my excuse that your father wasn't in his right mind when he wrote the will and had not left enough funds in the account."

Edwina felt her anger rising within her as she demanded, "How could you do such a thing?"

"Easily," Mr. Stanley replied. "I was tired of being poor when your family had so much wealth. It is my turn to be rich."

"But if that is the case, do you even intend to stop?" she questioned.

Mr. Stanley's expression darkened. "I have to. You mentioned that Lord Dunsby was going to start taking an active role in reviewing the accounts. I couldn't risk him discovering my treachery."

Edwina's gaze fell to the pistol in his hand and fear crept into her voice. "Do you truly intend to kill me?"

"I do. I am sorry that it has come to this," Mr. Stanley said, his apology sounding insincere. "Although, I did try to kill you once before. I startled that horse in hopes that you were trampled to death in the street."

Her eyes widened in shock and horror. "Why?"

"Because if you were dead, the questions surrounding your inheritance would go away," Mr. Stanley answered coldly. "Furthermore, it would release your dowry, which I could have stolen more funds from."

Edwina's breath caught in her throat as the full extent of Mr. Stanley's deceit and greed became clear to her. "You are a terrible person."

"The worst," Mr. Stanley agreed, his finger tightening on the trigger of the pistol. "I hadn't planned on shooting you, but I realize that this could work out in my favor."

Her heart pounded as she stared down the barrel of Mr. Stanley's pistol, knowing that one wrong move could be her last. "If you shoot me, the servants will come running," Edwina said, attempting to reason with him.

Mr. Stanley pursed his lips together. "You are right. I am going to have to muffle the shot." He walked over to the settee and retrieved a pillow. "This should do just fine. Now we will just wait until the music starts up again."

"You are never going to get away with this," Edwina stated firmly, trying to maintain a sense of control despite the fear gripping her.

"Who is going to stop me?" Mr. Stanley asked confidently with a smug grin, tilting his head towards the door where they could hear music playing in the distance. "Well, it appears that your time is up. The orchestra has begun the next set."

Edwina racked her brain as she tried to think of something to keep him talking but she was out of ideas.

And out of time.

Her breath caught in her throat as Mr. Stanley placed the pillow in front of the pistol and she froze.

But just as he was about to pull the trigger, the door swung open and Miles appeared in the doorway, his own pistol aimed directly at Mr. Stanley.

Edwina's heart leapt with relief at the sight of Miles, but she knew their situation was still dire.

"Put down the pistol," Miles ordered, his voice firm and commanding.

Mr. Stanley arched an eyebrow, a cruel smirk playing at his lips. "And why would I do that, my lord?" he scorned.

Miles stepped further into the room, his eyes still trained on Mr. Stanley. "Because you have lost. Do not make this any harder than it needs to be."

A dangerous glint entered Mr. Stanley's eyes. "Well, it appears that I have the advantage since I am holding a pistol aimed at Lady Edwina," he sneered. "If you don't put down your pistol, then I will shoot her."

Miles remained resolute, his grip on the pistol tightening as he stared down Mr. Stanley. "I will not allow that to happen," he declared.

"If Lady Edwina dies, can you live with that on your conscience?" Mr. Stanley taunted with a smug look in his eyes.

Miles didn't falter or lower the pistol but instead glanced over at Edwina and gave her a reassuring wink, providing her with great comfort. She didn't know how, but she knew in her heart that Miles would keep her safe.

Mr. Stanley tossed the pillow onto the settee and retrieved the leather-bound ledger from the desk. "I suggest we both put down our pistols and walk away from this unscathed."

"I cannot allow that," Miles stated resolutely, moving to stand in front of Edwina. "I have heard enough of your deceitful words and I refuse to let someone like you continue preying on those less fortunate."

Making his way towards the hearth, Mr. Stanley held up the ledger triumphantly. "If this book is destroyed, then all you have against me is your word. And what value does an earl's word hold in a court of law?"

"I daresay that it holds plenty of weight," Miles countered, his voice carrying the heaviness of conviction.

A gentle breeze drifted in from the open window, bringing the sound of Bennett's voice along with it. "I would think that two earls' words would carry even more weight."

"Yes, it would," Miles agreed before addressing Mr. Stanley once more. "And if you move to throw that book in the fire, I will not hesitate to shoot you."

Mr. Stanley gave him an amused look. "You will not shoot me."

Miles' gaze grew determined. "I most certainly will. You are a despicable man who deserves to pay for his heinous crimes."

Bennett climbed in through the window and pointed a pistol at Mr. Stanley. "You heard my friend. Put your pistol down."

With a dry chuckle, Mr. Stanley held his hands up. "This has all just been a misunderstanding," he said.

Edwina huffed in disbelief from behind Miles. "A misunderstanding? You were going to shoot me!"

"My cousin is right. We heard and saw everything," Bennett stated firmly. "You have taken advantage of our family's generosity for far too long."

"Is that what you think I am doing?" Mr. Stanley asked, his voice turning harsh and defensive. "No, my lord. I am simply taking my fair share. The only reason your family is so wealthy is because of me! I did this, not you. Not your father. Not even the late Lord Dallington."

Bennett took a step forward, unwavering in his stance despite Mr. Stanley's outburst. "That *was* your job, Mr. Stanley, but you are dismissed."

Mr. Stanley's face contorted with anger and he held the ledger up. "I will not give you the satisfaction of knowing the truth," he seethed, making a move towards the hearth.

Just as Mr. Stanley was about to toss the ledger into the flames, a loud gunshot rang out and shattered the tense silence in the room.

Chapter Twenty

Miles held the smoking pistol in his hand as Mr. Stanley dropped the ledger and his weapon before reaching for his wounded shoulder.

"You shot me!" Mr. Stanley shouted, his voice laced with pain.

Miles lowered his pistol to his side. "You left me with little choice in the matter," he said. "I could not let you burn the ledger."

Coming out from behind Miles, Edwina hurried over and retrieved the ledger. "I will be sure to give this to my uncle."

Mr. Stanley narrowed his eyes at her. "You ruined everything, you stupid chit."

A pained look came to Edwina's face as she met Mr. Stanley's steely gaze. "I don't know what happened to you. It is as if you are a different person now."

Bennett stepped forward and picked up Mr. Stanley's pistol. "That is what greed does to people."

Mr. Stanley scoffed. "And what do you know of greed, my lord?" he mocked. "You have wanted for nothing your entire life. I have had to scrimp and save just to survive."

As Bennett went to reply, the butler ran into the room with

four footmen behind him. His eyes roamed over the room in a panic until they landed on Mr. Stanley.

"We heard a gunshot," the butler said, bringing his gaze to Bennett.

Bennett kept his pistol trained on Mr. Stanley. "Send for the constable and the doctor at once," he ordered.

"Shall I retrieve Lord Dallington?" the butler asked.

"There is no need," Bennett replied. "Let him enjoy the soiree. I do not want to give the impression that anything is amiss." He lowered his pistol to the side. "Do you suppose any of the guests heard the pistol discharging?"

"It does not appear so, my lord," the butler said. "I do believe the music muffled the noise enough so as not to raise any questions."

Bennett nodded approvingly. "Good, now get him out of my sight."

The butler tipped his head before turning to the footmen. "Take Mr. Stanley to the servants' quarters and stand guard until the constable arrives."

After Mr. Stanley was forcefully removed from the study, Miles turned to face Edwina, his mind whirling with the fact that he had saved her from a certain death. He had come so close to losing her, and he had never felt such panic before.

Edwina's eyes held uncertainty as she said, "Thank you for coming when you did. You saved me… again."

If he were a smart man, he would just acknowledge her words and be done with it. But he couldn't seem to quiet the alarming thoughts in his head.

"What were you thinking?" Miles asked, his words coming out harsh. Too harsh. "You could have been killed!"

Edwina lowered her gaze. "I saw a light coming from the study and I went to investigate. When I saw Mr. Stanley in here, I didn't think he would hurt me."

"Well, you were wrong," Miles stated. "If it wasn't for me

and Bennett, you could have…" He couldn't finish his sentence.

"I know, and I am sorry," Edwina said, her voice contrite.

Miles took a few deep breaths, attempting to calm his pounding heart. "You can't take these types of risks, Edwina. Do you not think of anyone but yourself?"

Bringing her gaze back up, Edwina's eyes held a fierceness to them and he knew he had gone too far. "If it weren't for me, we would never have discovered Mr. Stanley's deceit."

Miles took a step closer to her. "It may have taken more time, but the truth would have come out."

"And how many people would have suffered during that time?" Edwina demanded, her gaze challenging him.

"Do you not realize how close you came to dying?" Miles asked.

"I do, but…"

Miles spoke over her. "No 'buts,' Edwina. Your actions were careless and foolish," he said, his words firm.

Edwina stared at him for a moment before her eyes started glimmering from unshed tears. Without saying another word, she ducked her head and fled from the room.

Miles watched her retreating figure, knowing he was a fool. He should have wrapped her up in his arms and never let her go.

Bennett cleared his throat. "That was poorly done on your part."

"I know," Miles said with a sigh.

"You should go after her," Bennett urged.

Miles huffed. "Yes, because this conversation went so well. I just came so close to losing her and it frightened me."

Bennett took a step closer to him. "Tell that to Edwina, not to me. She deserves to know the truth- all of it."

"And if she still rejects my offer?" Miles asked with a slight wince.

"Then at least you tried."

Miles glanced towards the door. "I don't even know where she went."

"If I know my cousin, she is in the rear of the gardens, next to the birch tree. There is a bench there that she likes to sit on," Bennett said.

With a grateful look at his friend, Miles departed from the study and with purposeful strides hurried down the path that led to the birch tree.

When he arrived, he saw Edwina was sitting on the bench and she was wiping the tears that were falling down her cheeks.

Not wishing to startle her, Miles said in a gentle voice, "Edwina."

Edwina's eyes went wide at the sight of him before she turned away. "Go away, Miles," she said, her voice filled with pain and anger. "I wish to be alone."

"That is fair," Miles admitted, stepping closer. "But I have come to apologize, and I am hoping that you will hear me out."

With her back still turned to him, she took a deep breath and let it out slowly. "I look a fright."

"To me, you have never looked more beautiful," Miles responded.

Edwina hesitantly turned towards him, her cheeks stained from tears. "Now I know you are lying to me. I just feel awful for what happened…"

Miles put his hand up, stilling her words. "You did nothing wrong, but I did. I was so afraid that I almost lost you that I took out my anger on you."

"I should never have gone into that study," Edwina said.

"If you hadn't, the truth wouldn't have been revealed," Miles remarked. "No one suspected Mr. Stanley was stealing from your uncle."

Edwina's eyes grew sad. "Mr. Stanley was always so kind to me. I never thought he would try to kill me," she said.

"Why would you? You have the kindest heart and I do not think you see the bad in anyone," Miles remarked.

"Perhaps I should start."

"No, do not let Mr. Stanley change the way you are," Miles insisted. "For you are perfect, just the way you are."

Edwina pressed her lips together. "I think not."

Knowing there was much that needed to be said between them, Miles gestured towards the bench. "May I join you?" he asked.

With a nod, Edwina granted her permission.

Once he was situated on the bench, he said, "I was wrong, Edwina."

Edwina gave him a baffled look. "About what?"

Miles met her gaze. "About everything," he replied. "When I lost Arabella, I thought my life was over. And then when John died…" He stopped. "Despite going through the motions, I was empty inside. Devoid of any hope. But everything changed when I met you."

"You helped me as well," Edwina said.

"You did more than just help me," Miles stated. "You brought my heart back to life."

Edwina gave him a weak smile. "You deserve to be happy, Miles. No matter where life takes you."

"But I finally know where I belong. For all my life, I have been making my way to you," Miles said. "I have tried to fight it, repeatedly, but I have fallen madly, irrevocably in love with you."

Emotions flickered across Edwina's face as she stared back at him. "But what about Arabella?"

"A part of me will always love Arabella, but my heart, my whole heart, will belong to you," Miles replied.

"I don't know what to say…"

"You don't have to say anything."

"… other than I love you, too," Edwina said.

Miles' brow shot up. "You love me?" he asked.

Edwina leaned forward and placed her hand over his heart. "I do," she replied. "You are engraved upon my heart."

Reaching up, Miles placed his hand over hers. "Marry me, and neither one of us will ever have to be alone again."

"Is that a proper proposal?" Edwina asked with a mischievous look in her eyes.

Keeping hold of her hand, Miles moved to a kneeling position on the moss-coated ground. "Lady Edwina Lockwood, would you do me the grand honor of marrying me?"

Edwina's lips twitched. "I have one condition."

"You can have anything you desire if you just say yes," Miles insisted.

"But you haven't heard what I want yet."

Miles grinned. "It doesn't matter, I will agree to it."

She returned his smile. "All I ask of you is to marry me at the chapel here at Brockhall Manor. It is where my father married my mother."

"I would have it no other way, my love."

Her smile grew, brightening her whole face. "Then, yes, I will marry you."

Returning to his seat on the bench, Miles cupped her right cheek and said, "I can't believe you finally agreed to marry me."

"All I wanted was your heart, Miles."

"And you have it."

"As you have mine," Edwina said.

Miles moved closer to her. "I promise from this day forward that you will always be *mine*, and I will always be *yours*. We will never be apart."

Edwina leaned closer to him. "Do you truly promise?"

"Yes, wholeheartedly," he replied, feeling her warm breath on his lips. "May I kiss you now?"

"I thought you would never ask…"

Her words had barely left her lips before he kissed her. In that precious moment, the world seemed to fade away as he lost himself in the intoxicating sweetness of Edwina's embrace. And in the kiss, he felt a silent affirmation of a love that would know no bounds. He experienced a love that would endure through every trial and triumph, guiding them through their journey together.

He broke the kiss but remained close. "Will you promise to always kiss me like that?"

"Why, did I do it right?" she asked.

A chuckle escaped his lips. "It was perfect, just as I expected it to be."

Edwina let out a relieved sigh. "Good, because I hope we can do that again, and often."

Miles pressed his lips to hers before saying, "I can assure you that I will never tire of kissing you. I daresay that it is my favorite thing to do now."

A clearing of a throat came from a short distance away.

Miles turned his head and saw Bennett, his arms crossed over his chest and an amused look on his expression.

"Are you two quite finished?" Bennett asked. "I merely ask because my mother wants to know if you two are ready to announce your engagement."

A line between Edwina's brow appeared. "How did she know we were getting engaged this evening?"

Bennett gave them a smug smile. "Why do you think my mother planned this lavish soiree?" he asked. "It was evident to everyone how deeply in love you two are- well, everyone except for Miles. It took him a bit longer to catch on than we anticipated."

Miles stood up and assisted Edwina to her feet. "It would appear that everyone has been conspiring against us," he said with a smile.

Edwina smiled back at him, her eyes sparkling with affection. "Indeed, but I have no complaints," she declared.

"Nor I," Miles responded. "This just means I can dance with you for more than one set."

Leaning in close, Edwina pressed her lips against his.

Bennett let out a disapproving huff. "Do show some restraint, Cousin," he chided.

With an unapologetic look at Bennett, she boldly stated, "Miles is my fiancé and that means I can kiss him whenever I want."

"And you will hear no complaints from me, my dear," Miles remarked.

Bennett looked heavenward. "This is going to be a long three weeks," he muttered under his breath.

Edwina felt as though her heart would burst with happiness. She was engaged to be married to Miles, and she couldn't wipe the smile off her face since they had announced their engagement last night. She eagerly looked forward to building a life with him, one where they would never have to be apart.

Martha's voice broke through her musings. "Are you pleased with your hair, my lady?" she asked, taking a step back.

Edwina turned her head to admire the elegant coiffure in the mirror. "It is perfect," she declared.

"You are happy," Martha said. It wasn't so much a question as a statement.

"I am," Edwina admitted.

Martha nodded knowingly. "Good. You deserve every bit of it," she remarked. "You should depart if you wish to join your family for breakfast."

With a grateful look, Edwina rose from her seat and opened the door, only to be greeted by a pleasant surprise. Miles stood leaning against the wall with a single red rose in his hand. As soon as he caught sight of her, he straightened up and his eyes lit up with adoration.

Miles closed the distance between them and presented her with the single rose. "I saw this rose and it reminded me of you."

"Thank you," she said, accepting the rose. "That was most thoughtful of you."

He gazed at her intently. "I hope that whenever you gaze upon it, you will think of me."

Edwina leaned closer to him, feeling overwhelmed by his love. "That will not be difficult since you are always in my thoughts."

"As are you in mine," Miles whispered tenderly.

Their moment was interrupted by Winston's voice echoing down the corridor. "Perhaps it would be best if you just eloped to Gretna Green. I won't say anything if it will make this stop."

Miles chuckled, his eyes still fixed on her. "I just came to escort Edwina down to breakfast."

"It looks like you were about to engage in something else," Winston said. He softened his words with a smile.

Edwina turned towards her cousin. "We are engaged to be married," she pointed out. "In the eyes of the *ton*, we are practically married."

"Yes, but we are not in London and these displays of affection are growing rather tiresome," Winston remarked.

"We only got engaged last night," Edwina said.

Winston smirked. "Yet my statement still stands."

Miles extended his arm towards Edwina. "May I escort you down to the dining room?"

"Yes, but you must allow me to give the rose to my lady's maid so she can put it on the table by my bed," Edwina replied.

It was only a moment later that they made their way

towards the main floor with a comfortable silence coming over them.

They arrived in the entry hall and White approached them. "Lord Dallington has requested your presence in his study," he announced. "All of you."

"I suppose breakfast can wait," Winston said. "I wonder what my father wishes to speak to us about at such an early hour."

It was only a few moments before they arrived at the study and Edwina saw Bennett and her uncle hunched over the desk, reviewing the ledger. Together.

Her uncle's head came up when they came closer to the desk. "Good, you are all here," he said. "Catherine should be down in just a moment."

As if on cue, her aunt stepped into the room. "I am here. You may start your apology."

Sitting back in his seat, her uncle shifted his gaze to Edwina. "Catherine is right. I do owe Edwina an apology, and it is long overdue."

Her uncle rose from his seat and came around his desk. He continued. "It is because of you that we learned of Mr. Stanley's treachery. Bennett told me what you did," he hesitated as he shifted his gaze to Miles, "what you both did. And it was nothing short of miraculous."

Edwina shifted in her stance, uncomfortable with the praise. "I didn't do much," she said.

Lifting his brow, her uncle remarked, "You saved this family from possible ruination. Your contribution cannot be understated."

"Thank you," Edwina murmured.

Her uncle sighed. "We have a problem though. Catherine told me that I have been doing a terrible job of being your guardian- and uncle. For that, I am truly, and utterly, sorry. But every time I gaze upon you, I see my brother inside of you and the grief washes over me. It is no excuse for my behavior, though." He closed his eyes, his voice betraying his emotions.

Edwina could hear the pain in his words and she knew he was in earnest. "I understand," she said.

Her uncle's eyes opened and they held a deep sorrow. "I promise that I will strive to be better with each passing day."

"I forgive you, Uncle. I just wish we could return to the easy relationship that we once had," Edwina remarked.

"As do I," her uncle said. "You are as kind and generous as your father was. I have never met a more genuine person. He would be proud of you. Just as Catherine and I are proud of you."

At the mention of her father, she felt tears form in her eyes and she started blinking them back. Miles gently placed a hand on the small of her back, providing her with immense comfort.

Bennett spoke up, drawing their attention. "Father and I have decided that we will work together to make our estate even more profitable."

"What of the village?" Edwina asked.

"We will ensure they receive what we promised, and our tenants will be given the needed repairs to their cottages," Bennett replied.

Winston stepped forward and said, "You might want to start with the vicar. Miss Bawden mentioned he was thinking about switching parishes due to the lack of funding."

Bennett tipped his head. "We will go speak to him at once and make it right."

Her uncle moved to stand by his wife. "We do have another problem that we need to address immediately," he stated. "I am grateful that Bennett brought it to my attention and I feel as if I must rectify the situation at once."

As her uncle reached for his wife's hand, he shared, "I understand that you saw something that you were not supposed to see… at least for now." He sighed. "But I cannot have you think the worst of me since I love Catherine with my whole heart."

"I love you, too," her aunt stated.

Her uncle offered his wife a private smile before saying, "The woman at the cottage is actually my sister. We have not spoken since she eloped with a man that was well below her station. She came to me a few weeks ago, battered and bruised, looking for a place to hide from her husband." He let out a heavy sigh before revealing, "Sarah could endure the beatings, but when her husband turned his hand on their son, she turned to me for help."

Her aunt interjected, "You must understand that no one can know Sarah is here. If her husband ever found out, it would be within his rights to take them away."

Winston crossed his arms over his chest. "You have enough influence in Parliament that we might be able to petition for a divorce."

"I doubt that," her uncle said. "Divorces are so rarely granted, and my sister made her choice many years ago, much to the disappointment of our whole family."

"We can still try," Winston pressed.

Her uncle bobbed his head. "Perhaps, but for now, we must go on pretending as if Sarah is not here. And I will be much more cautious when I go to visit with her and my nephew."

Edwina felt immense relief from her uncle's words, knowing she had thought the worst and had been wrong. The weight she had been carrying seemed to dissipate, making her shoulders seem lighter.

Bennett picked up the ledger and said, "We have one more thing to discuss with Edwina and then we can adjourn for breakfast."

Giving him an expectant look, Edwina waited for her cousin to continue.

"It is the matter of your inheritance," Bennett remarked.

Her uncle offered her an apologetic look. "Mr. Stanley has stolen a great deal of money from that account and I was foolish enough to believe his explanation for it. I had hoped to honor my brother's wishes but I knew that would take time. Which is why I never mentioned your inheritance. My plan was to turn the money over to you once you reached your majority," he said. "However, now that you do know, I promise that you will receive every pound you are entitled to. It just might take some time."

"Can we not just retrieve the funds that Mr. Stanley stole?" Edwina asked.

With a resolute nod, her uncle replied, "We will try, but it might not be as easy as that. There are many ways to keep funds hidden, but you must not worry about that. You will have your money. I promise you that."

Miles leaned closer to her. "That is your money that your father left you," he whispered. "You are free to do with it what you please."

She turned towards him and asked, "Do you truly mean that?"

"I do," Miles replied. "My estate is very profitable and we have more than enough money for two lifetimes."

Edwina felt her heart fill with gratitude for this man. How she loved him. With Miles by her side, it was as if all the pieces of her soul had finally found their rightful place.

Shifting her gaze back to Bennett, Edwina knew precisely what she wanted to do with her inheritance. "I would like you to use that money to help the village."

Bennett's brow lifted. "Are you in earnest?" he asked. "That is a small fortune."

Edwina reached for Miles' hand. "It is, but the villagers have suffered much by Mr. Stanley's hand. It will take some time- and money- to regain their trust again. Perhaps you could even open an all-girls' school."

"We will do so, but in your name," Bennett said.

Her uncle approached her, coming to a stop in front of her. His eyes were moist. "You are so much like your father, and I miss him."

Edwina dropped Miles' hand and embraced her uncle. "I do as well."

In a low voice, her uncle said, "I'm sorry, Edwina. You deserved better and I let you down. I promise to make this right."

Leaning back slightly, Edwina suggested, "Let's start over."

Her uncle released her and took a step back. "Thank you, Child."

Her aunt stepped forward and announced, "You must hurry and eat breakfast. The dressmaker is coming to fit you for a whole new wardrobe. You will need one befitting your elevation of status. You are to become a countess."

"I do not care about becoming a countess," Edwina said. "All I care about is that I am Miles' wife."

Miles grinned. "This will mean that you will need to start acting more countess*ish*."

"That doesn't have the same ring to it as 'earlish,'" Edwina teased.

"I am not as good at making up words as you are," Miles admitted.

Edwina patted his sleeve. "At least you are trying."

Miles reached for her hand and brought it up to his lips. "I will always try for you," he said. "You must know that."

"I do," Edwina responded, leaning closer. "And I promise I won't make up too many words."

"You can make up as many words as you want," Miles remarked, keeping a hold on her hand. "I just want you to be happy."

A broad smile came to her lips. "I am happy. Deliriously so," she admitted.

Miles' eyes filled with tenderness. "To love you is to

breathe, for without you, my life would be devoid of meaning or purpose."

"I love you, too," Edwina murmured, being transfixed by his gaze.

Winston let out a groan. "Just elope to Gretna Green already!" he exclaimed. "And leave me in peace."

"Absolutely not!" her aunt shouted. "Edwina needs to get married in the chapel after the banns have been posted."

Miles lowered her hand but didn't release it. "It might be best if I write about my undying devotion to you."

"I would like that," Edwina said.

Her uncle chimed in, "Shall we adjourn to the dining room?"

Everyone murmured their agreement and they filed out of the study. While they made their way to breakfast, Edwina met Miles' gaze and smiled. "Just so you know, I am yours, now and forevermore."

"Forever. With you. I quite like the sound of that," Miles said.

Epilogue

One year later

Miles cradled his newborn baby boy in his arms and his heart overflowed with a sense of gratitude. He couldn't quite believe the immense love that he already held for this little one. He was a father now, and he would do anything in his power to protect his son.

Edwina, still recovering from the labor, turned to face him on the bed. Her hair was tousled, and her appearance was a bit disheveled, but to him, she looked more beautiful than ever. How he loved this woman. She had given him a gift that he could never repay.

Glancing down at their baby, she said, "You have your son- your heir."

"It is true, but I would have been just as pleased if it were a daughter," Miles stated. And it was the truth. All he wanted was a healthy child.

"Well, there is always next time," Edwina quipped lightly.

Miles leaned in to press a gentle kiss to her lips. "You did well, my love. I do not think I could have gone through what you just did."

A small smile played on Edwina's lips. "I will admit that it was not exactly pleasant, but the reward was worth it. We have a son."

"Yes, we do," Miles said proudly.

The sound of someone clearing their throat drew Miles' attention. Dr. Mecham stood at the foot of the bed, holding his bag in his hand.

"Will that be all, my lord?" Dr. Mecham asked.

Adjusting the baby in his arms, Miles replied, "I would like for you to stay on for a few more days to ensure that my wife and child are both healthy."

Dr. Mecham tipped his head in understanding. "Of course," he said before he departed from the room.

Edwina eyed him curiously. "Must he really stay? He has patients in London that require his attention."

"It is wholly necessary," Miles replied. "I can't risk anything happening to you or our son."

"But he has already been with us for weeks," Edwina remarked.

Miles nodded. "And it was worth every penny. I wanted to ensure that you had the best care possible, and Dr. Mecham is one of the most respected doctors in England."

Edwina shook her head in amusement. "Our village doctor would have been just fine."

"Perhaps, but I couldn't take any chances with your well-being," Miles said. "You are my whole world."

"And now our world is expanding," Edwina remarked, shifting her gaze towards their son. "We need to come up with a name for him."

"I had thought once I saw our child, a name would come easily, but now that I hold him in my arms, I am at a loss," Miles admitted. "He looks like a baby."

Edwina laughed. "I tried to warn you."

Miles held the baby up. "Are you a Michael? An Adam? A William?" he asked. "I do not think I have a knack for naming babies."

"What about John?" Edwina suggested.

He sobered. "Are you sure?"

Edwina bobbed her head. "I think it would be a fine tribute to your brother."

Miles' heart swelled with emotion. "What about naming him Richard- after your father?" he proposed.

Leaning forward, Edwina gently moved the blanket away from their son's face. "We can name our next son Richard."

Tears welled up in Miles' eyes as he gazed at his wife and child, overwhelmed with love. "Thank you," he said softly.

Edwina rested her head against his shoulder, her eyes not straying from the baby. "There is no need to thank me."

"But there is," Miles insisted, kissing her forehead. "You have already given me everything."

"I am doing what any dutiful wife does," Edwina said, dismissing his praise.

Miles shifted on the bed so he could look his wife in her eyes. "This past year with you has been the happiest I have ever been. Every day I find that I love you more than the day before."

Edwina held his gaze, her eyes shining with emotion. "And each day, I fall deeper in love with you, Miles."

The door swung open and Lady Dallington appeared with a bright smile on her face. She approached the bed and asked, "How are you faring, Dear?"

Straightening up, Edwina replied, "I am well."

"You should rest," Lady Dallington advised. "I could take the baby until he is ready to feed."

"Oh, must you?" Edwina asked.

Lady Dallington's eyes held understanding. "Is it not amazing how something so small can completely change our world?"

"It is," Edwina agreed. "We have decided to name him John."

As if in response to his name being spoken, the baby stirred in his sleep, making Miles chuckle.

"Hello, John," Lady Dallington cooed, leaning in to get a closer look at the baby.

Miles spoke up. "I will hold John while Edwina rests."

"Very well," Lady Dallington conceded. "I will leave you be for a while, but I will come check on you soon enough."

Once they were alone again, Miles said, "Your aunt is right. You should rest."

"I don't think I can," she replied. "I can't seem to stop looking at John. It just seems too wonderful that we have a child."

"I understand, but do try to rest. From what I have been told, this is the calm before the storm," Miles stated.

In a hesitant voice, Edwina asked, "Do you think I will make a good mother?"

Miles took her hand in his. "My dear, you are the best of wives. I have no doubt that you will be the best of mothers."

"Do be serious."

"I am," Miles responded. "You, Edwina, will be a brilliant mother. Your kind heart and nurturing spirit make you more than qualified for this role."

Edwina's worries seemed to fade away as she looked at him. "I suppose I am just nervous."

"Raising children will be an adventure," Miles reassured her. "One that I cannot wait to embark on with you by my side."

The baby let out a soft cry, drawing their attention.

"Do you suppose something is wrong?" Edwina asked anxiously, her brows drawn together in concern.

Miles shook his head, smiling fondly at his wife. He could see the exhaustion etched on her face and he knew she needed sleep. "Rest, my dear," he encouraged. "I will ensure John is well taken care of."

A yawn came to Edwina's lips. "I am a little tired," she admitted. "Perhaps I shall rest for a bit."

As Miles settled onto the bed, holding their baby close to his chest and watching Edwina drift off to sleep, he knew he had everything he needed. Right here. In this room.

He didn't know what tomorrow would bring, but for now, he was content. Everything he had experienced in his life had led him to this moment. And it had been worth it. For what a glorious moment this was indeed.

The End

Next Book In Series

Bennett Lockwood, Earl of Dunsby, should feel nothing but contentment in his life, yet an unfulfilled longing tug at his heart. Despite past heartbreak, he yearns for a love match. When he discovers an injured young woman in the woodlands, he finds himself drawn to her, especially as she struggles to recall her past.

Delphine, Countess of Dunrobin, awakens to find herself in unfamiliar surroundings, her past shrouded in uncertainty. Grateful for her rescue, she leans on the Lockwood family for support, particularly Bennett, whose kindness captivates her.

As Delphine recovers, Bennett's feelings deepen, even as she resolutely declares her reluctance to marry. When visitors arrive to take Delphine home, Bennett senses danger in their motives and vows to protect her at all costs. With any chance of a future together now threatened, he must confront his own desires and decide whether to fight for love against all odds.

About the Author

Laura Beers is an award-winning author. She attended Brigham Young University, earning a Bachelor of Science degree in Construction Management. She can't sing, doesn't dance and loves naps.

Laura lives in Utah with her husband, three kids, and her dysfunctional dog. When not writing regency romance, she loves skiing, hiking, and drinking Dr Pepper.

You can connect with Laura on Facebook, Instagram, or on her site at www.authorlaurabeers.com.

Made in United States
North Haven, CT
04 September 2024